GIVE UP THE GHOST

ANGIE FOX

ALSO BY ANGIE FOX

The Dangerous Book for Demon Slayers

A Tale of Two Demon Slayers

The Last of the Demon Slayers

My Big Fat Demon Slayer Wedding

Beverly Hills Demon Slayer

Night of the Living Demon Slayer

What To Expect When Your Demon Slayer is Expecting

SHORT STORY COLLECTIONS:

A Little Night Magic: A collection of Southern Ghost Hunter and Accidental Demon Slayer short stories

Give Up the Ghost

The Southern Ghost Hunter Mysteries

Book 11

ANGIE FOX

GIVE UP THE GHOST

ISBN: 978-1-957685-03-8

CHAPTER 1

*I*t's a truth universally acknowledged, that every small town loves a good scandal.

And this was one for the ages.

It began innocently enough, on a beautiful Saturday evening in the fall, with the leaves overhead a wash of oranges, reds, and a few stubborn spots of green. I craned my neck amid a healthy crowd gathered in the town square as our local archivist, who also happened to be my sister, lifted the last item out of a time capsule that had been buried beneath the high school's flagpole since 1985.

Two large television screens stood by to broadcast the findings.

The mayor's elbow caught my arm as he leaned forward. Behind us, the press hovered, ready with cameras and notepads.

Melody's blonde ponytail skimmed the back of the white lab coat she wore over a simple green dress. We'd already seen the Air Jordan high-tops Stephanie Bunn wore when she won the Mad Max break dancing competition in the town square, as well as a boxed copy of the original Microsoft Windows 1.0, not to mention a game-used football signed by the entire 1985 high school varsity team. The crowd had *oohed* and *aahed* as my sister cracked each box open and shared the contents, her white silk gloves bright under the monitors that broadcast her smallest movement.

She held Darcy Johnson's secret apple pie recipe up for the television monitors, and a flood of cell phone photographs followed.

Betty Lou Thompson heaved a sigh from the special Sugarland Heritage Society section in front of us where she sat with her mother-in-law. "Secrets are meant to be secrets," she said, patting her blonde frosted hair.

"Not in Sugarland." The razor-thin Nellie Holcamp snickered from the first row.

In all fairness, Betty Lou was a city girl from up north around Nashville. She clearly hadn't been in Sugarland long enough to know better, and Mrs. Thompson had not schooled her properly. If Betty Lou had been local, she'd have understood we treated secrets like a plate of deviled eggs at a carry-in, made to be shared.

Besides, if you wanted things kept private, keeping them to yourself was a lot more effective than stuffing them in a time capsule. Now granted, these donations were originally supposed to be buried for one hundred years. And if they hadn't been stashed under the flagpole that needed to move to make way for the new high school football stadium, they would have stayed that way.

My boyfriend's arm brushed mine as Melody drew the last box out of its clear plastic wrapper.

Ellis Wydell was the deputy sheriff in our town and the best boyfriend I could ask for. Last week we'd unearthed the shocking truth about a skeleton that had been found in the time capsule, and I had a feeling he was looking forward to less drama moving forward. Still, he liked a good mystery as much as I did, and we both craned our necks to see the final object.

2

No bigger than a shoebox, the metal container lost flecks of rust as it slid from its wrapper.

"There are no markings on this one," Melody announced to the hushed crowd, "and no record of what club or organization left it." She eased back the rusty latch. "Everything else has been accounted for." The lid creaked as she lifted it. Melody let out a squeak.

The crowd gasped as Melody opened the box fully to reveal a book. Its image shone bright on the massive screen.

I was glad Nellie Holcamp's husband had remained at her side because she fainted dead away in his arms.

Ellis muttered a curse, while right in front of us, the genealogy club ladies from the Three Angels of the Tabernacle Blessed Reform Church of Sugarland crossed themselves and gave quick nods to Jesus in heaven to let this pass them by.

Because everybody—and I mean everybody—recognized what lay inside that rusted metal box. If they hadn't seen it themselves, they'd heard tell about it.

Now, a book might not sound like something to be afraid of, but *this* book was a legendary weapon in Sugarland. We all would be better off if that razor-edged sword had remained stuck and useless, trapped in stone—or in our case in a rusty box in a time capsule.

The book's sequined cover glinted under the bright stage lights. The skull and crossbones stitched onto the front cover appeared ready to cackle with delight as the initial shock of the audience gave way to frantic whispers.

My mouth went dry as I caressed the silver and gold filigree cross I wore over my heart. It had been my grandmother's, and it usually gave me comfort. Today, it wasn't quite up to the job.

Nellie Holcamp blinked furiously and struggled to raise her head. "It's Erma Sue's burn book," she moaned.

"I thought her reign of terror ended when she died," a woman in front of me gasped.

"They should have buried her with it!" another agreed.

"We don't want it," declared the preacher's wife. "Put it back in the hole!"

"At least keep it under lock and key," muttered a reporter behind me.

"We can handle this," the mayor vowed to himself.

"And here I was hoping to take some vacation," Ellis groaned.

"Run while you can," I said low under my breath. "I'll pack." We hadn't had a vacation in a while. Now would be a really good time.

"Excuse me." The mayor scooted past me toward the aisle on our left and made for the stage.

"It's just a book," scoffed the tan, over-muscled police officer who stood on the other side of Ellis.

Leave it to Duranja to trivialize something so important. Didn't the collective reaction of the entire town mean anything to him? I leaned past Ellis to enlighten the smirking deputy. "That is *not* just a book. It is the most notorious diary kept by the most cunning blackmail artist Sugarland has ever known."

The stiff-backed younger officer rolled his eyes. He never believed anything that didn't fit his agenda, especially if I was the one saying it.

"Let's just…agree to disagree," Ellis said, as if his colleague had a shred of a point, which he didn't.

Duranja would see soon enough. Or, if we were lucky, he wouldn't.

I blew out a breath and retied my ponytail. I shouldn't have expected an easy time with Alec Duranja. If we hadn't disagreed about the book, we would have come up with something else.

Nobody would mistake us for best friends.

According to him, I had corrupted Ellis's police skills with my ghost hunting. Never mind the number of crimes I'd helped solve.

And now he was dating my sister.

Well, Melody knew as well as I did—as well as we all did—how dangerous that book could be. Maybe his attitude about this discovery would put an end to their budding romance.

One could hope.

The mayor joined the library director at the edge of the stage while Melody lifted the book from its container like it might bite her. Poor thing. Duranja rested his thumbs under his police utility belt and appeared entertained by her reluctance to open the book, as if her completely reasonable sense of caution were some sort of cute quirk.

"She's under a lot of pressure up there," I pointed out.

He shot me a disbelieving scowl. "Why? She didn't do anything wrong."

That wasn't the point. Goody Two-shoes Duranja might be the type to think he was wild for eating one gummi bear out of the bin when he was six, but plenty of other people had faults they'd like to keep to themselves. And if any of those faults had shown themselves before Erma Sue died, they were probably memorialized somewhere in that book.

Erma Sue Bryce had carried that book with her everywhere, its pink feathers fluttering around the edges, the black rhinestone eyes on the skull glittering with a life of their own. And if you crossed her, she'd show you "your" page, filled with the secrets you didn't want spoken…unless you didn't plan to live in Sugarland anymore.

Erma Sue traded in secrets—hurtful truths that could destroy friendships, families, and lives. And she was very good at what she did.

Folks acted like they didn't know how she'd gotten the goods on so many people, like she'd done it by magic or something. But Erma Sue had been the premier hairdresser in town, which explained it all.

Around these parts, a woman's hair was her crowning glory,

and when it came to cut, color, and style, Erma Sue was a miracle worker. So the ladies still went to see her. They braved the lion's den and pretended she didn't have claws, that they didn't have anything to worry about because they were good people. What kind of secret life did you lead if you were afraid of stepping foot inside Two Sues' House of Beauty?

I crossed my arms over my chest.

Trouble was, ladies talked in that chair. Maybe not to tell on themselves, but sure as God made green apples, those ladies liked to tell on each other. And let's just say Erma Sue was a real good listener. Even if they didn't state their business outright, Erma Sue could put two and two together.

She was good at math, too.

"Even dead, she's not gone," seasoned reporter Ovis Dupree muttered behind me.

When Erma Sue passed, the biddies from Sugarland had volunteered in heaps and buckets to help her daughter clean out the house, but Twyla Sue had refused. They'd come with casseroles and stayed until Erma's one and only child eventually *had* to leave the room to attend to nature's call.

Together they'd searched every corner of that house, but nobody had found the book.

Now it seemed there'd been no book to find.

"Erma Sue must have put it in there herself," Ellis concluded, as if he couldn't quite believe it of her.

The time capsule contents had gone into the ground in the fall of 1985, six months before a heart attack struck down Erma Sue in the spring of 1986. I remembered because my friend Lauralee's favorite aunt had endured a lesser wedding updo, thanks to the untimely death of the only woman who could stack curls and roses seven inches high without the hairspray wilting the flowers.

Lauralee's aunt bemoaned her church picture to this day.

"Now it's back," the lady in front of me hissed, clutching her pearls. "She's back."

More and more people filtered up from the rear, filling the aisle to our left, unwilling to miss a thing.

"Come on, people. What can old secrets do?" Duranja protested, while at the same time it appeared Nellie Holcamp might faint again.

Ellis gave me a sideways glance, because I knew better than anyone what could happen when ghosts of the past spoke their truth. Scandal, blackmail, murder. We'd seen it all firsthand.

Duranja shot a judgy glare at poor Nellie. "It's nothing but a bunch of old gossip from the hair salon. Everything in there has to be at least forty to sixty years old."

For a person who'd lived in Sugarland his whole life, he sure didn't have much sense.

At my raised brows, he doubled down. "The only people who are going to care are the ladies in Harmony Springs Retirement home," he insisted.

"I care." A sweet, strained drawl rose above the crowd.

I couldn't help but gasp as Twyla Sue Bryce dodged her way through the crowd gathered in what remained of the aisle to our left.

She paused only to shoot a death glare at the startled officer. "She was my mamma." Twyla Sue's cheeks flushed, and her eyes glinted as sharp as the square-cut diamond studs in her ears. "You'd better treat her memory with respect."

"Now you've done it," murmured a woman as Twyla Sue clutched her red designer bag and continued her battle toward the stage. "If she's anything like her mother, she'll sting like a hornet."

"And bite like a junkyard dog," added the woman in front of me.

"Please let me through," Twyla Sue insisted over the din, admittedly not making much headway.

ANGIE FOX

"Twyla Sue has been nice to me," a woman offered.

"That's fine and dandy, but Erma Sue was the devil in pink pumps and pantyhose," snarked the lady next to her.

Cheeks red, Twyla Sue whipped around to confront the snickering matron. "You didn't call my mamma names when she let you pretend to God and everybody that you didn't turn gray until you were sixty," she declared, chin shaking.

The woman gasped.

"I knew it," Nellie called out, straightening like a shot.

I had to give Twyla Sue credit for sass.

And for the respect it gave her. The rest of the crowd at the front saw her approach and parted like she was the second coming of Elvis. Heads turned, and more than one person stepped back from the platinum-blonde storm in a bottle-blue wrap dress.

"This could get ugly," Ellis said under his breath, stepping forward, motioning to Duranja to follow him.

He was going after her.

"Do you need me?" I could do…something.

"No," Ellis said quickly.

"Relax," Duranja urged, refusing to budge. He held his shoulders stiff as he scanned the crowd. "It's not like she's going to make a scene."

"She's already making a scene." How could he not see it? And I'd bet my aunt Sally there was a bigger duck fit coming.

Ellis worked his way through the crowd while I forced myself to keep breathing. I hadn't had much experience with Twyla Sue, but she'd always been plenty polite and kind to me. She'd never criticized me when I'd gone through my own scandal. She'd never ruled the town like her mother, or taken advantage of any knowledge gained in the beauty chair.

Well, until a minute ago.

Still, I couldn't entirely fault her for a moment's outburst.

Nobody liked to hear smack talk about their mamma, even if some of it might be deserved.

But if Twyla Sue got hold of that book while she had anger in her heart? Well, I couldn't see it going well.

Ellis kept his distance, but he stayed on her.

The beautician was a sight to behold, her gold bracelets glinting in the afternoon sunlight, her perfectly wavy locks streaming over her shoulders. She was model tall, and her silver stiletto heels refused to sink into the soft grass.

She strode up the stairs and onto the stage. To my shock, the mayor himself stepped aside and gave her a loving pat on the shoulder. She nodded her thanks, tears glistening in her eyes, before stalking toward my stunned sister at the microphone.

"My mamma's diary is not a sideshow display," Twyla Sue declared. "Now, give it to me," she ordered, holding a hand out for the book.

Melody made a quick step back, bumping the camera. It shook and swung around for a close-up of Twyla Sue's flushed cheeks and trembling bottom lip.

"I'm not going to let you or anyone mock her or desecrate her memory," she vowed.

Feathers shook as Melody gripped the book tighter. "Believe me, I'm not mocking her," she insisted, "and I'd never want to cause you pain." At the same time, she couldn't just hand over artifacts to anyone who asked, especially not the burn book.

"You might not judge her, but everyone else is." Twyla Sue sniffed, refusing to look at the crowd. "Now hand it over."

"I'm not sure I can do that. This is an artifact from the time capsule," Melody stated, holding her moral ground.

Twyla Sue ground her jaw. "It's my family heritage, not yours." I said a little prayer for Melody. It wasn't a good idea to mess with a woman who did hair for eight hours a day in four-inch spiked heels with teeny tiny buckles.

Melody looked to the library director, who stood with eyes

wide, rooted to the spot. Her gaze veered to the mayor, who held Ellis in check with an outstretched hand.

His jowls quivered as he gulped. "Best give it to her, Melody. We all know it was her mamma's, and people have a right…"

"She would have wanted me to have it," Twyla Sue said, plucking the book from Melody's gloved hands. "Thank you, Mayor."

"But—" Melody began. She looked to Ellis, who shook his head. We could all see the mayor's point.

Twyla Sue turned to the stunned crowd, gripping the book to her chest. "Now is a good time for you all to start being a lot more charitable toward me and my late mother." She straightened her back and quickly wiped a tear. "It's not too late to make amends, you know," she added before her expression went cold. "For some of you, at least."

She strode offstage like she owned the place.

And maybe now she did.

CHAPTER 2

*O*n a balmy evening not too long after, Ellis and I tried
to find a little escape where we could. I would have
preferred Tahiti or Guam or any tropical island far away from
the whisper networks currently on fire over "the book," but a
sunset picnic at Lovers' Leap would have to do.

"Goat.cheese?" I asked, spreading a cracker and offering it to
my handsome boyfriend.

He tipped his head forward and ate it from my hand in a way
that would have been cute and charming if everything had been
normal.

I tried to smile. Tried not to notice the stiffness in his shoulders or how he carefully avoided the subject on both our minds.

It wouldn't do any good to dwell.

Nearly a week had passed with Sugarland living under the
shadow of impending social doom. And while Ellis and I did
our best to get away and relax, it felt as if we were picnicking on
top of an active volcano. I could almost feel the rumbles.

"Grape?" he asked as he returned the favor.

I let the sweetness burst over my tongue. I mean, so far
everything had been fine.

We were fine.

Still, I had no doubt Twyla Sue would use the book.

She'd all but said so.

I sighed. At least my sister and I were too young to be shaken down by the late Erma Sue. Ellis, as well.

Not that we had any quarrel with Twyla Sue or her mamma.

Thank goodness.

I'd already suffered the distinction of being Sugarland's social pariah. It had begun when I'd canceled my wedding to Sugarland's favorite son, who also happened to be Ellis's younger brother. It got worse when I started dating Ellis. We grew close on my first ghost hunt and *not* when I was with his brother, although tell that to the biddies who thrived on scandal. Letting the town know I could see ghosts hadn't helped either.

I was still recovering my reputation. Or perhaps I'd forever be known as an odd duck. In either case, the wheels of the Sugarland gossip mill could crush a person, and I wouldn't wish it on my worst enemy.

I took a sip of homemade dandelion wine. I'd bought it at my neighbor's farm stand, and it was the perfect sweet, floral treat for a casual evening.

Ellis had parked his patrol car on the road that edged a wide swath of grass and trees overlooking the river. As we listened to the water cascading over the rocks below, we'd set up a blanket with our charcuterie and various little treats. After a brief inspection of our light dinner, my pet skunk, Lucy, wandered off to chase butterflies.

She was exceptionally cute today in a custom harness my mother made. She'd covered it in green silk and attached yellow and white Lucy-sized glittery butterfly wings. My little girl was the outdoorsy type, and my mother liked to spoil her.

Ellis barely noticed Lucy's evolving fashion. Instead, he

stared out at the reds and golds streaking the darkening horizon, deep in thought.

"We're relaxing, right?" I asked.

"Yes." He sipped his wine. "Sure," he added in a weak attempt to be chipper.

"Look at that," I said, nudging him to notice Lucy, my sweet black and white ball of fluff, who leapt after a fluttering yellow insect, her own wings catching the breeze. She landed without much grace, scattering pinecones and scaring herself for a second in the process.

That earned a snort from my all-too-serious boyfriend.

But it was halfhearted at best.

"You're not relaxing." I cringed. "It's okay. I'm not either. Pretending everything is fine isn't working, is it?"

"No…" He sighed, closing his eyes briefly. "There've been three fights this past week. One at Bob's Bar. Two at the retirement village." He leveled his gaze at me. "Charity Franklin assaulted Merry O'Toole with a Connect Four board while at the same time Merry allegedly attempted to throttle her with a half-knit dog sweater."

Oh my. "That's…unfortunate." Also some tight stitching on Merry's part. "My knitting"—what little I'd tried—"would never hold up to strangulation."

"Verity…" Ellis raised his brows.

"Right." Not the point. "Besides, we're not talking about that tonight."

"Sure," he answered, unconvinced.

It had been his suggestion we get out of town and spend a romantic evening watching the sunset and then lying out on a blanket under the stars. I'd made him stop on the way up the hillside so we could collect wildflowers for the centerpiece of our picnic.

I'd woven a flower necklace for Lucy. Now I was working on

a bracelet for myself as a light breeze scattered the first leaves of fall.

I glanced to Ellis. "As long as we're on the subject, the entire Fall into Reading Book Club at the library is convinced Melody *gave* Twyla Sue the book." As if she'd had a choice. "One lady had the nerve to suggest she should have chased Twyla Sue down and taken it back by force."

Ellis drew a hand through the soft grass. "People are edgy. I've written more tickets this week than I ever have. Whatever Twyla Sue's doing or not doing, she's stirring people up."

"The line is out the door at the hair salon," I said, taking another—medicinal—sip of dandelion wine.

Twyla Sue had the book under glass at Two Sues' House of Beauty. I couldn't decide if it was a savvy business move or a threat. Probably both.

Ellis eyed me as he rolled up a slice of salami around a pickle. "Duranja's had to go over there every day this week to clear the crowd out of the street. Sidewalk traffic only."

"And only paying customers with appointments can get close to the display case," I added. "I hear if you tip well, she'll let you hold it."

Her appointments would be booked out through next year at this rate.

Everyone wanted a peek at Sugarland's most notorious blackmail book.

The head of the library had appealed for its safe return, but the city lawyer had announced this was Twyla Sue's family heirloom, and she had rightful ownership.

Nobody else in Sugarland could think of a plausible reason to keep a daughter from her late mother's things. Or perhaps they didn't dare incur the wrath of Twyla Sue.

The *Sugarland Gazette* did a two-page feature on her and her salon, with glossy color photos for the weekend edition.

"She probably has stuff on Ovis Dupree." He'd been the lead

reporter for as long as I could remember, and I'd never seen him do such a royal puff piece.

"I hear she hasn't had to buy a dinner out all week," Ellis said ominously.

Okay, well… "It could be that's all she wants it for." One could hope at least. "She's got the publicity now, the business. People are talking nice about her mamma…at least to her face."

Ellis held his jaw tight enough to crack walnuts. "Verity…"

I lingered on a sip of sweet wine. "Well, her mamma was downright cruel. There's no use pretending otherwise. But Twyla Sue doesn't need to let the power go to her head. She can be a better person."

"Your problem is you think everyone is as kind natured as you are," Ellis said gently. He slipped his hand into mine. "You've got the biggest burn book in all of Sugarland," he said with a loving squeeze. "You can literally talk to dead people and get secrets all the time."

True. It was how I solved so many mysteries.

Still… "You know, and more importantly all of Sugarland knows, I'd never use that to hurt people."

He eyed me. "Twyla Sue would. She said so onstage for everyone to hear."

I nodded. He was right.

For a moment, I envied my little skunk, whose biggest concern appeared to be the second butterfly that had landed on her tail.

"It's not a matter of if," Ellis said grimly. "More like when. I saw the look in her eyes. That woman is trouble."

"Speaking of which…" Lucy, after a running leap, had inserted herself into the hollow base of a nearby tree trunk, with only her tail sticking out.

I climbed to my feet. A few bees dove in circles nearby. Lucy liked to chase bees as much as she did butterflies and had been stung on the nose before. I bent to scoop her out, but as soon as

I touched her silky fur, she dashed all the way inside the hollow tree.

She'd never learned her lesson. Or more likely, she was too brave for her own good.

"Lucille Desiree Long!" I admonished.

Ellis crouched behind me. "She's fine. There would be more bees if there were actually a nest in there."

"Yes, well, gauzy wings don't fare well against tree bark," I said, going to my knees. I could no longer see her inside the trunk. "I think she climbed up," I said, reaching a hand in, loath to encounter anything but a skunk. And even if I managed to find her back end, I wasn't sure how I was going to get her out.

"I've got her," Ellis said with a grunt.

I sat back on my heels as he walked around from the other side of the tree, my little girl tucked in his arms.

"Thank goodness," I said, hurrying to take her.

He handed her over with a chuckle. "Looks like the trunk is mostly hollow. There was a hole on the other side."

I brushed tree bark out of her fur and off her wings, which were bent at impossible angles. "What's this on her nose?" It was gooey and brown and...

Ellis pulled a Ziploc bag out of his pocket. "Peanut butter mixed with oats."

"That you carry in your pocket," I finished.

He shrugged, not the least bit embarrassed. "I knew I'd be seeing her today."

She had Ellis wrapped around her little paw.

"I like doing things for her. And for you."

I grabbed a belt loop on his jeans and dragged him closer. "I can see why she leapt into your arms."

He'd gotten to me too. And he knew it, judging from his sly smile as I pulled him in for a sweet, tender kiss at sunset.

Maybe we were in for a night to remember after all.

Ping.

Ellis's phone chirped loudly and vibrated against his leg.

He kept kissing me.

Ping.

Ping.

It was his day off.

Ping.

Ping.

I was going to murder whoever wanted to talk to him right now.

Ping.

Ping.

I pulled away. "You'd better get that."

Then we could get back to important things.

Stone-faced, he took the call. "This is Ellis." His expression grew darker as he listened. His jaw clenched. "Right. Hold tight. I'll be there in five minutes."

"Be where?" I demanded.

Pretty much anywhere in Sugarland would take five minutes.

"I'm sorry," he said, stuffing the phone back into his pocket. "There's trouble at Twyla Sue's hair salon."

Well, we knew sooner or later somebody besides her regular customers was going to want to get a look at that book. "What kind of trouble?"

He fished out his keys. "Twyla Sue is dead."

CHAPTER 3

*I*t took me a split second to process it. "Twyla Sue is dead?" I'd known that book meant trouble. I'd just figured Twyla Sue would be the one causing it. "Someone killed her?"

"We don't know that yet," Ellis said, ushering us to the car. I was still holding Lucy. She sensed the tension and tried to climb my shoulder. She liked to have a good vantage point in times of trouble. "Come on," Ellis urged.

We didn't bother to pack the picnic. I had Lucy, and that was all we needed.

"You're not dropping me off at home," I insisted, glad I'd kept my sandals on. "You're taking me with you."

He opened the back door. "I am, because we need to be the first ones there." He helped me get Lucy settled into her carrier. "You and Lucy can wait in the car."

We both knew that wasn't happening.

Well, maybe Lucy would stay put. She'd be asleep on her blanket before we made it down the hill. She'd had a busy evening.

Mine was about to get busier. "How can we be the first ones

to the scene if work is calling you in?" The police station was downtown, only a few blocks from Twyla Sue's salon.

I slid into the passenger seat of his patrol car, and Ellis gave me a long glance as he fired up the engine. "I—" He began backing out. "Let's just drive."

"Ellis?" I prodded.

He clutched the steering wheel as we barreled down the hill.

"That wasn't the police dispatch calling," he said in a rush.

"Who in four counties is calling you about a dead body before calling Sugarland PD?" I asked, my hair whipping my cheeks while I stabbed the button to raise the car window.

Ellis was a good, upstanding guy you could count on, but this was a little much.

"It's complicated," he muttered, eyes trained on the darkening strip of road ahead.

That answer was about as satisfying as a salad for lunch.

"Hold on one holy minute," I said. Ellis was as by-the-book as they came. He got on me all the time for skirting protocol and doing things my own way. And now he was definitely up to something squirrely, not to mention holding something back. "If whoever called you isn't calling the police, let me do it. I'll call the emergency number right now." He was too busy driving like he belonged in the Indy 500.

"I am the police," he reminded me.

He wasn't acting like it. He refused to even look at me, as if he was processing something heavy. Or worse.

We turned the corner onto the highway like the car was on rails, and I had to hold on to the door lest I end up in his lap. Lucy's crate slid halfway across the seat in the back, yet a quick glance showed her snoozing away, one furry foot mashed against the metal crate door.

Oh, to sleep like a skunk, I mused as we raced down the back road on the way to downtown Sugarland. Most places downtown closed at five o'clock, and it was well past six. Sure, a few restaurants would be cheerfully lit amid the streetlamps trimmed with faux leaves and mini pumpkins; however, this street was all shops and daytime businesses.

Ellis slowed a hair, but the street lay deserted. There were no pedestrians, no storefronts open as we passed the Twinkle Toes Dance Studio and the new Knitting with Class. I was on high alert by the time we turned up Third Street toward Two Sues' House of Beauty.

The front of the salon boasted two large picture windows framed in black trim. A sleek silver fixture over the door directed the light sideways rather than down, making the shiny white-painted brick exterior appear almost wet.

The sidewalk stood empty. A pair of ruby red hibiscus in hammered silver pots flanked the glass front door, which was etched with a single rose and the words *Two Sues' House of Beauty* in fancy script.

I glanced to Ellis, who slammed the car into park and braced himself for a split second before flinging open his door. "Stay here."

Bless his heart.

I watched as Ellis strode up to the glass front door and covered his hand with a handkerchief before grabbing the handle. He yanked hard and discovered it was locked.

Well, now he truly needed me.

"There's a door in the back," I called, already half out of the car.

"How do you know?" he asked, frowning as I locked the car behind me and jogged over to join him on the sidewalk.

"I got my hair done here for my engagement photos." That didn't improve his mood, considering I'd been engaged to his younger brother at the time. "Your mother was adamant, only Two Sues' would do." Virginia Wydell was a big fan of Twyla Sue's salon, and she'd insisted I have only the best. I'd been her treasured daughter-in-law-to-be...until I'd canceled the wedding and incurred her wrath, but that was a different story. "There's a back door to the alley that they keep open for the cross breeze. We might as well try it—" I said, ending on a gurgle.

Silver chandeliers in the hair-cutting area blazed bright. Hair products lined the shelves of the glass display case that also served as the reception desk, but that wasn't what caught my attention. Nor was it the small shrine to the deceased Erma Sue, complete with flameless candles flickering amid silk rose petals. A bit creepy, no?

I gasped instead at the familiar blonde figure crouched on the floor next to the counter.

And in an instant, it became crystal clear who had called Ellis, and why he didn't immediately inform police dispatch.

"Ellis Graham Wydell, you're covering for your *mother*?"

Ellis's mother, Virginia Wydell, matriarch of Sugarland, queen of the social set, and pain in my behind, bent over Twyla Sue's red designer bag, tossing out lipstick, a wallet, and several silver pens as she rifled through the dead woman's purse.

Ellis saw it at the same time I did.

"What the hell?" he muttered as Virginia frantically motioned for him to enter the store. When he didn't, she rushed to the door with blood on her hands. There was no mistaking it. She left crimson smears on the glass as she fumbled with the lock.

I had a feeling Twyla Sue was not only deceased, but dead in a very bad way.

"What took you so long?" Virginia demanded, her hair mussed, more blood spattering her buttery yellow suit and skeletal legs. Her haughty demeanor remained disturbingly intact as she clutched the dead woman's purse like a toy we might take away from a toddler, completely ignoring the motionless feet clad in silver stilettos that I could now see behind the counter.

"Is that Twyla Sue?" I choked, rushing for a better look.

The pool of blood lay like a crimson halo beneath the dead body of Twyla Sue, her cream shift dress stained from the gash across her neck. A pair of bloody scissors lay on the floor near the counter.

Ellis let out a small sound I'd never heard him make before. "I've got to call this in," he stated, almost to himself, as he pulled out his police radio.

"Stop." Virginia dropped the purse and held out a bloody hand. "It's not what it looks like!"

"I'm sorry, Mom." He held the receiver to his mouth. "Hello, Chief?"

Virginia stood stunned.

Ellis locked eyes with her as he watched the color drain from her face. "I need to call in a murder."

CHAPTER 4

*V*irginia stared at Ellis as if she couldn't believe her own son had called the police to the scene. Well, *more* police to the scene.

"You tell them this is something you are going to handle on your own," she ordered, daring him to challenge her. "We do not need to make a bigger mess of things."

She'd broken two French-manicured nails, and even more startling—she didn't appear to notice. I'd never seen Virginia's eyes so wide, or her normally flawless platinum hair tangled at her shoulders.

"What were you looking for?" Ellis pressed, his tone not quite official, but still lacking the softness of the dutiful son.

"Nothing," she said, waving away the question like she would a bug. "It isn't here…" Color flushed her cheeks. "The book isn't here. Look," she insisted, "somebody stole it right out of the case."

The sliding door at the back of the display case lay open, the silver key dangling from the lock.

"Twyla Sue could have removed it herself," I pointed out.

At the behest of her killer.

"You keep your mouth shut," Virginia ordered. "Why is she here?" she demanded to her son.

Oh, please. "You're acting like he brought a date to a murder."

Wait. He kind of did.

Ellis didn't answer. He'd moved past her and now crouched over the body, studying it. I didn't know if he was checking out the position of the wound, or how Twyla Sue fell, or whatever else he'd been trained to see as an officer of the law, but Virginia didn't like it one bit.

She let out a frustrated huff that failed to cover a hint of desperation. And I only noticed it because in all my life, I'd never seen her remotely afraid.

Her breath came quick. "The killer stole the book. You have to find him right away." She waved a hand, as if dismissing Ellis's examination of the body, protocol, and anything else that didn't suit her. A lock of hair fell in front of her eyes. "Don't waste time with the rest of the department. It's obvious what happened here." She spread her arms wide, displaying the pale, toned skin of her inner arms. If anything, all it did was highlight the blood smearing her fingers. "She let him in, so it had to be someone she knew!"

Ellis surveyed his mother as he stood, keeping himself between her and the body. "Why are you here?"

She dropped her arms. "Twyla Sue sees me after hours. Saw me," she added quickly with a wild fling of her hand, as if she couldn't quite believe she was making that correction. "I've been her client long enough that she keeps the shop open so I can have my hair done in peace." Her fevered gaze strayed down to the woman lying dead on the floor and locked on her bloody neck. "Oh, my God." She brought a hand up to her mouth, and I swore I saw tears glossing her eyes before she turned away.

Ellis studied her every move. "How'd you get in?"

Virginia waved the hand she'd used to cover her mouth, her

eyes on the floor. "She leaves the back door open for me. My Cadillac is parked in the lot right next to hers."

"You stay here." Ellis pointed to the floor, taking off for the rear of the shop.

"What?" she called after him. "You can't expect me to wait while you do...whatever you do. I need to get home. This is too much. I need a hot bath and a brandy!" she added as if he owed her a favor, a reward, or perhaps a marching band tribute for calling in a murder. Her gaze whipped to me, and she gasped. "He's leaving us here with a body."

I didn't have the heart to point out she'd been here alone with the body and had used the time to go through the woman's purse. In fact, there was no telling how long she'd been alone with Twyla Sue—before or after the beautician's death—before she'd called her son. The shop most likely closed at five o'clock, along with the rest of downtown Sugarland. I checked my watch. It was six thirty. Virginia would have had more than an hour to be alone with Twyla Sue. And she obviously hadn't spent any of that time on her hair.

Before this, I would have thought Virginia Wydell capable of anything short of murder. Now, perhaps I'd have to revise my opinion.

After all, Virginia lived and died by her reputation, and Twyla Sue had come into possession of the burn book. This was the book that had exposed the elementary school principal as a thrill-seeking shoplifter. Better yet, I should say former principal—she'd fled to Phoenix in shame. It outed a "war hero" and VFW officer as a fraud who had served overseas at a resort in Bali instead of the jungles of Vietnam. And people still talked about the day we learned that Jimmy the mailman used to break into houses along his route whenever he wanted to eat lunch or take a nap. It hadn't been all that hard for him. Nobody in Sugarland locked their doors.

Erma Sue had blackmailed them all for years until they ran

out of money or offended her in some other way. Then she used the dirt she had on them.

There was no telling what Erma Sue hadn't revealed yet, especially about a long-term client like Virginia Wydell. And Erma had known Virginia before she'd become the belle of Sugarland. Ellis's mother had grown up poor, although she did her best to make sure nobody remembered that.

And if Twyla Sue had threatened to expose Virginia in any way? Well, some would kill to keep their secrets.

Virginia began to shake.

She was in shock, that much was clear—but was it from what she'd walked in on or what she'd done?

She brought a hand to her chest, smearing blood on her silk top. "Does Ellis think I did this?" Her gaze iced over. "Do *you* think I did this?"

He seemed to believe she'd been up to something, as did I.

"Tell me what happened," I said, careful to keep between her and the body. It wasn't going to be my fault if she destroyed any evidence. And maybe I could help get to the bottom of this.

"Don't play junior detective with me," she sneered. "My friend is *dead*. I've been coming to this salon since I could afford a stylist who knew what to do with a pair of scissors." Her gaze flicked over me and stopped at my simple, straight hair, curled at the ends for my date. "You should try it sometime."

And she was back to her normal self.

We stood in silence for several minutes after that, with me fighting the urge to touch the lovely waves I'd curled into my hair before my date with Ellis, and with Virginia glaring at various parts of my person and clearly finding them insufficiently polished and therefore below par.

At least I was keeping her occupied.

Virginia was typically coiffed and styled within an inch of her life. At the moment, she looked like a guilty, unhinged mess.

The rear door of the shop slammed closed, and Ellis walked

26

into the main part of the salon. He wore gloves and a grim expression. "The burn book isn't in her car or yours. You really need to start locking your Cadillac."

"Why would I do that?" Virginia asked as if he'd suggested she join the Future Farmers of America.

We could at least agree on something. "This is Sugarland." We'd been raised proud that we didn't need to lock up anything. I mean, it wasn't like Jimmy was still delivering the mail.

The sigh was clear in Ellis's eyes. "Yeah, well, there's no sense taking unnecessary risks. People get killed in Sugarland. At least they do these days," he added to himself.

I resented his negativity.

Even if what he said happened to be true. Lately.

A squad car pulled up outside, the lights casting harsh flashes of red and white over the muted interior of the shop. Duranja slid out and began barking orders into his police radio.

Virginia stared in horror. "What did you do?" she demanded. "I told you not to call the law!" she hissed to Ellis as Duranja snapped on a pair of plastic gloves and eased the glass front door open.

Ellis's report must have gone out over the police scanner, because the street was soon illuminated with the headlights of various cars and trucks full of onlookers parking along the curbs on both sides.

It was like we'd announced a carnival, a tractor pull, and a street fight all in one.

I went to the glass for a closer look and saw how the parallel parkers blocked a lumbering city maintenance truck loaded down with enough wooden barricades to hold back a small riot. The truck finally made it to the front of the shop and ground to a stop with a screech and a hiss, blocking in the squad cars.

"You see what a spectacle this is?" Virginia demanded, taking a step back, then two, before she spun and made a beeline for the back door, her heels clicking against the polished wood floor.

"Stop!" I called.

She couldn't just walk out on a murder scene with blood on her hands.

But, as usual, nobody and nothing stood in her way.

I fought the urge to chase down and tackle my almost-past-maybe-future mother-in-law. The police would handle her. And if they didn't? I could take her. Especially from behind.

Even if Virginia did simply discover the body like she'd claimed, she couldn't just wash her hands of this. She couldn't control it or insert her own rule of law like she did to any other person or situation she didn't like.

Ellis crossed his arms. "Mom, they're securing the back door, same as the front," he stated, a little sad. Or maybe a little tired. Probably both.

"You—" She whipped around to give him a parting shot as Junior Officer Collins walked in through the back door and nearly ran into her.

"Is that blood on your hands?" he asked, going for a closer look. "What are you doing walking around loose?"

"I am a witness," she declared, attempting to scoot around him. "I am an upstanding citizen of Sugarland. I am technically your boss!" she added when he refused to let her pass. "You look at county records, young man. I'll bet I pay half the taxes in this town."

"Only the better half?" Collins quipped as Ellis ran a hand over his eyes. "You'll need to come with me, ma'am." Collins took hold of her arm and began escorting her away from the rear exit.

"Let's all calm down," Ellis said, taking charge of his mom, wrapping an arm around her and leading her away from the junior officer, who was now openly scoffing at the queen of

Sugarland. "You've got to respect the law," Ellis said under his breath.

"Like it's ever done you any good," she said, shaking off his grip. But she didn't make another break for it as he led her toward the glass windows at the front of the shop. She shot me her deadliest glare, then gasped as she caught the commotion behind me.

I turned.

There was a bit of glare on the glass, but I could still see that police were making good use of the barricades. They'd blocked the entire street in front of the hair salon and cordoned it off with bright yellow tape, but that didn't keep the crowd from pressing up against the barriers. There had to be at least thirty people gawking by now, with more cars pulling up farther down on both sides of the street.

If Twyla Sue's book had fired up the lookie-loos, no telling what a killing at her shop would do.

I cupped my hands near my eyes and peered out. I spotted Fred Portman and Dave Mosser, who were always some of the first on the scene. Then there was Dominique Riddick and Bart Roan. They'd stayed out all night at the funeral home fire of 1996. And it looked like Earl and Lisa Kent had brought their dinner with them. At least I hoped they didn't normally travel with a full pizza.

Then, as if he'd ordered up a Hollywood entrance, Senior Detective Pete Marshall's cruiser made a shrill *whoop-whoop* noise as he drove slowly forward, easing his way through the crowd.

The two junior officers outside pulled back the barriers enough to let the chief pass into the center of the action. He left his lights blazing and let his barrel chest lead the way as he shoved out of his cruiser like a modern-day Wyatt Earp dismounting a stallion.

Pete Marshall had to be in his early sixties, but he moved like a man twenty years younger. He'd gained some pep in his step since our sleepy town proved to be not so sleepy anymore. Tonight it showed as he strode for the front door of Two Sues' House of Beauty.

Cell phone cameras lit up the night, but he ignored the crowd like he'd gotten used to the paparazzi. Most would say his swagger was warranted. His department had solved every murder the town had seen since he'd taken charge. Well, with my help.

Unfortunately, Marshall didn't see it that way.

And then I realized between the almost complete dark outside and the blazing lights inside, we were in a fishbowl.

The bells at the front door jingled as Duranja opened it for the detective and let it slam shut.

"You," Marshall growled, sauntering past the deputy and catching me with a beady eye. As if he *always* caught me at murder scenes.

He only *mostly* caught me at murder scenes. "I had nothing to do with it this time," I insisted. "I was just on a date."

He shot me a disapproving grunt.

"Evening." He nodded to the two officers. "Whadda we got?"

The jagged furrows in his weather-beaten forehead deepened as Ellis related the events of the evening. They exchanged a few quiet remarks, after which Ellis nodded slowly, and Duranja appeared stricken.

Marshall walked straight past me like I wasn't even there and stopped in front of Virginia. He pulled a pair of silver handcuffs out of his back belt. Then he said, "You need to come along with me."

For a moment, she appeared too shocked to react.

Then all hell broke loose.

The crowd outside—which had doubled—let out a collective roar as Virginia whipped away from the chief. She hauled off and looked about to slap him, or perhaps she was thinking about making another run for it. He swiftly caught her outflung right hand, then her left, and in seconds had cuffed them both behind her back with a firm *snick*.

"You can't do this to me!" She fought the cuffs like a caught trout. "Don't you know who I am? Ellis, do something!" she ordered. When he didn't move, she set her jaw hard. "I'll call your father." Her eyes pleaded at Ellis, then went cold. "I'll call my son the *judge*." She whipped around to glare daggers at Detective Marshall. "I'll have your badge."

Detective Marshall gripped her by the arm. "I advise you to cool it."

Outside, the crowd began climbing the light posts to get an unobstructed look. And wow, they were on the rooftops across the street.

The crew in charge of the barricades let them. I didn't blame them a bit. There was no way to stop everybody, and they wanted to see what was happening as much as the rest of Sugarland did.

Detective Marshall looked to a stone-faced Ellis. "You're off the case." Then to Duranja, "Secure the scene." He grabbed hold of his radio. "Clear the exit," he ordered the officers outside.

"You have the right to remain silent," he said, dragging Virginia toward the door.

"You can't do this!" she shrieked, her knees folding. "Ellis! Stop him!" Marshall hauled her up. Cameras flashed.

"Anything you say can be used against you in a court of law."

Virginia lost a buttery yellow pump. The chief kept going.

The eager crowd spilled up to the edges of the barricades, where crack reporter Ovis Dupree stood at the very front. He'd secured a spot right next to the door, his camera up and ready to take a volley of pictures for the *Sugarland Gazette* as the detective led Virginia outside.

Ovis caught Virginia with her mouth open, dress bloody,

and hair flying every which way to Sunday as she fought going through that door.

A torrent of camera flashes lit up the sky as the senior detective forced her out like a Roman centurion dragging some poor soul to the coliseum floor to feed them to the lions. The miracle of Virginia Wydell arrested and brought low in front of the masses had to be captured for posterity.

In true Virginia fashion, she recovered herself enough to cast a haughty glare at Dave Mosser, and his ilk before the chief planted her firmly in the back seat of his patrol car. And it could have been the gleam of the lights, or the exertion from her struggle, but I thought I saw a fat tear roll down the ice queen's cheek as the door of the squad car slammed shut.

CHAPTER 5

"**You** did the right thing," I said as Ellis navigated the long driveway toward my home.

"I know." His eyes flicked to the spindly peach orchard I'd planted the year before. "I just wish it felt that way."

Ellis had always tried to do right by his family despite the way they'd treated him over the years. He'd been the duty-bound son, the black sheep, the one who had chosen the military and then the police force over the easy money to be made as part of his family's immensely successful law firm. They'd never let him forget the way he didn't fit in. And now I feared they never would.

He adjusted his grip on the wheel. "I mean, my mom reached out to me. She counted on *me* for the first time in her life, and I turned her in."

"You didn't have a choice." A woman had been murdered, slashed to death with a pair of scissors, and Ellis had made a promise to uphold the law. He wasn't a man to compromise his beliefs or justify a cold-blooded killing, no matter the circumstances.

More than that, he was a good person. He felt an obligation

to do the right thing. He felt it down to his bones. It was one of the things I loved about him.

I glanced to him and took in his resolute profile, strong jaw set firm, the moon casting soft light over his cheekbones.

I unlatched my seatbelt and scooted closer. "It'll work out," I promised, placing a hand on his leg.

I just wasn't sure how.

I'd left my porch lights on, and they greeted us with their warm yellow glow as we drew closer to the antebellum home that had been in my family for generations. Too bad life couldn't be as simple as doing the right thing then returning to my comfortable old home.

We'd had a devil of a time leaving Two Sues' House of Beauty. The gawkers had remained in the street even after the chief's cruiser parted the crowd with Virginia in the back seat.

They'd stayed for what was basically a crime scene behind glass, better than any detective show on TV. That, and everybody wanted a word with Ellis, as if he could tell them exactly what had transpired to land the matron of Sugarland in the back of a squad car.

Ellis placed his hand over mine. "I should have kept driving when that reporter stood in front of my car," he ground out, easing down the gravel drive along the side of my house.

"Yes, and then Ovis Dupree would write a story about what it's like to be run down by a police officer."

He didn't need to be in the newspaper along with his mother.

We reached the small parking area in back of the house, and Ellis shut off the engine.

"What's done is done," he said, more to himself than me.

He heaved himself out of the car and took a second to gather himself before gently cracking open his back door. He gazed down at the sleeping skunk curled up in her blanket, tendrils of her floofy tail escaping the door of the cage.

She picked that moment to roll over onto her back with a contented sigh, wantonly displaying her soft, round belly.

"Okay, I needed that," he said with the ghost of a smile.

He lifted Lucy's carrier from the car without waking her. I slipped my hand into his as we strolled past my late grandmother's heirloom rosebushes and up the back porch steps.

There wasn't anything I could say or do to make it better.

I was just thankful he knew Lucy and I were on his side.

When we reached the top of the stairs, Ellis paused.

"Do you want to stay?" I asked, brushing a kiss over his lips.

"I'd better not." He set the carrier down, regret settling over him like a dark cloud. "I just got my mom arrested," he said as if he still couldn't quite believe it. He dug a hand down the back of his collar. "I think I need to make a few phone calls to the family, maybe see if I can make her more comfortable back at the station."

I understood. "You did the best you could."

He nodded.

Perhaps it wasn't the ideal time, but I had to ask. "Do you think she did it?"

He gave me a long look as the question hung between us.

In all the years I'd known her, Virginia had proven herself to be ruthless. She'd shocked me time and again with her cruelty—from her attempt to bankrupt me after I'd called off the wedding to Ellis's brother, to the perverse joy she'd taken in buying my grandmother's necklace at auction so she could wear it in front of me.

She'd never paid the price, never really been called out. Virginia ruled half of Sugarland by fear. The rest admired her seemingly perfect life.

Would she risk it all by killing her hairdresser and then calling Ellis while she was still at the scene?

Ellis still hadn't answered my question. Rather than press-

35

ing, I posed another. "What could be in that burn book that would make Virginia kill?"

He winced like I'd slapped him. "I don't know. My mother doesn't exactly confide in me."

There had been years when she'd barely talked to him.

"I'm sorry," I said quickly, not sure if I was apologizing for asking or for how he'd been forced to grow up.

I had a bad habit of thinking out loud. Virginia could very well be innocent. There was the brutality of Twyla Sue's death to consider. Virginia didn't usually do her own dirty work, and the blackmailer's daughter had died savagely.

Ellis ran a hand through his thick, dark hair. "My mom wouldn't have called me unless she was desperate," he said, holding back his verdict. "And you of all people realize that finding a body doesn't mean you're the killer."

True. "If it did, I'd be guilty of a lot."

That earned a hint of a smile from my boyfriend. "Still, this isn't the time for her to be cagey with me. I need to know everything that happened before we arrived." He shook his head. "I need to talk to her off the record."

That might be tricky. Sure, Detective Marshall had taken him off this case, but he was still an officer of the law. "Are you allowed to do that?"

He dropped his hand. "No." He gave a small shrug. "Morally, ethically, I have to follow the letter of the law. Even when she called me from our picnic. You saw…" He gestured weakly.

"I'm so sorry," I said, wrapping my arms around him.

He let me hold him for a moment. "I know." He rubbed my back absently before dropping a quick kiss onto the top of my head. "I'll call you tomorrow."

"All right." My heart hurt for him as I watched him walk down the stairs and toward an impossible task. "Call me sooner if you need me," I urged.

Virginia Wydell might deserve whatever she had coming to her, but her son didn't.

Lucy rustled in her carrier, and I bent to let her out. "I wish there were something I could do," I said, easing her butterfly wings through the door so she could make her way down to the backyard.

No doubt she'd want to answer nature's call before we turned in for the night.

"Let me at least help you," I said, attempting to remove her wings. But before I could reach the Velcro strap, she shook me off and toddled away from the steps leading out to the yard. "All right. You can leave your pretty wings on," I conceded, closing the carrier, preferring to watch Ellis drive away.

He'd be all right.

I'd see to it personally.

I stared after him so long, I failed to notice trouble brewing on my own porch.

Instead of making her nightly trip down to the yard, Lucy had come to an abrupt halt behind the white-painted porch swing. She stood with her gaze fixed at an empty spot near the side rail.

"Go on down and do your business," I prodded. "Let's not dawdle." It had been a tiring evening, and I was looking forward to changing into my jammies.

Lucy grunted and stamped her feet, all the while staring at...nothing.

"What is it, sweetie?" I asked, joining her. She sometimes liked to chase fireflies, but I didn't see a one. In fact, I saw nothing to capture the skunk's rapt attention.

I felt a prickle of unease. She certainly wasn't taken in by the gangster ghost who haunted my property. Frankie the German was visible to both me and Lucy, oftentimes when we would rather avoid him.

Let's say it plain. Frankie wasn't the best houseguest.

Still, he had the ability to show me the ghostly side of Sugarland, and that came in very handy for solving mysteries.

Nobody ever thinks about hiding their actions from the dead. And you wouldn't believe the history that gets warped and changed over the years. I'd learned the truth behind a lot of events—and people—in town.

Lucy let out a throaty gurgle and scraped her claws against the white-painted wood.

She was definitely seeing something, or some*one*.

"Hello?" I asked, wishing I had Frankie's power to see the other side right then. He had to lend it to me, and he didn't always do it willingly. For one thing, giving me energy tended to drain his. For another, well, the ghost could be downright cantankerous.

Frankie hadn't gotten over the fact that I'd accidentally grounded him onto my property for eternity. No matter how many times I offered my sincere apologies, he thought I should have known better than to dump out a filthy old vase over my rosebushes and rinse the dirt into the soil. I mean, how was I supposed to know the vase from my attic was actually a memorial urn, and that rinsing his ashes into the soil had planted him onto my two acres for good?

I never would have imagined it possible until he went and mustered up the energy to go all scary specter on me. And that was after I'd filled his urn with water and added a nice, fat rose blossom.

My skunk spun in a circle and stomped her feet with a grunt.

Okay, this was weird. Normally Frankie would have shown himself by now, probably complaining about the way Lucy tended to snub him. "Frankie?" I glanced behind us, hoping to spot the ghost. "Are you around?"

He liked to hang out by the apple tree, which was also Lucy's favorite spot. But not a soul stirred out in the yard, at least as far as I could tell.

And while I couldn't see ghosts without the help of my less-than-cooperative, seemingly permanent houseguest, Lucy certainly could.

"What is it, girl?" I asked the skunk, who had begun to weave in a tight figure-eight pattern, her butterfly wings flopping with the churning of her squat little legs. "I certainly hope it's friendly," I said, with a tickle of alarm.

I'd met both kinds of spirits and could do without either tonight.

So of course, Frankie picked that moment to pop his disembodied head out from the plank floor.

I let out a shriek. Lucy squealed and swiped a paw through his head.

The dead gangster rolled his eyes as if *we* were the problem.

"You don't have to sneak up on us like that," I snapped as he slowly rose out of the porch.

Frankie wore the pin-striped suit he'd died in, with cuffed trousers and a fat tie. Although he appeared in black and white, I could see through him. Just barely.

"You said you'd be gone tonight," he sneered, tipping his fedora down to cover the round bullet hole in his forehead. It was the shot that had killed him, and he was sensitive about it.

"I came back," I informed him. "I live here, remember?"

Lucy retreated toward the porch rail. Frankie was about the only individual, living or dead, whom Lucy actively avoided. No matter how nice he acted toward her, Lucy did not like my ghost one bit, which drove him kind of crazy.

But it wasn't her obvious disdain for him that caught my attention. It was the fact that she didn't leave entirely. She'd backed herself into a corner. As a former wild animal, she should know better.

"Babe?" I saw through the ghost to my little skunk, who

appeared to be leaning up against thin air as if needing the security of…someone else?

"What is she seeing?" I squinted as if it would help me determine it. "She's acting like there's someone there."

Frankie had the nerve to raise his brows and try to look all innocent. He hadn't been innocent in a hundred and twenty years.

The gangster straightened his tie. "Maybe she likes the porch rail."

I shot him a droll look.

Lucy sniffed the invisible object next to her. And if that wasn't strange enough, Frankie had come up out from under the porch. He didn't tend to hang out with the dirt and the spiders. If anything, he should have been lounging in the shed Ellis had built for him out by the pond.

I stared him down. "You're not digging tunnels under my house, are you?"

"Why? Is there a bank next door?" he chuffed.

"Searching for buried treasure?" I tried again.

"You wish," he shot back. "Why do you always think I'm up to something?"

Because he usually was.

"Can't I just be hanging out?" Frankie drew his hands out to the sides in an innocent act that wasn't fooling anybody.

"No." Frankie liked to spend his every last eternal second causing trouble.

"I'm going to be twice as mad when I find out on my own," I declared, stalking a wide circle around him to try to catch my skunk. Touching a ghost was bone chilling at best and downright soul rattling at worst. "Luckily for you, I don't have time for your shenanigans tonight. I have enough trouble with Virginia being arrested for murder."

"Go Virginia," Frankie said, ten kinds of impressed.

"Really?" I asked over my shoulder as my skunk danced sideways away from my grasp.

"You always remember your first time," the gangster said fondly.

"Yes, well, Ellis is heartbroken," I said, straightening, giving myself a break and Lucy a chance to calm down and pry herself away from the porch rail. "He turned his mom in."

"You can't trust the fuzz," Frankie said, as if we finally agreed on something. "Now why don't you head on inside and rest?"

"No." My suspicion notched up a rung. Since when did Frankie ever want to give me a break?

"I *really* think you should," he ground out, glancing behind him.

"The catch is, if Virginia did kill Twyla Sue, she would have taken the book and left. But we found her at the scene instead, going through Twyla Sue's purse." At Frankie's raised brows, I explained the events of the night.

Frankie glanced around uncomfortably and dug for a cigarette. "Why are you talking to me about this?" he asked, plucking a silver cigarette case from his inside jacket pocket.

Because Ellis was too focused on his mother to break down the facts with me. Besides… "You're a criminal; you know how they think."

"Okay," he said, tipping a smoke onto his bottom lip, "but blackmail is more of a motivational program than a crime."

That type of thinking was what had gotten him shot in the forehead.

Still, I wanted his input on this, so we'd let it slide. "So now the daughter is dead," I said as he lit up his smoke. "Possibly killed by Virginia. And the book is gone."

He took a drag. "So she's either really bad at murdering or really good at hiding the book," Frankie concluded.

Stars. We hadn't searched the shop. "I'm sure the police are on it," I said, hoping I was right.

"Why don't you take your skunk into the house and think about it tomorrow," he said, directing a fleeting look over his shoulder.

"You know what we need to do," I said, an idea formulating. "We need to see if we can find the ghost of Erma Sue."

"I'd rather not," he said, smoke trailing out of his nose.

"If not her, then someone she knew well. You and I need to learn why she put the book in the time capsule and who might have killed her daughter in order to get hold of it."

He pointed his smoke at me. "Stop and think about it. You and I don't care." He ignored my surprise and took a drag. "It's good for you that Virginia's in jail. She's getting what she deserves, even if it isn't for the right reasons."

"I admit there's a part of me that enjoyed seeing her arrested," I conceded, "and a big part of me that thinks she belongs behind bars." But I had to be practical. "As soon as her lawyers get involved, they're going to start twisting and bending the facts until we won't know what's the truth anymore. And they'll for sure make Ellis look terrible for calling the police on her. We need to learn what happened tonight, or Ellis will never find peace with what he did." Knowing him, it would eat him alive.

Frankie dipped his chin and stared at me. "So you've interrupted my evening—"

"On my porch."

"And now I'm supposed to help your evil, possibly future mother-in-law get out of jail in order to make some cop happy?"

Yes. "You need to do it for me," I stated. "I've given you a home."

"More like a prison," he said, taking a drag.

"I've put up with Friday poker nights."

"You need to stop suggesting we make it a book club," he said, pointing the cigarette at me.

"You've gotten me shot at more than once."

"You need a little fun in your life." He shrugged.

Frankie never, ever did anything the easy way. "I'm not even pressing you on what you're clearly hiding from me right now on this very porch," I pointed out.

"Yeah, but you'll peek as soon as I let you see the ghostly side." I opened my mouth to protest, but he cut me off. "You've done it before."

When he'd tried to open an illegal racetrack in my backyard? Yes. It had drawn half the Union Cavalry, not to mention every outlaw, pioneer, and gangster ghost within a fifty-mile radius. I was still finding ghostly cigar butts on my lawn, and Lucy hadn't taken a dip in the pond since.

"So what are you hiding right now that's so terrible I can't see?" I demanded.

Then I realized Frankie had put himself between me and Lucy. Even stranger, my skunk had tolerated his presence for a whole five minutes. She typically fled when Frankie made an appearance. Instead, she was doing that funny circle-eight again.

"Show me now, or I'm going to call in an exorcist," I snapped. It was one thing to play games with me, but whatever he had going on was affecting my skunk.

He froze for a split second. "You don't know any exorcists," he gruffed, taking a quick drag. But his hand shook. Whatever he had going was important to him.

"I have a phone book." Actually, I didn't. But I had Google.

"I'll make you a deal." He took a drag. "We'll track down this Erma dame *if*"—he held up a finger—"if she's still around and *if* you promise I can keep what I have going on, on your porch."

"So there *is* something on my porch!" I gasped.

No wonder Lucy appeared so intent on checking it out.

"I can't promise until I see it," I said, crossing my arms over my chest.

"I want your word," the ghost countered.

He knew I was good for it. And eager to learn what I could to help Ellis.

But I really, really didn't like to make promises to Frankie sight unseen.

And I'd be willing to bet whatever he had going would last a lot longer than my talk with Erma Sue, if she was even still in Sugarland. Some ghosts moved on immediately. Some stayed for a bit, but I was counting on Erma Sue hanging out for going on thirty-five years.

It was a stretch.

"Deal?" he asked, a little too eager.

I thought of Ellis's face tonight when his mother had been arrested, how he'd felt all the years he'd been an outsider in his own family. How this evening's events would make it worse.

I wasn't just bargaining for a onetime chat with the ghost of a blackmailing gossip. I was bargaining for Ellis's freedom as well. When I looked at it that way, granting Frankie a favor didn't seem so unreasonable.

"We will find Erma Sue or a ghost who can help us," I clarified, "and if we do, you can keep whatever's on the porch." I said it quickly before I could change my mind.

"Forever?" Frankie pressed.

"Forever," I agreed, knowing I'd most likely regret it.

At least I had a pretty good idea where we'd find Erma Sue.

As for the rest? "Show me what I just agreed to," I bid the ghost.

And with a triumphant grin, he did.

CHAPTER 6

rankie's power washed over me like a hot, prickling rain. My head went light, and my limbs numbed as his energy seeped down deep, through muscle and bone. In a million years, I'd never get used to the feeling. Or the sight. The surrounding air shifted like molten glass, waking up my senses to what lay on the other side.

The ghostly version of my porch shimmered in black and white, and my mouth fell open as the back end of a ghostly horse shimmered into view right in the middle of my hanging swing, its tail flicking ghostly flies.

"Frankie!" He'd tied a huge phantom horse to my porch rail. "Move this animal at once." He could tie it to his shed. Or better yet, get it off my property entirely.

"You said I could keep what I have going on, on your porch," Frankie said, with smug satisfaction. "Forever."

I did, didn't I?

I'd figured he'd rigged up a moonshine still in the corner, one the cops would eventually confiscate. Or maybe he'd nailed together a stage for a jazz band and a couple of dancing girls—spirits who would zip out of here when the job was done. I mean, the party couldn't go on forever. Not even Frankie had that kind of stamina. "I didn't know you were talking about a live animal." Well, a dead one. But alive enough.

The horse appeared quite at home in a nest of scattered hay, with a wash bucket filled to the brim with water, a barrel loaded down with enough feed for five horses, and a ball of twine hanging down from a string in the ceiling.

I stared as the immense animal bobbed for the ghostly carrots poking out of the twine.

"Meet Frisky Pete!" Frankie announced, with ta-dah arms.

"A horse?" I countered, still trying to wrap my head around it. I mean, this was a commitment. Of course, Frankie wouldn't think far enough ahead to realize it. "You want to keep a *filly* on my porch forever and ever?"

"Stallion," Frankie corrected.

Knowing the gangster, this was only the beginning. "You are not opening up another racetrack in my backyard," I declared.

The last one had gone over like a lead balloon, with ghostly hooligans on my property day and night—drinking and gambling at best, casing the joint at worst. And that was before we considered the effect on poor Lucy.

Frankie held up a finger. "Frisky Pete is not a run-of-the-mill racetrack horse. He is a champion!" he announced. "A champion I plan to race." He held the ball of twine steady for the horse, who couldn't seem to pluck a carrot to save his life. "But don't get uptight. I'm not racing him on any loser track you could have in your backyard."

Funny. "As I recall, that 'loser track' was *your* grand enterprise."

"Not anymore," Frankie said as if it were ancient history and not something he'd tried last year. "I'm thinking bigger now. Don't you see?" he prodded, plucking a carrot and offering it to Lucy, who sought refuge near the porch rail. She couldn't eat a ghostly carrot anyway. "I'm a hotshot owner now." He fed the carrot to the eager horse. "I'm going to race Frisky Pete with the big dogs. This is my secret training facility."

He gestured to my yard, and now that I was tuned in, I could see large wooden balls littering the grass, glowing gray in the night.

"What are those?" I demanded, pointing at them.

"Horse toys," the gangster snapped, as if I should have known. "For fun. You do know what fun is, right?"

"I do." And this wasn't it.

The gangster had also dredged up a rusted old starting gate, both ghostly and ugly, from who knew where, and sweet heaven... "*That* is a racetrack!" I said, pointing to the circle of dirt he'd dumped all around the pond.

"Training facility," he corrected.

Yeah, well, the joke was on him because I'd said he could keep whatever was on the porch, not the monstrosity he'd created in my yard.

"What did you mean before when you said this is your *secret* training facility?" I cross-examined the gangster. With Frankie, I'd learned to pay attention to the details. "You stole Prickly Pete, didn't you?"

"Frisky Pete," Frankie corrected as if that were the issue.

"You stole him, and you're hiding him in plain sight on my porch until his owners show up and start a gang war." This was it: the one big, dumb thing he was going to do that would ruin my family land. Because once you attracted ghosts to a property, they could be darned near impossible to get rid of. And try stopping an eternal gang war.

Lucy would never sleep again, and it could ultimately drive me bonkers as well since too many ghosts in one place can make it unlivable, even for people who aren't tuned in.

"Like I would start a gang war," Frankie balked, probably out of habit, because a split second later, he tilted his head. "Okay, I would. We haven't had a good one in years. But in this case, I bought this stunning animal outright in a trade for Len the Hammer's car. That I stole," he clarified.

"So now Len the Hammer is going to show up with his friends. And start a war."

"Len started this, not me," Frankie shot back. "I only stole Len's car because he cheated me at poker. But look what I got for it—a true winner!" he said, stroking the horse, who ignored Frankie and kept trying for another carrot. "Frisky Pete took first in 1932 at the Tennessee Timbers at Overtown Downs."

"Sure. He's a lovely animal." In truth, I knew nothing about horses. At least this one appeared happy enough. "Still, you can't keep a horse on my porch."

Frankie appeared as shocked as if I'd told him Lucy had to move out. "You said I could keep him here. Forever!"

"I did, but we can find some place better," I determined, taking a step toward the nickering animal. "He belongs in a ghostly barn." Perhaps one on the other side of town.

My foot squished in something foul. A bone-jolting chill ran up my leg, and I looked down to see I'd stepped in ghostly horse poo.

"He likes your porch," Frankie countered, stroking the animal, who began scratching his hooves against my heirloom wood. "And what's it to you?"

"Well, for one thing, it smells like a stable out here, and now I do, too." Shivering, I scraped my strappy sandal over the floor, trying to get the manure off.

"That's the smell of money," Frankie said with relish. "And you're the one who asked to be tuned in."

Sure, I would only get the full effect when I was able to see the ghostly side, but that was often enough lately. Besides, I'd meant what I'd said about not attracting more ghosts, much less agreeing to another permanent one.

I mean, yes, it had been my idea to place Frankie's wooden shed by my pristine pond. He deserved to feel at home. And I didn't even mind his gangster friends popping by now and again. He deserved to have a social life. I especially liked his girl-friend, Molly. She was the one who lit him up, the reason he'd had energy to spare these past several months.

But this horse on my porch? It was a step too far. This was encroaching on my home. I liked my actual house ghost-free. I mean, I'd agreed to a favor, but this was too much.

And per usual, Frankie hadn't thought it through. "So what happens when Len the Hammer chases you down for his car and finds a horse instead?"

Frankie considered the question. "I'll tell him—truthfully— that I don't have his car. And then I will hope somebody else stole his hammer because I've seen what he can do with it, and it's not pretty."

"That's a terrible plan." I winced.

Even Frankie had to see it.

"Lucy's happy," he pointed out.

My skunk was currently dancing a figure eight around the horse's legs. I'd have been terrified if the horse could actually kick her. A mere touch would be uncomfortable for both of them, but my skunk appeared to consider it a game.

"Look," Frankie prodded, as if he were the practical one, "Len's car will go back to him eventually anyway. It always does." Ghosts could only permanently keep what they'd died with.

"Well, in that case, won't Frisky Pete go back to his owner as well?"

"Of course not," Frankie said as if I'd suggested something barbaric. "Ghost animals have free will. They own their souls, not somebody else." He ran a hand down Pete's flank. "Frisky Pete loves me. He'd never leave."

"You've had him for a day. Unless…" No. I mean, how long could he hide a horse?

"A day is all it takes when the chemistry is right," Frankie lectured, stroking the animal. "Besides, Frisky Pete's former owner went to the light, so he doesn't have anybody else," Frankie said. He released a contented sigh as the horse nosed his shoulder. "He needs me."

That was up for debate. I hated to point out the obvious, but this was too ridiculous to let pass. "You still need to worry about Len showing up."

"Only *if* he finds out it was me who stole his car," Frankie said. "And if he asks where I got this magnificent animal, we'll tell him Frisky Pete is your family horse that you keep on the porch."

"You want to tell him I keep a dead horse on my porch," I said, my tone level.

"Ghost horse," Frankie corrected, shooting me the hairy eyeball. "Don't be difficult." He turned back to Frisky Pete. "Just look at that mane," he said, stroking the horse. "Feel it. We'll watch it fly as he leaves all the other horses to eat his dust."

"I'm not going to pet him," I informed the ghost. It always hurt to touch the dead, and I wasn't going to get attached to an animal that was definitely not staying. "In fact, I'm going inside. Come with me, Lucy."

But she refused to move. Her fascination with the ghost horse kept her riveted to the porch.

"Time to pull out the big guns," I murmured to myself, cracking open the door to the kitchen.

Frankie could pull his schemes. Lucy could refuse to cooperate. But I had my own secret weapon in the kitchen. I'd baked an apple cinnamon skunk crumble this afternoon, in anticipation of tonight's picnic. When Ellis had mentioned he was bringing fresh fruit for Lucy, I'd left the baked goods at home. Time to put it to good use.

I ducked inside.

"Lucy!" I called, showing her the pan of cinnamon skunk crumble from the doorway.

My skunk swooned over homemade treats, and she didn't know I'd snuck in a helping of Vita-Skunk nutrition formula. She raced for me so fast I feared she'd storm straight through one of the ghosts.

"Lucy's a natural!" Frankie crowed, admiring her speed as she claimed the taste I held down for her.

"This way," I cooed, luring her inside like a Greek siren and slamming the door on the horse and the gangster.

Too bad I could still smell the 1932 champion. Much to my dismay, the scent of horse hide and manure did not blend well with the smell of cinnamon and apples.

Lucy didn't seem to mind. Her nails clicked on the wood floor as she danced at my feet.

I should have gone back outside and made Frankie take back his power, but truly, I'd had enough of that ghost for the moment. And I'd like to keep an eye on the horse.

I made Lucy a plate, and she ate it with gusto. She'd worked up quite an appetite since the picnic.

Lucky girl.

My appetite was shot. While she finished her treat, I made a cup of tea with honey to settle my nerves.

Sighing, I leaned up against the kitchen island to take a sip. I didn't know what I was more rattled about—the dead body we'd discovered or the horse on my porch. Both came as unexpected surprises, and I wasn't sure what to do with either.

So I settled for taking care of what I could.

I put Lucy on a leash and led her out front to do her business.

"Sometimes, we can only take care of the basics," I told her as we eased out the door.

She'd begged for more skunk crumble, but eating more before bed would only keep her up. My skunk was nocturnal as it was. No sense adding an overload of sweets and inviting a sugar rush.

ANGIE FOX

The night was infinitely more peaceful out in front of the house. My land stretched on both sides of the long drive, and the peach orchard I'd planted last year appeared spindly in the moonlight.

I let Lucy wander on her leash to enjoy the breeze as I looked up at the blanket of stars. We'd figure out what to do about the horse. And the murder. I'd set this all right…eventually.

And if I couldn't?

Well, there was no sense thinking that way. It wasn't like I had a choice.

My cell phone rang, and a quick check showed it was Ellis.

Thank goodness.

"How are you?" I asked, almost dropping the phone as my skunk yanked hard on her leash and tangled it around the nearest tree trunk. "Whoops Lucy's trying to strangle herself on a peach tree."

Ellis hesitated. "Why are you walking her out front with a leash?"

Because I didn't want her wandering anywhere near the ghost horse on my back porch, but I also didn't want to add to Ellis's worries. "I'm just getting her some practice." Lucy wasn't the greatest with a leash. "How's your mom doing?" Jail had to be tough, especially on a woman like Virginia.

"She's out already," he said, as if he couldn't quite believe it.

I almost dropped the leash. "Did your brother let her go?" Ellis's older brother was Leland Wydell IV, the most malleable judge in three counties, but I'd figured he had his limits.

Apparently not.

Lucy tugged me deeper into the trees.

"Leland recused himself," Ellis said quickly. "The judge is a friend of my dad's. He didn't even set bail."

"Wow," I said, wishing it had come as a surprise. "Talk about clout." Even murder couldn't stick to Virginia Wydell.

"Mom has a pretty solid alibi," Ellis interjected, bursting my growing bubble of outrage. "She was chairing the Sugarland Heritage Society harvest tea in front of about fifty people until shortly before she called me. In fact, the last photograph of her was taken twenty minutes before her call." He hedged. "It's not a big window to kill someone."

Yes, but it took only about five minutes to get anywhere in Sugarland. Ten tops. How long could it take to slash a person with scissors?

"Have they determined the time of death?" I asked, trying to cut Lucy some slack as she inspected a tuft of grass.

"The coroner is working on it," Ellis said crisply.

Yet they'd already let Virginia go.

I stared up at the moon. She probably wasn't a flight risk—she loved Sugarland as much as I did. But unlike me, she had a passport, a safe full of cash, and membership in a private jet club.

Not to mention she'd already tried to bolt from the hair salon.

"Verity, I hate to ask," Ellis hedged. "I know my mom hasn't exactly been good to you."

"Understatement of the year," I answered, feeling my shoulders tighten. It was a good thing I loved him. "You want me to look at the ghostly side."

He seemed relieved I'd said it first. "For me, not for her."

It was the only way I'd do it.

"I've already updated Frankie, and we're going to try to talk to Erma Sue," I explained. "I figure it's the next logical step."

"It's a good place to start," he agreed.

"I'm hoping she was watching over Twyla Sue and saw what happened to her, or perhaps she can tell us who Twyla Sue interacted with in the days prior to her murder."

It took months, sometimes years, for a person to return as a ghost, if they ever came back at all. But I had town lore in my

53

favor. Rumor had it that Erma Sue haunted her old salon after she'd died. In the months after her passing, more than one patron reported the beauty chairs felt prickly. And they'd lost a stylist after she swore something inside her drawer kept nipping at her fingers.

Twyla Sue had remodeled the place, and that seemed to help. Still, even if Erma Sue didn't see what had happened to her daughter on the night of the murder, she might know who would most likely kill to get their hands on that book.

There were a lot of possibilities, I decided as I stared up at the stars, and they all began with Erma Sue.

"Verity," Ellis said, his voice trailing off. "I know I can always count on you, but...thank you."

"I know." He didn't need to thank me. "I'd do anything for you." Not for Virginia, but for him.

Lucy began jumping to try to catch a firefly. I hoped she'd done her business first. I'd been too busy focusing on Ellis to pay her proper mind.

"I haven't ever seen Erma Sue around town, but I've heard rumors among the living that she haunts the salon." She'd started the business, and it had been her pride and joy.

"I don't think I can get you in there," Ellis said. "I'm off the case."

And it was a crime scene. Although that hadn't always stopped me before.

"I took the liberty of finding Erma Sue's last known address," Ellis said, "It's 7 Battery Hill. She lived there thirty-six years."

That was one of the houses in the old, fancy neighborhood just north of downtown. "How did a hairdresser make enough to own one of the big old mansions?" I asked aloud, before realizing. "Oh, wait. Blackmail."

"She died in the house as well," Ellis continued, "in the upstairs master bath."

Ghosts liked to haunt their death spots. It was worth checking out.

"After Erma Sue died, her sister lived there for a couple of years. She was a legend with the police department because she was always reporting strange noises. My old boss believed her, said the place was haunted to the gills."

"That's great news," I told him.

"Yeah, the best," he said with markedly less enthusiasm.

"Did Twyla Sue ever live there?" I asked, curious about the haunting.

"She did until she graduated high school. But once she started working full-time in her mom's shop, she moved out."

"Maybe she was avoiding the ghost," I reasoned.

"Let me go with you," Ellis said quickly. "Erma Sue was ruthless. Her spirit could be dangerous."

"I'd like that," I told him.

"We'll go tomorrow," he vowed. "I'll set it up."

"Tomorrow," I agreed, squaring my shoulders at the thought of encountering the legendary Erma Sue.

The truth was Ellis couldn't protect me from the other side. Not when I was tuned in and he wasn't. But I appreciated the support. After all, there was still a living killer on the loose.

I hung up with Ellis and looked down at my frolicking skunk. "Looks like we have a busy day ahead of us tomorrow."

CHAPTER 7

*M*y day began earlier than I'd planned.

It seemed a horse on the porch made a certain skunk in the house restless. Sure, Lucy was nocturnal. Most of the time I could sleep through her regular nighttime antics. It wasn't unusual to wake up with her toys in my bed or to sleepily dodge them on the stairs leading down to the first floor on my way to breakfast. I could get both of us fed with my eyes barely cracked open.

But when a skunky screech pierced the air shortly after dawn, it jolted me awake.

"Lucy?" I called, instantly regretting the decision to move my futon upstairs to my grandmother's old bedroom.

Downstairs, the windows rattled, and Lucy let out a strained cry.

I threw back the covers. She didn't sound good. And she definitely wasn't playing.

"I'm coming, sweetie!" I called, sending a toy banana flying as I scooted out of bed and hurried for the stairs.

This was it. Len the Hammer must have discovered it was Frankie who nipped his car, and he was out for revenge. With a dozen of his most murderous friends. And of course I still had Frankie's power when I'd zipped inside the house last night. I'd wanted to keep an ear out for him and whatever else he might try to pull. Then I'd forgotten about it entirely.

I was probably lucky I hadn't woken up with a ghostly horse head in my bed.

"Lucy, come here," I ordered, despite the odds. When had Lucy ever come on command?

I reached the foyer, gray in the early morning light. Grabbing the newel post, I made a sharp turn toward the back of the house.

Leave it to Frankie to start a gang war on my porch. He didn't care about the sanctity of my home or my peace of mind.

He didn't worry about my skunk.

Grunts echoed from the kitchen, followed by a squeal and a stomp.

Lucy wasn't afraid enough of ghosts. Sure, she couldn't stand Frankie—maybe my skunk was smarter than me—but it would be just like her to try to defend our home from the mob.

I'd never forgive myself if something happened to her.

"I've got you, baby!" I called, charging down the hall. My house was usually very safe and free of ghosts—save for the one in my shed—so it was easy to forget when I was tuned in to the ghostly side. It used to happen less often, but now that Frankie was with Molly, he had enough power to keep me plugged in twenty-four seven.

I skidded into the kitchen to find Lucy hunched on the sill of the vertical window that looked out onto the back porch. I watched in horror as she let out a high-pitched cry and flung herself against the glass.

"Baby!" I ran for her as she fell back and landed on the hardwood.

Before I could rescue her, she rolled and popped back up. She gave a skunky snurfle before stomping her back feet and racing toward the windowsill once more like a kid at an amusement park.

A giant horse's nose snorted against the glass on the other side, creating a wet snot mark that the ghostly animal then proceeded to trail all the way up the glass.

I reached for my skunk, who dodged out of my way and hopped back up onto the windowsill. She ran her nose over the glass and grunted happily.

Frisky Pete rubbed his head against the glass, rattling the window.

Lucy stomped her feet and swished her tail with abandon.

I whooshed out a breath and planted a hand on my hip. "You're playing?" I asked as Frisky Pete slopped his giant horse tongue against the glass, displaying a mouth full of teeth.

Lucy leapt against the window, catching it with her back feet instead of her head, then pushing off and sticking the landing on the floor with a roll and a snort and a satisfied foot stomp.

"You woke me up," I informed the unapologetic skunk. She didn't even have the courtesy to look guilty. Instead, she trotted over to the door and waited for me to open it. "And I'm rewarding you," I added, letting her out into the yard to do her morning business.

Frisky Pete huffed against the window and gave it another lick.

I'd never be able to wipe the smudges off the ghostly side.

And Frankie wouldn't do it right, assuming I could convince him to do it at all.

"You're a bad influence," I informed him, but he wasn't listening. He'd ambled after Lucy, who'd waddled down the steps.

The horse didn't make it far, since he was tied to my porch. He'd have to settle for his overfilled feed bowl and his hay...and a brand-new, obnoxiously large squishy ball.

Frankie had been busy overnight.

But Frisky Pete's favorite toy appeared to be Lucy, who finished in the yard faster than I'd ever seen and immediately returned to her obnoxious friend, who nosed his new ball in her direction.

"Come on inside," I coaxed, opening the door for her. "I've got some more apple cinnamon skunk crumble. As much as you want," I added, despite the fact it would ruin her diet for the day.

Lucy darted between the horse's legs and stayed there, perched on her back legs, completely enamored with her new partner in crime. He tossed his head back and let out a happy nicker.

"The world's gone crazy," I declared to no one in particular as I closed the door and went to put the coffee on.

It was too early to call Ellis, so I did two loads of laundry and cleaned the kitchen until it sparkled. Then I got myself fixed up and ready for the day ahead.

I was just about to try my boyfriend when he called me at nearly nine o'clock.

"I hope I didn't wake you," he said as I drew a hand down the long avocado green phone cord in my kitchen.

Oh, that ship had sailed. "You're not a skunk in love with a horse," I remarked without thinking.

Ellis paused. "Say that again?"

"Never mind."

Hopefully working to find Erma Sue's spirit would be easier than dealing with the party on my porch.

Ellis cleared his throat. "Listen, I'm about to get called into a briefing, but I wanted to let you know I won't be able to get out and look for Erma Sue until later on tonight."

"Seriously?" I asked, letting it slip before I remembered my manners. "I mean—"

"I understand," he said, sweet as he was. Ellis of all people knew the urgency. "We've got some smugglers working Route

41, and the state highway patrol is asking us to check a few things out for them. And since I'm not officially on the Two Sues' murder case..."

"Of course." I twirled the phone cord harder in my hand. I mean, he had a job, and it was important. "I might go drive past Erma Sue's house in the meantime, just to get the lay of the land."

"Verity." His tone went dark. "I looked into the place. It's empty and up for sale. No one is supposed to be in there. Don't forget we're dealing with a killer."

"You weren't making your point at all until you mentioned the killer," I said in all practicality. Ellis and I had had issues in the past with me thinking it was a dandy idea to slip into vacant houses. I saw it as convenient. He viewed it as illegal.

Technically, he was right. And Duranja had threatened to arrest me the next time he caught me ghost hunting where I shouldn't be. Therefore, I'd vowed to myself to only break in when absolutely necessary.

"I promise I won't go in there alone," I conceded. Maybe Erma Sue liked to hang out on the front steps or in the garden.

"Tell me you mean that," he cautioned as if he could hear the wheels turning in my head.

He'd gotten to know me too well.

"You have my word," I assured him. We both knew I'd never go back on it.

Still, there was no reason I couldn't have a quick look-see at the property where Erma Sue had lived and died. The house might be empty, but it was in a historic neighborhood on a public street. And I'd have Frankie with me.

While we were at it, we could take a drive past Two Sues' House of Beauty. I'd like to see if anything had changed since the night before. Plus, if Frankie was on a ghost hunt with me, he wouldn't have time to make that horse any cozier.

Because it wasn't staying.

I'd most likely find my reluctant houseguest in his shed, and after the morning I'd had, he owed me a trip into town. I fetched my purse and keys and opened the back door to the sight of Frankie cantering Frisky Pete around my pond with Lucy the skunk scampering happily behind.

"Look at his gait!" Frankie hollered, jogging along next to him. The gangster held his hat on his head with one hand while clutching Frisky Pete's rope lead with the other.

The horse took advantage of his distraction and stopped cold. Frankie kept trotting until the taut lead snapped him back.

"Good horse," he said, stumbling a bit as he recovered. Frisky Pete began munching on the sweet, tall grass growing along the edge of the pond. Frankie gave him a rub on the neck. "A champion knows when to refuel."

"Right," I said, navigating around the presents Frisky Pete had left on my porch. "Listen, while he's refueling, let's go take a look at the house where Erma Sue died."

I already had the gangster's power, but I also wanted his opinion. Frankie had a century's worth of firsthand knowledge of the ghostly plane, and he'd helped me out of close calls more than once.

"Stay," Frankie ordered the horse, who showed no signs of moving. "I suppose I can spare part of the day," said the ghost, who had nothing but time. "But first, Frisky Pete needs his bath and a brush. Then while he finishes drying, I need to muck out his stall."

"Oh, for Pete's sake." I tossed my hands up.

"Exactly," Frankie said, without a trace of guile.

Not what I'd meant.

That would take hours. Worse, Frankie had caught me in my sweet spot because even if Frisky Pete was a ghost, he was still an animal that needed love and care.

"Fine," I snapped, wishing I could argue.

Whatever angle Frankie was working, I didn't like it. And he always had an angle.

Yet, I was glad the horse was getting attention.

"Can't Frisky Pete live at the Heritage Society with Molly?" I suggested. From what I remembered, they had a cow and at least a few horses. "I'm sure she and her friends wouldn't mind."

Frankie looked at me like I'd asked him to leave Frisky Pete out in traffic. "Molly and the girls have enough animals to take care of." He stroked the horse's neck. "So many that Frisky Pete might not be special."

"Oh, brother."

Frankie tied the horse to a long training rope so the horse could wander. I wondered what else he'd installed on my property that I hadn't noticed yet.

Lucy stayed outside, basking in the sun with the horse while I used my frustration as fuel to clean the entire house. I might not have complete control over my yard, but my utensil drawer had never been straighter or more crumb-free. The lint catcher in my dryer looked new. And my bathroom could have doubled as a surgical ward.

Finally, at half past noon, I had what I wanted—a ghost in my car and a trip to see the house at 7 Battery Hill. Even better, my skunk had worn herself out trying to impress Frisky Pete and now lay fast asleep under her favorite apple tree.

Sometimes it's the little things.

"You did good." I glanced over at the ghost in my passenger seat. Frankie wasn't always the most responsible guy, but I had to admit, he'd taken excellent care of that horse.

Not that we were keeping it.

The gangster chuffed and wrinkled his nose at my choice of local radio stations. "The news?"

"Shh…" I made the turn onto the highway that led into town.

"I don't want to listen to the news unless I'm in it," the gangster said primly.

"It's the bottom of the hour, and I want the latest scoop," I told him as the local public radio announcer ran down a list of things I already knew about last night's murder before coming around to the fact that the police had searched the beauty parlor for the missing burn book and come up empty.

Darn it.

"The police are stuck," Frankie concluded. "You're lucky you have me."

"We just need to figure out who would want to steal the burn book," I said to Frankie as we headed north on Main toward downtown.

"Pretty much everybody," he said, loosening his tie. "Heck, I'd steal it if I could."

I slowed while the car ahead of me pulled aside to park. "You just like stealing."

"True," he said as if I'd just flattered him. "I mean, yeah, for sure ask Erma Sue what she saw or heard, but also get her to tell you the juiciest tidbit in the book."

"And who it implicates," I said, finishing his thought. "It would at least give us some place to start looking."

"*Us* meaning *you*." Frankie stretched a hand out through the glass window of the passenger seat to catch a breeze as I turned left toward Third Street. "I only agreed to help you connect with Erma Sue. Then I'm done. I have a horse to race."

I'd worry about that later after I navigated the traffic jam outside Two Sues' House of Beauty.

Parked cars lined the street up and down like they did... hardly ever.

"Keep an eye out for Erma Sue," I said, slowing to match the crawl of the white Nissan ahead of me.

"What does she look like?" Frankie asked, scanning the crowd.

"Skinny blonde," I said, slowing for a woman pulling a red wagon loaded down with snacks and a cooler.

"That narrows it down," the gangster grumbled.

"I'll pull a picture up on my phone once I get a second," I promised, stopping to let a family of four cross in front of me.

"What is this? A parade?" Frankie snorted.

Might as well be.

"Up ahead is where Erma Sue worked," I said, glancing at him. "Also where her daughter died last night. With any luck, we'll see Erma Sue there." Ideally outside next to a potted hibiscus.

Although I hadn't promised Ellis that I wouldn't enter the beauty shop.

The only trouble was that it was a crime scene and not at all deserted. Yellow police tape blocked the doors. The inside appeared dark and abandoned, but that didn't matter to the crowd of two dozen or so gathered on the sidewalk.

A few remaining barricades blocked the good citizens of Sugarland from spilling into the street, and I spied Duranja manning the door. He spotted me in a flash, as if he had some kind of acute anti-Verity radar. When he locked in on me, he frowned.

As if I were the problem.

I gave him a little wave, which he ignored.

Hey, I tried.

Despite the glacially slow speed of traffic, I couldn't see much in the darkened shop. The people standing in front of the windows didn't help either.

"Want to pop inside?" I asked the ghost. "I can meet you around the corner."

He looked at me like I'd asked him to jump into a pit of snakes. "I don't like haunted places any more than you do. And I'm not wandering into some girlie beauty parlor by myself. For all we know, we're wasting our time."

"Fine." I stopped cold, tossing an apologetic wave to the soccer mom in the red Toyota behind me. My 1978 avocado green Cadillac was as huge as it was old. I'd inherited it from my grandmother and affectionately referred to it as the land yacht. Unfortunately for the traffic situation in Sugarland, nothing was getting around this monster. I did a quick search on my phone and found a newspaper picture of Erma Sue.

"That's her," I said, tilting the phone toward my ghost. "Now take a look inside the shop," I added, leaning back so he could get a better view. Frankie could sometimes locate spiritual signatures that I couldn't see even in the best of conditions. "Is Erma Sue inside?"

If she was, I had a fun conversation with Duranja in my future.

Would you mind me slipping into your crime scene for a quick chat...

Duranja gritted his jaw and waved me on. Fancy that. It was my turn to ignore him.

Hmm...maybe this was why we didn't get along.

A quick glance in the rearview mirror showed the woman in the red Toyota busy rubbernecking right along with us. There was nobody behind her.

I adjusted my bag on the seat next to me, listening to Frankie's urn clank against the flashlight I carried with me. You never knew when you'd need one.

Frankie's eyes squinted as he observed what only he could sense inside the darkened shop. "Give me a minute..."

Bing!

A text popped up on my phone.

Oh, yay. It was from Duranja.

MOVE.

"You're blocking me," Frankie said, peering into the darkness.

I leaned back in my seat and texted a reply to mister bossy himself.

Sorry. I do not text and drive.

I shouldn't tease him, but it was kind of fun a second later when he turned red.

"Okay, yeah. I can't locate any souls inside," Frankie murmured, his gaze still trained on the shop.

Interesting. "Not even live police officers?" I asked as Duranja stood spread-legged and stiff-kneed, angry texting as if his life depended on it. I'd assumed he'd come with a few others. "You'd think they had work to do in there."

"Nobody," Frankie said, sitting back. "I can smell the fuzz a mile away. Trust me."

I did. At least with this.

Meanwhile Duranja had shoved his phone into his pocket and had begun stalking toward my car.

"This will be fun," I said to myself. Trouble was, we still had one more thing to do, and I wasn't eager to have this conversation in front of nosy, judgy Duranja.

I braced a hand on the back of the bench seat and turned to my ghost. "Last night, I didn't have your power, so I couldn't get an otherworldly look at the spot where Twyla Sue died." Fresh death left behind soul traces, which were remnants of the deceased's energy that lingered for a short time when the person departed. In the past, we'd been able to tell a lot from those markers. "I don't see any soul traces now, even with your power."

Then again, I couldn't exactly get a good view of the spot behind the counter.

"They're faint," Frankie said, closing his eyes, feeling his way as Duranja rounded the barricade.

I really wished I could pull away.

"Red streaks mean anger," Frankie murmured.

Yeah, then Duranja was going to have red streaks coming out of his ears soon.

"Violence," the ghost continued.

"I could figure that from the scissors," I said, a little saltier than usual because Duranja was almost upon us. "Anything else?" I asked, starting up the car just as my phone rang.

I wouldn't have answered for anybody except Ellis.

And it was Ellis.

"Hey, sweetie!" I killed the engine.

Technically I wasn't being rude, considering a pair of older ladies had skirted the barricade to talk to the woman in the red Toyota. And there was still nobody behind her.

"Duranja says you're parked in the street out front of the beauty shop," Ellis drawled.

The officer's angry scowl and beady-eyed glare now filled my window.

"Duranja is a tattletale." I rolled it down a crack. "I was just getting ready to leave, but now I'm on my cell phone."

Duranja barked out something or other, but I'd rolled my window up.

"Is Erma Sue inside the shop?" Ellis asked, guessing my intent.

"No, and I heard the police didn't find her book last night."

"We're going with the assumption that the killer has it." Ellis sighed as Duranja began knocking on my window. "Which will hopefully clear my mom."

If it didn't get her arrested again.

"Frankie's looking at the soul traces now." Duranja's knocking grew more insistent.

Heavens.

"Why did he tell you to call me if he didn't want me talking to you?" I asked Ellis. Loudly, so his friend could hear.

Ellis cleared his throat. "You don't have to get along with Duranja—" he began.

"Good," I said, staring Duranja down, "because every time I discover a murder, he assumes I did it."

"To be fair—"

"Because he thinks Frankie isn't real and I'm a fake and that I corrupted you with my womanly wiles, and—"

"You're welcome to corrupt me any time you want," Ellis broke in.

The grin in his voice almost made me smile too. I dug in the glove box for my hands-free headset and noticed Frankie deep in thought.

"Just remember—Duranja is dating your sister," Ellis coaxed as I yanked out the tangle of wires and plugged it in.

"I'm trying to forget." I adjusted my hands-free headset as a delivery truck pulled up behind the Toyota. "Okay. I really do have to go."

I started the engine back up, and with a wave to Duranja, we were on our way.

"That was kind of fun," I admitted to Frankie. When he didn't respond, I glanced over to find him sitting with his shoulders stiff, arms folded over his chest. "What is it, Frank?" Oh, shoot. "Did I pull away too soon?"

I shouldn't have let Duranja distract me like that.

The gangster cocked his head to the side. "You're going to think I'm nuts."

I already thought that.

"Tell me what you found," I said, keeping an eye on the road as we made our way north through downtown.

"What did Frankie find?" Ellis asked in my ear.

I'd forgotten Ellis was on the phone for a second.

"Oh, wait," Ellis continued. Voices erupted from the police radio in his squad car. "I've got to go."

"Be safe," I said before we hung up.

"You too," he warned.

I'd try. Truth be told, I didn't always like it when Frankie grew so serious. "Tell me," I prodded.

Frankie drew a hand over his chin. "Inside that beauty shop, there's that display case."

"Yes, I saw Twyla Sue's body behind it," I confirmed.

68

"In the case," Frankie said, waving me off, "there's the shelf with the candles. I'm assuming that's where she kept this book you keep talking about."

"Yes." I pulled over in front of Cool Beans Coffee. "How did you know?"

He turned to face me. "There were faint traces of energy under that place, too. You'd never be able to see them. And they weren't connected to the spot where you found the dead lady on the floor." He drew a hand through his hair, knocking off his hat and not noticing. "But somebody loved that book with their heart and soul."

"Twyla Sue?" I wondered. "I don't think she loved it so much as she loved her mother. And maybe she wanted to use it." I thought for a moment. "And how can an object have any kind of soul trace?"

"It shouldn't," Frankie said, distinctly uncomfortable.

A part of me hurt thinking about it. Even if Twyla Sue had been a potential blackmailer, she didn't deserve to die over a book.

"Let's see if we can find her mom," I said, starting the car up again.

We didn't have to go far. Erma Sue's old neighborhood stood just north of downtown.

"You're getting a lot of mileage out of me today," Frankie grumbled as if he'd just discovered how helpful he'd been and resented it.

"A deal's a deal," I reminded him.

I let him mutter to himself while we drove past a pair of snarling lion statues a few blocks north of downtown. The gates were new, at least according to local standards. They'd been erected in 1924 to mark the entrance to one of the town's historic neighborhoods. Each lion stood atop a thick limestone base done in art deco style, with pink marble accents and round bronze lights dripping green patina.

Mature trees lined the street, and beyond them stood large homes, most constructed at the turn of the last century. They were solidly built and sat far back from the street, behind stretches of grass and artfully placed landscaping.

It was a far cry from my country neighborhood. Most of the houses near me had cropped up as we'd sold off bits of the farm.

"This trip counts as our deal," Frankie said stiffly as we passed 1 Battery Hill, a white stone home with a green tiled roof.

"Our deal was for you to help me find and question Erma Sue," I reminded him. "We're allowed to make more than one trip."

"Then I'm allowed to have more than one horse," Frankie concluded.

"Don't even think about it."

He rubbernecked when we passed a gray stone home with an honest-to-goodness turret. "I went to a few parties there back in the day. Maybe you could drop me off, and I can see if they know Erma Loo—"

"Erma Sue. And no deal. You and your friends were dead before Erma Sue ever lived here." He was helping whether he wanted to or not.

And with Frankie, that typically meant *not*.

"You didn't have to go bringing my lack of life into it," the gangster grumbled as we pulled up in front of 7 Battery Hill.

The red-brick colonial revival looked like a dollhouse, with a large yellow-painted porch and matching dormers. Potted ferns hung at precisely spaced intervals, and antique gas lanterns flickered along the white stone path that cut through the perfectly manicured lawn. Ghostly potted topiaries flanked the entrance to the porch, but that was the only indication of the presence of spirits.

So far, at least.

A real estate sign stood in the yard. On it, a blonde with a toothy smile pointed to the Divine Finds realty group name and logo, and... "Oh my goodness. Look!" On top of the sign rested a placard that read Open House. "We don't have to sneak inside. We can go in with the real estate agent!"

"You say that like it's going to be a good time," Frankie snarked.

It would be. Finally, I had a way to get information that didn't require breaking and entering or a police escort.

I punched in a quick call to Ellis and told him the new plan.

"I don't like it," he said. He sounded like he was running. "That house turns over all the time ever since Erma Sue died. Nobody's lived there for more than a year or two. After her sister inherited, she swore she saw Erma Sue's reflection late at night in the glass shower door."

"That's a good thing, right?"

Although I supposed not if you wanted to take a shower.

"That place is haunted in a bad way," he warned.

"I understand." It wasn't as if Ellis could protect me from ghostly threats. Besides, it didn't seem like he'd be able to go with me anytime soon. "I'll be fine," I assured him. "I have Frankie."

"That's not a comfort," Ellis said.

"I heard that," Frankie snorted. "I've saved you lots before."

And only some of the time had it been from situations Frankie had dragged me into.

In any case, I'd have to rely on my ghost sidekick. For better or worse. "I'll call you when I'm done," I promised Ellis before we hung up.

With Erma Sue's burn book at large, I couldn't pass up an opportunity to make progress in my investigation right away.

Yet, as I slipped out of the car, I spotted a curious sight in the yard. I froze for a moment and wondered if I was about to step into more trouble than I'd realized.

CHAPTER 8

The sharp-dressed blonde from the real estate sign braced one hand on a stately old oak tree, her eyes wide and her mouth slack. Pink splotches dotted her face and neck, and she shook all over.

"Are you all right?" I asked, slamming my car door and hurrying across the lawn toward her.

"This is a ghost hunt, not a do-gooder rescue mission," Frankie snarled in my ear. "Don't get distracted by the dame!"

"Why don't you go case the place?" I murmured to him, knowing he'd be unable to resist.

I was right.

"Ha!" he crowed in triumph. "Just remember you said that," he added by way of parting as he streaked past me and around the back of the house.

Maybe he wouldn't get into too much trouble.

Maybe he'd even be able to track down our ghost.

And as long as I was wishing, maybe Erma Sue would invite me up onto the porch for a chat.

In any case, I couldn't follow him. It wasn't as if I could just slip through the wall. I needed to attend the open house as soon as the real estate agent was ready to open it.

On the upside, it seemed I would be welcome. The moment the blonde on the lawn spotted me, she straightened her tailored red jacket and pasted on the same toothy smile from her marketing headshot.

"Verity Long, as I live and breathe!" she chirped, brushing off her hands as if she had been merely leaning against the tree to pass the time.

She obviously knew me, but for the life of me, I couldn't remember her name. Of course, that wasn't our biggest problem at the moment. As I drew closer, I saw her hose had torn, and a bloody knee poked out from under her red pencil skirt. She hobbled toward me, favoring her injured leg, although she tried her darndest to pretend otherwise.

"Oh, my goodness. You poor thing." I hurried to close the distance between us so that the poor woman didn't have to do any more walking than necessary.

"Oh, I just knocked my knee on the porch rail a few minutes ago," she said as if it happened all the time. She clasped both my hands in hers the moment I reached her. "Daphne May," she said by way of introduction, pretending for both of us that her name was on the tip of my tongue. "I was three years behind you in high school."

"That's right," I said quickly. The name did ring a bell. "There was a Charlie May in my graduating class."

"He's my brother." She grinned. "I also live in the same building as your sister, Melody. Apartment 2F," she added as if I might feel the need to visit. Yet another reason to love Sugarland.

"Well, it's great to see you," I said, wondering why a real estate agent didn't own real estate in town. "This is your listing?" I asked, looking past her to the early twentieth-century home.

"It is, and it's the most gorgeous place you've ever seen," she gushed. "Six bedrooms, eight baths. There's a chef's kitchen and a newly updated solarium—it's perfect for a single girl who is looking to invest in Sugarland history."

Sure. I needed a solarium. Not to mention eight bathrooms. I mean, I'd made headlines last year for solving a lucrative ghost-hunting case at a Great Gatsby-era mansion. Still, she had to realize this was out of my price range. "It's quite a house, but you know how attached I am to the home I inherited from my grandmother." I didn't want to lie, and there was no sense getting her hopes up.

If anything, her smile grew brighter. "Maybe you and Ellis want to share a home of your own, start off fresh." She winked.

"I'm not sure if Ellis is the solarium type," I admitted, carefully avoiding any discussion of my relationship.

"Well, this place is surprisingly affordable," she added brightly. She tucked a lock of hair behind her ear and leaned in as if we were sharing a secret. "I can't believe I snagged the listing. It'll be the third house I ever sold and by far the grandest. You're lucky it's still available because this house is going to sell itself!" She gestured toward the house like a *Price Is Right* model and topped it with a big Hollywood smile.

Yet she'd made no move to get me out of the yard and into the house.

I crossed my arms over my chest. "Is it haunted?" I asked, ready to address the elephant on the lawn.

She opened her mouth, then snapped it shut. "Of course not!" She rallied, with a pish-posh of her hand as if the entire question were absurd. As if she hadn't been injured on the property this very afternoon. I mean, whom did she think she was talking to? "It is delightfully quirky," she assured me, "just like Sugarland."

"Right." Only Sugarland was safe.

Well, except for all the murdering lately.

"Please, please, don't go around saying it's haunted," she pressed, nearly begging. "If you do, I'll never be able to sell it."

I hated to break it to her, but this place already had a reputation, at least among the Sugarland PD.

I scanned the darkened windows of the grand old house, looking for signs of afterlife. Maybe the late Erma Sue had merely given the Realtor a scare, one that had caused her to trip. Or maybe Erma Sue was more dangerous than I'd realized.

There was only one way to find out.

"I'll go on in and take a peek," I said, starting toward the front door. I'd just have to be careful.

Very careful.

"For sure!" Daphne said, her eyes going a little wild, glancing toward the street as if she'd rather run in the other direction. "This house was built in 1914 by riverboat captain Cornelius Jones as a wedding present for his daughter, Jane," she said, moving stiffly toward the cheerful yellow porch. "It's nearly five thousand square feet with all the original fireplaces in working condition."

I hated to force her back inside when I had no intention of buying. But she'd advertised an open house, a literal invitation for me to poke around, and I intended to use it.

"I can go in by myself if you'd rather wait on the lawn to… greet homebuyers," I suggested.

Maybe seek out some first aid.

Plus, I really didn't want her watching me talk to ghosts, especially given her stance on the haunting.

"Oh, no! I'm all yours," she promised, pressing her glossy lips together in thinly masked terror. "I'm on you like a tick until you see every nook and corner of this place."

"You really don't need to set foot back in that house." There would be a few places I'd like to explore in private, like the bathroom where Erma Sue had died.

"Nonsense." Daphne grabbed hold of my arm in what would

have been a friendly gesture in these parts, except she clung like a heroine in a horror movie. She began walking me toward the house. "I can't wait for you to fall in love like I have."

Not a ringing endorsement.

"You say it's not haunted at all." Clearly, I was her human shield.

"The last three agents said it's most definitely not," she vowed as if she were trying to convince herself as well. "They were all much more experienced than me."

They'd known when to get out.

To Daphne's credit, she barely hesitated before gamely tackling the stairs up to the wide, planked front porch. She kept a tight hold on my arm, dragging me with her as she bent to straighten a toppled wicker chair. "Isn't this the perfect spot to sit outside and enjoy a lemonade in the evening?" she managed.

Perhaps if you were among the living. On the ghostly side, the chair had a hole torn through the seat. Daphne replaced the cushion.

"You have a funny look on your face." Her fingers tightened on my arm. "Are you not in love yet?" she asked as if she expected a ghost to come flying up out of the porch.

It wouldn't be the first time that had happened to me this week.

"You can always repaint the porch if yellow isn't your color," she said, her voice trembling only slightly.

"The yellow is lovely," I assured her, blinking until the vision of the damaged chair receded. At times, it could be hard to juggle seeing two worlds at the same time.

Daphne nodded and forced a smile. "The custom oak front door is original to the house and made from trees grown right here in Sugarland," she said, cracking it open for me.

Not that I would ever consider moving, much less to Erma Sue's house, but I kind of loved it based on that door.

We stepped into a massive parlor with a soaring ceiling and

a staircase topped with a sculpture of an angel holding an orb. I immediately sneezed as I was hit with the overwhelming smell of gardenias.

"Excuse me," I said, eyes watering from the impact. "Do you smell that?"

"Oh, you might be allergic to the wood polish. I dusted a little this morning," Daphne lamented. "I'm sorry."

It wasn't that. "It's"—my sinuses tickled, and I let out a mighty sneeze—"gardenia."

Her eyes scanned the room as if expecting an attack. "People say it always smells faintly of flowers here in the entryway, but I can never tell."

"Faintly?" I repeated, wishing I could open a window.

I was able to extricate myself from Daphne's grip long enough to wipe my eyes and blow into the hankie from my purse. Upon recovery, I realized the assault of gardenias wasn't the strangest thing about the place. Ghostly marbles littered the massive, soaring staircase in front of us. Dozens and dozens of them. And worse, at the bottom, large, otherworldly shards of glass stood glued to the floor, pointy sides up.

"What is this place?" I asked, realizing too late I'd said it out loud.

"Pretty impressive, right?" Daphne asked, nodding a few too many times. "There's a sign-in sheet this way," she said, walking straight through the treacherous shards, beckoning me to follow.

"Give me a sec," I said, picking my way along the edge of the foyer, trying to be casual about it. No sense explaining what I saw on the ghostly side. It would only upset the Realtor. It was hard to imagine, but perhaps Erma Sue wasn't the dominant ghost in the house. If she was, I couldn't fathom why she'd do this to the place that, from all accounts, had been her pride and joy.

Daphne had stopped in front of a marble-topped table at the

side of the stairs, wringing her hands as she watched my cautious approach. "Err...are you all right?"

"I am if you are." I cut too close to a shard, and the sharp bite of glass made me wince. "I'm just taking in the full scope of the room."

Her chin shook as she attempted a smile and failed. "Your ankle is bleeding," she said, her voice ending on a squeak.

A thin trail of blood streaked down my leg and created a crimson stain on my white canvas shoe. "I must have knocked it on the porch," I said, borrowing her excuse.

"Must have." She aimed for a little laugh and missed.

"Unless the house is haunted," I said, giving her one more chance.

"Definitely not," she vowed as if wishing made it so.

I wasn't going to burst her bubble. I avoided the rest of the glass and left my name and number in the first slot on the sheet, pretending I didn't notice that the sheet had been dated two weeks prior and mine was the first entry.

"Not getting much traffic today?" I asked, leaving the pen on top of the sheet.

"It's been slow." She cleared her throat. "But I love a challenge! It only takes one person to fall in love with this house, and after that everyone else will be sorry they didn't snag it first."

At the moment, I was sorry I hadn't snuck in the back.

"If you don't mind, I'd like to explore a little on my own," I said, wondering how much it would hurt to kick the ghostly marbles off the stairs. If I could dodge my way past all the glass.

This was where Frankie would have come in handy, but of course, I saw no sign of him. I should have endured his snarky comments and refused to let him out of my sight. But there was nothing to do about it now.

The most likely place to find Erma Sue would be in the master bathroom where she'd died. A lot of ghosts liked to haunt their death places. And I had a lot of questions for the not-so-dearly departed hairdresser.

If I could get rid of Daphne, maybe I could call for Frankie to clear the way.

I would have to hope he answered. Frankie tended to ignore me when he was having fun. He was like Lucy in that respect.

"Those stairs tend to be...slippery," Daphne said, casting an apprehensive glance that way. "Let me show you one of the house's best features first," she rallied. "On to the kitchen!"

I'd wanted to attend an open house, not a tour.

But I also didn't need her seeing what I'd have to do to get up the stairs.

She led me under a gorgeous archway flanked by tasteful hanging lamps. A ghostly bucket hung on strings between them, with the handle attached to a wire.

"Hold up," I said, stopping cold.

"These are original Tiffany lamps," Daphne said approvingly as if I'd had the good taste to stop and admire them.

I followed the wire from the bucket down the wall to where it crossed over the hallway at ankle height, forming a ghostly trip wire.

For the life of me, I didn't get the point of it. Erma Sue was known for blackmail, not booby traps. Then again, she had probably made a whole lot of enemies, and some of them were bound to be waiting for her on the other side. Perhaps this was her idea of ghostly security measures. Heaven knew Frankie had pulled some similar stunts around my property.

I vowed to pay attention and move slowly. Erma Sue had rigged her house for maximum pain, and I'd really like to get out of there in one piece.

"I hear this place changes hands quite often," I said. I was starting to see why. Most people could sense ghosts on some level, even if they couldn't see them.

Think of the prickling feeling you get at the back of your

neck when something is *off*. The uncomfortable sensation as if someone is directly behind you. The quick glance over a shoulder to reveal...nothing.

In Erma Sue's former home, add in the unexplained scent of flowers and the slipperiness of the main staircase. Even if it was impossible for a regular person to activate the ghostly trip wire, walking under a loaded supernatural trap would trigger a certain discomfort.

"This is where you're in luck," Daphne assured me. "Everyone who sells this house does an upgrade. So what we have here is a rare combination of classic elegance and state-of-the-art updates."

Yet nobody stayed.

"Are you ready to see the kitchen?" Daphne asked with the tone I used to give Lucy her apple cinnamon skunk crumbles.

"Sure," I said with markedly less enthusiasm. "But let's go slow," I suggested, stepping over the trip wire and vowing to keep my eyes peeled for any more traps. "I want to take it all in."

CHAPTER 9

"I promise you've never seen anything like it," she said, steeling her shoulders as she led me into a massive, newly remodeled kitchen.

"The thing is—" I hated to lead her on. And despite what Ellis thought about me taking too many risks, I didn't want to see any more of this house unnecessarily because—oh my word —wire coat hangers wound around every kitchen knob and handle in the room on the ghostly side. It was like some bizarre, monstrous art project.

"I see you're admiring the custom metal drawer pulls and handles," Daphne said proudly. "The notorious Erma Sue Bryce added these, and they were kept during the remodel." She led me to cabinets by the sink. "These were made custom for her by the old Sugarland metalworks. One of a kind. Look closely and you can see little bees. *B* for Bryce and bees." Daphne ventured far enough to open a drawer. "Ouch!" she said, yanking her hand back. "Static shock," she added with a little laugh.

"Right." I followed the wires to where they disappeared under the sink. "Can I have a peek under here?" I asked, not really asking as I toed the sink cabinet open with my foot.

A ghostly car battery sat in the space below, leaking acid, the wires wound around its terminals.

This wasn't fun anymore. Daphne might get a little pinch, but those of us tuned in on the ghostly end could get electrocuted. And sliced in the entryway. And doused with whatever was in that bucket in the hall.

I didn't know what was happening, and I didn't care. Okay, I cared. But I couldn't afford to worry about it. I needed to find Erma Sue—if she was here, I needed to talk to her about the book—and then I'd leave and try to forget I'd ever stepped foot in this place.

"Check out the pantry," Daphne said, crossing the room. "It goes all the way under the main stairs, so there's plenty of storage," she added, opening a polished wood door, with an etched frosted-glass window. Spiders poured out on the ghostly side. Thousands of them.

This was worse than I'd thought.

"To be honest, I'm not house shopping. Not one tiny bit," I said quickly before I changed my mind. "I just saw your open house sign, and I'm snooping. Hard."

She froze in a mound of ghostly spiders, her chin wavering. "I think this place is haunted."

"Yeah, it is. Big time," I said, edging out of the kitchen and toward a pair of French doors.

The real estate agent looked like she was about to cry. "It just feels so icky in here sometimes." Ghostly spiders scrambled over Daphne's shoulders and fell to the floor.

"Oh, honey, get away from that pantry," I urged.

She nodded and began walking stiffly toward me. On some level, she felt the creepy-crawlies. I knew she did. "All the former owners have talked about strange things happening. No one else would take the listing." A tiny spider crawled through her hair. "Now I'm in over my head."

"Daphne," I began. "Excuse me," I added, brushing the spider from her hair, feeling the cold, gut-wrenching sting of the other side and pushing through as I swept the spiders from her shoulders. "You have…something on you."

"That's just how this house feels," she said, vibrating with it. "Slightly…haunted. But sometimes people like haunted things, right?" she asked, wringing her hands as she rallied. "I mean, that could actually be a selling point in the right context. Don't you think? Imagine cooking on this amazing Viking gas range the current owners just added." She took a shaky step in that direction. "It's gas with six burners."

"Wait. Don't touch it." It was probably wired to explode. Not that it would hurt Daphne, but I'd rather not catch the blowback.

She halted in the center of the kitchen, shaking. "The Tiffany sconces on either side of the door to the backyard are original, and they don't break even when the door flies open on its own. Someone has to think of that as an advantage," she said, with more hope than conviction. "There are lots of haunted places that aren't bad to be around."

True. "Only this one is." I loathed to say it. I felt sorry for the poor girl, but… "This haunting is bizarre."

As if prompted by my words, a strange metallic rattle echoed from behind the French doors leading to the next room.

"That's the solarium," Daphne said, frozen to the spot.

"Did you hear that too?" I prodded.

"Yes," she said in a small voice.

I shivered as a ghostly spider crawled over my shoe. "I'd be glad to take a look around and tell you what you're up against." After this kitchen, I was looking forward to the bright, plant-filled room beyond. Even if it was haunted.

"That would be…" Tears erupted at the corners of her eyes, and she sagged against the gourmet center island. "This place won't move, and it's my only big listing, and I can barely afford my rent right now much less hire a ghost hunter, or even admit the place is haunted, or it'll just confirm the rumors, and nobody will come see it, and I'm done. I'm done."

"One step at a time," I said, trying to give her some measure of comfort. I needed to find the ghost who haunted this place. "I'm not going to charge you," I promised her.

I heard the distinct rumble of Frankie's groan from inside the solarium. "Leave it to you to say that."

Oh, good. I'd been wondering where he was. "Frankie?" I called, hesitating in front of the door, scanning it for booby traps.

"Leave me alone. I'm concentrating," he said from the other side.

He was supposed to be helping me find Erma Sue.

"There was never a Frankie who lived here, but there was a Felix," Daphne offered. "About six years and four owners ago. I'll get the doors for you," she added, screwing up her courage. "They tend to stick."

"Be careful," I warned as she snaked around me, a tad guilty for making her touch them. But if she sprung a ghostly trap, at least she wouldn't feel it.

Much.

We'd fetch my wandering housemate, and then he could help me get upstairs.

"I'd be grateful for anything you could do to help," Daphne said, giving the doors a sharp tug. They didn't budge. "This listing is my chance to turn things around, to make a mark in Sugarland real estate." She yanked again. "If I could just get a good story that would explain things to people so they didn't have to be scared," Daphne added, wiping her hands on her skirt, hope tinging her words. "Like Erma Sue is just being her quirky self or something, that would be great."

"To be honest, I don't know what to think about Erma Sue," I said, noticing ghostly water on the floor under the counters, right where a person's toes would be when they reached for the wired handles.

Daphne shot me a nervous glance. "I was inside the solarium watering plants this afternoon, and I swear something tripped me. I banged my knee against the old birdcage."

"Show me," I said.

She nodded, and I saw her swallow. "I'm trying," she answered with manufactured enthusiasm. I felt for her. I truly did.

"It's hard to miss," she added, and with a wild yank, the doors sprang free.

We peered inside the sun-drenched room, and I took a moment to admire its gorgeous steepled skylight. Tasteful white wicker furniture, the cushions decorated with birds, added brightness to the plant-filled space. A wrought-iron bistro set stood next to a small gurgling fountain, and tiny white lights twinkled in the trees.

Finches chattered and perched inside a massive built-in birdcage on the far end.

"Who's feeding these birds?" I asked. The place was vacant.

"I am," Daphne stammered. "The former owners jumped in the car one day and drove to Pittsburgh. They haven't been back since. I'm taking care of the birds."

"Okay, good." At least the animals appeared well, although she should probably get them out of there. "That's real nice of you," I added, trying to reassure her, the words catching in my throat as I watched in horror at what lay on the ghostly side.

The ghostly birdcage stood empty, bars rusted and brown. A makeshift metal tube thrust halfway through the cage, scarcely the width of a man. It narrowed as it reached the center. Sharpened nails jabbed into the tube, rendering it smaller and more treacherous, but that wasn't what worried me.

My housemate Frankie hovered inside, growing smaller and

smaller as he inched his way into what was most certainly a trap.

"Frankie!" I called.

"I really think it's Felix," Daphne said, crowding next to me.

"Shhh!" Frankie hissed. "I've almost got it," he said, his attention laser focused, body impossibly long, as he reached for a bottle of Old Rip Van Winkle bourbon hanging on a string.

"It's a trap," I said, rushing for him, wishing I could yank him out by his ankles, but he was already too far in, and touching him would zap us both. Plus, the nails were way sharp, and I had no idea if they were connected to a charge or what this trap was set to do.

The string led to a pulley that connected to a trapdoor over the exit, and naturally, the ghost was completely ignoring me.

"You really see a ghost?" Daphne stammered, on me like sauce on ribs.

"A very dumb one," I told her. In more than one hundred years on this Earth, Frankie Winkelmann had never learned to look before he leapt. "Get out of there," I ordered. "Or at least find another way in." He was doing it the exact wrong way. If he should even be there at all—which he shouldn't. "Glide out backward and avoid the nails altogether by going through the main bars."

"Can't," he grunted, focused on inching through the tunnel. "The bars are electrified. This tunnel, too. It's all electrified. This is the only way in and out."

"Then back out right now." It was just a bottle of booze for heaven's sake. "Go drink with your friends at the speakeasy. I'll drive you there. In fact, I'll drive you to any speakeasy you want as soon as we're finished."

He inched a hair farther inside. "This is Old Rip Van Winkle. It's made with wheat instead of rye, so it's smoother. Tastes even better when you steal it."

Seriously? "It's wired!" What part of *bad idea* did the ghost not understand?

"Now you're making it more fun," he mocked, reaching for the bottle. "Besides, I'm excellent at stealing."

"I'm never letting you out of the house again," I muttered.

"Watch and learn," he challenged. "I'm gonna hold the bottle straight while I use my pocketknife to cut the string and—eeeyah!" The second he gripped the bottle, it flew up and took him with it, straight through the electrified tunnel of nails.

"Frankie!" I ran for the cage as the trapdoor slammed closed and a lock snapped shut.

CHAPTER 10

*F*rankie hung from the top of the birdcage, still clutching the ghostly bottle. "I should have seen that coming," he admitted.

He'd lost his hat, his suit coat was full of smoking holes, and I could have sworn I saw ghostly energy sizzling up and around one ear. I felt it, too. Energy zipped up and down my arms like an electric shock waiting to happen, and the hair on my head and arms stood at attention.

"Oh, Frankie." I rubbed my arms, willing the energy to settle. I didn't know how we were going to get him out of there. "Just drop the bottle. Maybe try to muscle your way through the electric bars." It sounded bad even to me—and no doubt it would feel worse—but we still had to find Erma Sue.

"I'd rather try to sweet-talk the dame," he said as a frigid wind swept through the room. "The ladies love me."

That was it. The electric shock must have boiled his brain.

Daphne shivered as the temperature in the room plummeted. "Did I leave a window open?" she asked weakly.

"I'm afraid not," I said, my ghost's spiky, erratic energy

making me twitch as a very striking, very angry spirit descended from the ceiling.

She wore her hair in loose curls, like a young woman, but her cheeks were hollow and her eyes sunken into the bone. Her cap sleeves and flowing gown fluttered, and I shivered. The wind went positively polar as she descended.

She appeared like a skinnier, more haggard version of the Erma Sue I'd seen in photographs. Still, her resemblance to the blackmailing beautician was unmistakable.

I pasted on my sweetest smile. "Hi there, Erma Sue—"

"Quiet!" she hissed.

With a gasp, I realized I could see my breath.

"I have to go!" Daphne wailed before running out of the room.

I understood the urge. I did. But I didn't have the luxury of fleeing. Instead, I steeled myself. I wasn't sure what to do next, but I had a trapped housemate and a job to do.

"Well, well, well..." The ghost's voice crackled. Hair floated around her shoulders. Her eyes narrowed as she halted opposite the gangster in the cage. "I've caught a thief."

"He doesn't mean it," I insisted. Erma Sue hurled a wrought-iron garden chair straight at me. I dodged it. Barely. I let out an involuntary shriek as it clattered to the floor behind me and toppled a ghostly potted palm.

Frankie still hadn't let go of the whiskey. "May I say you are looking radiant today?" He winked at the ghost.

Heavens. He was going to get himself fried and me zapped to next Sunday before he left me trapped with an angry ghost.

She stared blankly at him for a moment before her anger roared back. "Get your paws off that whiskey!"

My thoughts exactly.

"As soon as I'm done stealing it, I'd be glad to share," Frankie said as if he were at a party and not dangling in a haunted trap with smoke drifting out from under his collar.

Erma Sue waved her hand, and the door of the cage flew open. "Get out!"

This was Frankie's chance!

Of course, he didn't take it.

"Care for a smoke?" Frankie asked, digging his free hand through a hole in his jacket and pulling out his silver cigarette case.

She raised a hand again, but I interrupted. This was my chance, too, and I wasn't about to pass it up. "Erma Sue—" The ghost directed a death stare at me, and I lost my train of thought for a second. "Hi," I said, recovering and trying my best to be conversational. Most folks could be respectful when treated with respect. "The truth is, we're here to see you."

She snarled low in her throat, and I felt it down in my bones. "I'm *not* Erma Sue." She advanced on me. "I'll *never* be Erma Sue."

All right. "My mistake," I conceded. Only the family resemblance was uncanny. "You must be...her sister," I said as pleasantly as I could, hoping she didn't realize I couldn't recall her name. It wasn't because I was scared. I was more than a little terrified. It was just that nobody talked about the sister. Nobody told stories. Or showed pictures. Or...anything.

Erma Sue was the star.

The haggard spirit's face twisted with rage as she hit me with a sudden, chilly blast of energy. "Say my name."

"Ahh…" I began, rubbing the goose bumps that had erupted up my arms. My grandmother would have known, as would my mother. It was quite the Sugarland faux pas to forget a name, but in this case, she could hardly blame me. "I'm sorry, but you'd passed by the time I could have met you."

Her anger sizzled over me in a dark, prickling wave. "You know about my sister, and she died first."

There was that.

I was suddenly very sorry I'd drawn her attention. "I'm just here to—"

"Stop!" she ordered Frankie, who had been trying to untie the whiskey. The bottle flew across the room and into her hand. "Gangsters..." She rolled her eyes. "They never learn."

She didn't even have a horse on her porch.

"Believe me, I know," I blurted before I could change my mind. "I have to live with this one." She looked at me like she would eye one of the spiders in her kitchen. "Verity Long," I added, hoping she might not be so eager to toss another chair at someone she knew on a first-name basis.

"Rowena Samburski," she said automatically.

"That's it," I said as if it had been on the tip of my tongue.

"Don't lie," she ordered.

"I'm sorry my gangster friend caused you trouble," I mustered on.

"I'm not," Frankie snarked. "That's some damn fine whiskey, and I stole it fair and square."

"We're looking for Erma Sue," I added, keeping my focus, refusing to debate.

Rowena closed her eyes briefly. "We're all looking for Erma Sue," she rumbled. She shook her head and cracked open the bottle of Old Rip Van Winkle. "Ahh..." She took a swig and let it slip down her throat. "Why do you think I went through all this trouble?"

"Now you're just *trying* to torture me," Frankie groaned.

The ghost made a point to cap the bottle in front of him.

Wait. "So you rigged the house." It made sense, given her whiskey trap.

The corner of her mouth tilted up. "I did more than that." She tipped the nose of the bottle at me. "I accidentally trapped Erma Sue in the gardenia bush in the backyard. Grounded her." She chuckled.

"Of all the dirty tricks..." Frankie swore under his breath.

"How?" I asked. I'd never met a ghost who had been grounded like Frankie. Let's face it—my gangster was one of a kind.

She smirked as she toyed with the cap on the bottle. "My sister hated that gardenia. Always talked about chopping it down, but she was too busy going to lunches and parties and letting everyone suck up to her. So when she died, I figured I'd bury her under it."

How sweet. "That had to be against a million different health codes."

"The tough part was stealing the ashes out of the urn on Twyla Sue's mantle," Rowena huffed. "Good thing Twyla Sue couldn't tell the difference between craft sand and the real deal, although who would look?" She shrugged. "I smuggled Erma Sue out in a Ziploc and scattered her ashes around that stupid bush. I hosed them in good. I wanted that bush to live a nice long time." She chuckled. "I didn't know it would ground her to the property until I'd been dead a few years and decided to stop by." A grin broke through. "Served her right."

"So now you've got her stuck in this booby-trapped house," I started. I never thought I'd think it, but poor Erma Sue.

"Even the grounds are wired, right down to that stupid gardenia," Rowena sneered. She dropped the look when she saw my stunned reaction. "Hey, my *amazing* sister tortured me my entire life. Erma Sue was the beautiful one, the smart one. The vicious evil one who stole my boyfriends because she could." She pointed a bony finger at me. "Erma Sue told me how ugly I was and how I needed to lose weight. I developed an eating disorder because of her, and she made fun of me for it. She deserves more than spiders in the kitchen and marbles on the stairs."

"I'm sorry," I said. I truly was. Nobody deserved to be treated that way, especially by a sister who was supposed to love them.

Melody and I had our disagreements from time to time, but we loved each other unconditionally.

She smoothed her hands over her scrawny torso, her ribs visible underneath her flowing gown. "I wanted to be pretty, so Erma Sue did my hair. She 'got busy' and left the chemicals on too long. She fried my hair until chunks of it started falling out! She said it was a common mistake, but it never happened to anyone else. Just me." Her chin shook. "I saw her smiling later when she told her friends about it."

"I—" I didn't know what to say. "That's awful." I'd hug her if she weren't slightly unhinged. And a ghost.

She jutted her chin defiantly. "She used to call me the invisible one, and she was right. I was nobody in my own town." She pressed her thin lips together. "She never let me forget."

"You don't have to live like that anymore," I said gently. Yes, she'd been mistreated by Erma Sue. Terribly. It seemed a lot of people had. And Rowena certainly never deserved it. Still, she had her whole afterlife to think about. She didn't have to dwell on the past. "You can start again. You have…forever to make friends and enjoy all the things you missed when you were alive."

"Erma Sue liked to steal my friends from me." Rowena ran her fingers along the bars that held Frankie. "As soon as I thought somebody liked me, she'd turn on the charm, and that would be it. She couldn't stand to see me happy." She clenched her fingers into fists, and the room chilled. "Erma Sue enjoyed watching me cry."

"And now you've dedicated your afterlife to hurting her," I concluded. It was an awful way for both of them to spend eternity. I mean, Erma Sue might be able to escape to the ether from time to time. It was an in-between place where ghosts could rest and recover, but they never could stay for long.

"I'm the dominant one on this side of the veil." Her mouth

twisted brutally. "Strong emotions are powerful, and I've got enough rage to rule this house forever."

"It's good to have goals," I ventured. This really wasn't going the way I'd hoped.

"You don't know how many times I got her on the stairs." Rowena snickered. "Her upstairs bathtub is completely electrified and wired straight to her beloved dressing table." Her gray cheeks darkened with pleasure. "She's too afraid to venture anywhere near."

Yikes.

I couldn't imagine being trapped in a house like this. "So she's hiding," I reasoned. I wondered if there was a way for me to get Erma Sue out of there, at least until her sister calmed down and stopped abusing her. But no. She was grounded. Stuck.

"When she comes back, I'm going to trap her with Old Rip Van Winkle." She grinned at her whiskey trap.

"I don't know how she could resist," Frankie admitted.

Wait. I'd missed something big. "If Erma Sue is grounded, she's somewhere here in the house. Or at least on the property, right?"

That was how it was for Frankie at my house.

"She was." Rowena twisted the whiskey bottle in her hands. "Until one day, she escaped. I don't know how."

Hold the phone… "She ungrounded herself?" I managed.

Frankie shrieked.

"Yes." Rowena smashed the bottle on the floor. "She did. Hell, I'm still trying to figure out how I grounded her, but the diabolical twit did it. She got away!"

"Oh my word," I said to Frankie, who looked like he needed to start breathing into a paper bag. "Do you know what this means?"

"It means I can smoke and drink and live and do whatever I want," he said, bracing his hands on his knees. "I'm gone! I'm out of here!" He gasped. "I can be out on Main Street robbing an armored truck quicker than you can say, 'Freeze, mister!' I can ride Frisky Pete off into the sunset!"

Not yet. But for the first time, I had hope we could actually set him free. Now we really needed to find Erma Sue.

She had to know what she'd done to escape. She was cunning. She was smart.

She was gone.

"Oh, we'll get Erma Sue," Rowena said as the shards of the broken bottle flew back together, bringing the whiskey with them as they formed back into a whole bottle in her hand. "She'll come home one of these days. She might even have a little rage of her own built up, and she'll think she can take this place away from me. She'll try. Mark my words."

"I'm sure that'll be lovely," I said, my mind still spinning. But I couldn't wait for Erma Sue to brave her way back. I had a murder case to solve. And unlike Rowena, I didn't have all the time in the world.

"She loves Old Rip Van Winkle," Rowena said, glaring at the bottle as if anything connected to her sister was rotten.

"It must be tasty," I said automatically. It had sure gotten my ghost. But we needed to return to the matter at hand. "Do you have any idea where Erma Sue might be now?" I asked, just to be sure.

"Yes, but it's not like I can drag her home," she ground out. "I'm not *that* strong."

"Maybe I can track her down," I said, glancing at Frankie, "if you tell me where she is."

"Yeah," the gangster said, straightening. "That's Verity's talent. She can...bring ghosts different places," he added, lying like he was born to it. Which he probably was. "I didn't want to come here today, but voilà."

The ghost's forehead furrowed. "She bent a gangster to her will?"

"I'm Frankie the German," he informed her as if she should know his name. "Men fear me. Women love me. Verity…is in a class by herself."

Rowena stared at him, as if deciding whether or not she should team up with a live girl and the ghost who'd tried to steal her Old Rip Van Winkle.

To be fair, she was right to be suspicious. Frankie wouldn't know the truth if it bit him, and I had no intention of delivering poor Erma Sue up to Rowena to be tortured again, no matter what kind of person either one of them had been in life.

Rowena frowned and drew up to her full height. "Don't cross me," she warned.

"We'd never," I vowed.

"Except when there's Old Rip Van Winkle in the mix," Frankie added. "Then I can't promise anything."

Maybe it was that bit of honesty that snagged her.

In either case, she ground her jaw and relented. "My evil sister is haunting her old beauty chair."

I brightened. "At Two Sues' House of Beauty?" I'd heard stories about strange occurrences at the salon after Erma Sue died.

"Not exactly." She chuckled. "That's where she went at first. Twyla Sue made a shrine out of that stupid chair and covered her mom's station in flowers and pictures. It was pathetic."

It sounded nice to me.

"They had a grand old time for a few years. Until I died. Then a few thumbtacks on the chairs took the la-di-da out of those ladies." Rowena smirked. "Not to mention mouse traps in the beauty desk drawers and snakes in the salon sinks. The place was a nightmare after that, even for the living."

"Oh my." So that was what happened. She seemed to expect praise for her craftiness, but I couldn't quite muster it.

"Twyla Sue tore out all the old stuff and redecorated. She couldn't fathom what had gone so wrong," Rowena crooned.

"Now Erma Sue is haunting her chair in a storage locker with a bunch of old hairdryers. She doesn't even have the sinks anymore. Twyla Sue donated the wash area to the preschool!"

"Remind me to never tick you off," Frankie said under his breath.

"Too late," she retorted. "I'd go after that place, too, but she's so attached to that chair, it gives her enough power to hold me off." She chortled. "She can have her fifteen-by-fifteen slice of paradise."

"So you're pretty sure Erma Sue is in her daughter's storage locker?" I pressed.

"You'd have thought she died clutching that chair." Rowena chuckled. "It's pathetic."

"What if we can get her to come out?" I asked.

She stopped grinning. "That would be nice. Very nice indeed," she purred. "The storage facility is down by the railroad tracks."

"You mean It's Not Junk on the southwest side of town near Route 4." I nodded. "I'd almost had to get an apartment down there after Virginia Wydell tried to ruin me."

"That's the place," Rowena said with a snap of her fingers. "The locker belongs to the salon. Erma Sue kept an extra set of keys hidden under the drawer in the antique phone cubby built into the hall outside the kitchen." She glided through the bird-cage bars and began retying the bottle into the trap. "If you see her, send her back home to her sister."

CHAPTER 11

"I think we just made an enemy," I said, sparing a glance at Frankie as I hightailed my 1978 Cadillac down Route 4 toward It's Not Junk public storage.

"You think too much." The gangster dug in his suit pocket to retrieve his silver cigarette case and drew out a smoke. "Far as I'm concerned, we hit the jackpot."

"We did." Freeing Frankie would be a game changer. But we had to do this right. "I mean, we're headed to the old warehouse down by the railroad tracks to meet up with the town's most notorious dead blackmailer. And if we don't deliver, her booby-trap-happy sister will revenge haunt us for fun. We're the real winners here."

"Revenge is fun." Frankie shoved the smoke onto his bottom lip and struck a match.

Had he learned nothing during our time together? I turned off onto a service road. "Let's just...take it down a notch." We had a lot to figure out before we could celebrate.

"Gangsters don't slow down. We accelerate." He lit his smoke and shook out the match. "We catch this dame, and I could be free tonight." He tossed the ghostly match stub out through the window next to him.

"We need a solid plan first," I warned, taking a bump in the road too fast and sending us airborne for a second.

We landed with a teeth-rattling thud.

Frankie didn't notice. He took a hard drag and blew the ghostly smoke out all over my passenger side.

He was lucky I had bigger things on my mind.

We barreled past a rundown gas station. "Erma Sue is crafty," I said, adjusting my grip on the wheel, fingers aching from the pressure. "If we're not careful, she'll figure out her sister sent us to find her." I mean, we had the keys. That was a decent clue. "It's not as if we can pretend we just happened by. She'll be on her guard."

"So we sneak up behind her and throttle her," Frankie snipped.

"Absolutely not." I rounded the corner and made a turn past the old apartment building next to the tracks. "We want Erma Sue to talk."

"Right." Frankie took another hard drag. "We can throw her in the trunk, drive her over the railroad tracks a couple dozen times to loosen her up, then throttle her."

He was going to screw this up.

"We need to get her on our side," I insisted, spotting the cinder-block storage building up ahead on the left. "There has to be a way to reason with her. Or bargain." Heaven knew I'd had to do that enough with Frankie. "Maybe there's something Erma Sue wants in exchange for information. That's been her currency in the past."

Frankie looked at me like I had a screw loose, the ash growing long on the end of his cigarette. "The trunk is way faster. Don't worry. Your tires can take it. And it'll get the job done." He took another rough drag. "Stop messing with a system that's been putting concrete boots on wiseguys since 1922."

"That's not how the world works anymore."

"Watch and learn, kid," he scoffed.

"Says the ghost who can't leave my house without a babysitter," I shot back.

"That was a low blow," he grumbled as if he expected me to apologize. We whizzed past the railroad tracks, a blur in the window behind him as he took another drag. "Look, I'm about to track down a dame who can tell me how to get unstuck. This is all I've wanted since I got washed into your rosebush, and you expect me to get tangled up in the details."

As if I were the dead weight. "We wouldn't have the first clue about Erma Sue ungrounding herself if I hadn't won over Rowena." Sort of.

"You wouldn't have had a chance to sweet-talk her if I hadn't tripped her whiskey trap," he shot back.

Yeah, he was a real hero. "Hey, I'm all for breaking into a murder victim's personal locker," I pointed out.

"Visiting," Frankie corrected. "We have a key. You don't get credit for a break-in."

"Fine." I wasn't going to argue the finer points of skirting the law.

It suddenly occurred to me that this trip to see Erma Sue would be sort of, maybe, definitely a violation of the deal I'd made with Ellis. We weren't entering an abandoned property per se. But it wasn't like we had consent from the property owner to go inside.

Although technically Twyla Sue was unable to give permission, so…loophole?

I was beginning to sound like my gangster.

It wasn't as if I could convince Frankie to wait. I didn't want to stop, either.

I made a hard left into a crumbling parking lot and cringed as my beloved avocado green land yacht bottomed out.

At least we were the only car at It's Not Junk.

The place did not seem to do a heaping lot of business, judging from the weed garden springing from the parking lot, not to mention the paint peeling from the sign. I parked at the spot closest to the side door and slipped out of the car. "Let me do the talking."

Frankie blew a few smoke rings as he exited straight through the passenger door. "I know how to handle the ladies."

"Sure." I tried the first key on the ring marked INJ. "You did just great back there with Rowena."

"You gave away my bottle of Old Rip Van Winkle," Frankie said, offended all over again as he glided straight through the door I was trying to open.

I tried a second key. "It wasn't your bottle, it was bait. She had you dangling from her hook like a prize marlin."

"I almost had her where I wanted," the gangster said, popping his head through the wall as I cracked open the door. "Unlike you, I'm subtle."

"Subtle as a shoot-out." I stepped inside and wrinkled my nose at the smell of dust and mildew.

"Now that would be fun," he mused.

I flicked the switch by the door, and after a long second or two, industrial lights flickered on overhead. A stark gray hallway stretched out ahead of us, broken by a series of black-painted doors. "This reminds me of a prison," I murmured.

"Nah," Frankie said, surveying the hall. "Prison smells better."

That was slightly comforting. After all, there was a certain police officer who'd love to lock me up for the night if he caught me trespassing in the late Twyla Sue's storage locker. But "better" than a rank combination of basements and feet still left plenty of room for bad. For the first time, I hoped Duranja was over at my sister's.

In any case, we needed to get in and out quickly.

Unfortunately we'd neglected to ask Rowena which storage locker belonged to Twyla Sue. With a long line of doors ahead of us, it seemed we might be here a while trying to find it.

"Don't worry," Frankie said, popping his head through door number one. "When this works and I get free, I'll still let you tag along from time to time."

"*If* you get free," I said, inserting a key into door number two across the hall. "Rowena doesn't know how Erma Sue managed it. Erma Sue herself might not know either." We couldn't get cocky. If Rowena was telling the truth, and if Erma was behind one of these doors, *and* if the ghost could (and would) help us… well, we'd take it one step at a time.

"Don't even think it," Frankie snapped. "Not after what you've put me through."

We each took a side as we made our way down the lonely hallway.

"It hasn't been all bad," I muttered to myself, trying the next door and the next. I mean, I still couldn't believe we might have found a way to free Frankie. It was great. Terrific. I'd always said I wanted him to be free, and I did. He deserved to have his own afterlife. But part of me would miss him.

I glanced across the hall to find him glaring at me.

Sometimes.

"If I see one more dusty old treadmill, I'm going to scream," Frankie said, holding his hat as he shoved his head through the door of another storage locker. "Only crazy people would spend their afterlives here."

"Unless maybe she's grounded again," I ventured, trying a door with a band of wood rot at the bottom. "I mean, if Erma Sue figured out part of the secret to grounding and ungrounding, maybe she got away for a little bit, but the grounding followed her and trapped her here."

Frankie gaped. "Do you get off on coming up with horrific scenarios?"

I was just trying to be practical. "There are worse things than being grounded on my property."

"Can you stop talking now?" He moved on to the next locker. "Let's just...find this dame and throttle her until she tells me how to get free."

"Ah, back to the throttling," I reasoned as the door clicked open.

We both froze.

Frankie drew his gun.

"Diplomacy, Frank," I said as he barreled through the wall next to the door.

He was going to ruin everything.

"Frankie!" I flung open the door and flicked on the light.

Erma Sue Bryce sat alone on a pink salon chair, reading a decades-old *Glamour* magazine. She appeared the same as the picture that had hung for years in her salon—her hair styled in perfect layers, her lips glossy, and her false lashes model perfect.

She wore a sleeveless party dress and an earnest expression I hadn't expected.

"Well, hi, sugar." She slid off her beautician's chair, and the stacked boxes and sheet-draped lumps of furniture behind her began to glow with ghostly light. "Welcome to New Sue's House of Beauty."

A chandelier formed out of the mist and covered the naked bulb on the ceiling above. On the ghostly side, the sheet-draped lumps transformed into the beauty salon stations as they'd appeared at Two Sues' House of Beauty before Twyla Sue redecorated.

The *Sugarland Gazette* had done a full spread in the newspaper this past weekend.

I stood looking at a spitting image of the original, if you didn't count the real-life StairMaster in the corner or the stacked boxes along every wall. And, well, instead of a vibrant, active salon, it was only Erma Sue, clutching her magazine. Alone.

She'd focused on Frankie instead of me.

Frankie, who was pointing a gun at her head.

"Hey now—" I dodged a ghostly standing hair dryer and scooted next to him. "Shoot her and you're just going to have to wait longer to ask your questions." A bullet wouldn't kill her, but she'd be passed out on the floor for a good while.

"I hate when you're right," he said, holstering his gun. "Good thing there's always throttling."

Before he could make a grab for her, the beautician zipped out of his reach and materialized behind her beauty chair. "What is this?" Her voice took on a hint of steel. "A dead gangster and a live girl?"

"Rowena sent us," Frankie said, looming over her.

"We just want to talk," I said quickly, inserting myself between them before the gangster ruined it all.

"You mean trap me again," she snapped, glaring at the ghost.

"Kind of the opposite," I said as Frankie cracked his knuckles.

"You come any closer, and I'm gone," she threatened. "You'll never see me again."

"Then why are you still here?" he sneered, closing in again.

Probably because she didn't want to leave us alone in her shop.

Dang it all. He needed to learn how to read a room. I mean, she was obviously comfortable here among her things. And we were right next to Erma Sue's famous beautician's chair. It was made for nice long talks.

"Frankie, stop," I ordered. "Or the horse goes."

"Hey now." He pointed a finger at me. "You promised!"

The deal was for him to *help* me talk to Erma Sue, not drive her away.

I turned to the beautician. "We're here because we need your professional opinion on something. Have you ever seen a gangster with such a helmet head?"

She froze, unsure of our angle. "It's hard to see it with the hat."

Then she'd have to take my word for it. Frankie rarely showed his bullet hole. "I've known him for years, and his hair barely moves."

"I agreed to help, not to be insulted," Frankie said, eyeing Erma Sue. "And that's the style," he said, touching his hair. "It's slicked back."

"Old-fashioned," she tsked.

"Just like him," I agreed.

"Why you gotta make this personal?" Frankie balked.

As if the throttling he'd wanted to do wasn't personal.

"Oh, I get it," Erma Sue said, lighting up. "His bad hair makes him grumpy."

"You'd be grumpy too if people talked about you like you weren't *standing right here*," he informed her.

"Can you do anything for him?" I asked the beautician. "I mean, if anyone could, it would be you."

Frankie rolled his eyes. "Shoot me now."

If it kept him in the chair, I'd pick up the gun and do it myself. We were making progress.

Erma Sue studied him with a critical eye. "If I didn't have such an open schedule, I'd kick you out for your attitude."

"Good thing you love a challenge," I said, perky as I could.

"No." Frankie backed up. He saw where this was going. "Absolutely not."

I saw only one way to get the beautician talking, and that was with somebody in the chair. I wouldn't be able to stand the chill of ghostly hands and scissors near my hair, so Frankie would have to take this one for the team. "We made a deal, Frank," I said, using the same argument he had for keeping the horse on my porch.

"Don't call me Frank." I could see the wheels turning as he tried to come up with a way out.

I pasted on my brightest smile and squeezed as close to him as I could. "You're screwing up your chance to be free," I said into his ear. "If you want to learn about ungrounding, and you want to do it now, then get. In. The. Chair."

He stiffened as he recognized the logic of my words.

"You first," he balked, his voice going hoarse.

Nice suggestion, but… "I'm alive. Erma Sue doesn't serve live clients anymore." She couldn't touch me without getting a shock.

Frankie began breathing heavily despite the fact he no longer needed to draw any breath. "Fine," he hissed, not budging an inch. "How hard could it be?"

He still hadn't moved.

"Be brave," Erma Sue teased, not helping matters. "A style refresher does a man good."

"I like my hair the way it is," he muttered under his breath, gliding to the chair like a man facing the guillotine.

"Yay, go Frankie," I said, trying to lighten the mood as the beautician whipped a cape onto him.

"Now the trouble is that you're dead," she said, securing the cape and plucking the hat off his head. "So your haircut won't last as long." Ghosts tended to revert to how they appeared when they'd died. "However"—she brightened—"I can put a lot of energy into a cut, and mine tend to last for at least a few weeks."

"You're so talented," I said, proud she'd found a way to serve her ghost clients so well.

She winked at me.

Frankie gripped the arms of the chair and cringed like a

two-year-old as Erma Sue began wetting down his hair with a spray bottle. "Okay, ahem." He cleared his throat. "Tell me how you got ungrounded," he ordered with the finesse of Genghis Khan.

She dug a comb through his hair. "You *have* been talking to my sister," she said, her voice steely and her movements sharp.

"Easy." Frankie winced.

"You have a lot of pomade in here," Erma Sue remarked, flicking her comb.

"Even Rowena admits you do the best hair in town," I told her as Frankie's eyes bulged at me.

"Oh, Rowena's hair always turned out *interesting*." She snickered. "She was the only one I could never quite get right," she added breezily, but I couldn't miss the smug satisfaction behind her words.

The gangster's hair came down in long strands. I hadn't realized how much he'd slicked it back.

"I'd appreciate it if you'd pass the word that I'm open for business," Erma Sue said. Her comb got stuck, and she reached for the spray bottle again. "I mean, I've been trying to get New Sue's Salon going, but I haven't had a lot of luck getting customers."

Now that did surprise me. "You had the busiest book in town back in the day." Although her new shop was a bit off the beaten path.

"That's because I'm the best," she said, combing Frankie's long bangs over his eyes. "And some of my customers died with truly terrible hair. They need me now more than they did when we were alive."

"Not me," Frankie said from under his mop.

"It's not like you can plan when to go," I pointed out. "Or much else for that matter. But tell me—how did you escape from that gardenia bush?"

She chuffed and picked up a pair of scissors from the

counter next to her. "Tell Rowena nice try. I'm not letting her trap me again." She sectioned off a portion of hair. "And next time she wants to threaten me, she'll have to come down to my place here and do it herself!" She sliced off a huge hunk of Frankie's hair, and the gangster let out a shriek.

It would grow back.

"We're not trying to help Rowena," I insisted, wondering how I could gain her trust. "You can ask any of the ghosts in Sugarland. They'll tell you we barely know Rowena." The rumor mill could actually work in our favor this time.

"I'd rather not." She drew her mouth tight. "I'm not exactly tuned in to the Sugarland social set anymore," she said, getting her comb stuck again. Out came the spray bottle. "I can't walk the streets of downtown Sugarland without ghosts pouring drinks out over my head. And worse. The deceased ladies of the Sugarland Heritage Society pretend I'm some kind of strange ghost they can't see," she added as if she still couldn't quite believe it. "But I know it's all an act. It's just a childish snub. And when I tried to venture out to the homecoming parade this year, I was run over by a 1968 Impala."

"The nerve," I said, shocked, but not overly surprised at how she'd been treated. She'd been feared and despised while she was alive, and that kind of behavior tended to have consequences, even on the ghostly plane.

Sensing my sympathy, she clucked, "That ghostly Impala took a victory lap, and people cheered." Her face fell, and for a brief second I saw her vulnerability. "It hurts!" She sliced off a chunk of Frankie's hair as if trying to cut away her own pain.

"Is that really necessary?" the gangster demanded.

At least I could see his face now.

And I didn't want to say it to Erma Sue, but I found it ironic to hear her talking about the pain of being ostracized when she didn't seem to worry about that happening to anyone she'd hurt or blackmailed.

"All my former clients who *said* they loved me?" She angrily combed out another section of hair. "The old biddies play cards and don't invite me." She sprayed Frankie's head with the water. "If I show up, they say they have no space at the table. And on the off chance there is a space, they claim someone's sitting there, only they are invisible!" She kept spraying Frankie's hair until the ends dripped. "Bet they all had a real laugh when they heard what my sister did to my dream house."

"I think I'm done with the cut now," the gangster offered. "Where you're at is fine."

"Don't you move. It's only half done," she said, spraying him down more.

"I do have something to tell you," I said gently. No doubt she'd be upset at the news of her daughter's death, but maybe she would find comfort in knowing she'd soon have someone who loved her on the ghostly side of the veil.

Might as well start from the beginning. "Your feathered journal," I began, "was in the 1985 time capsule we dug up for homecoming."

She froze. "Who put it in there?"

"We all figured you did," I said, surprised.

"No." She ground her jaw and went back to digging through Frankie's hair. "It was stolen. I never let on because obviously that would have been a disaster."

It certainly would have. "Nobody has stepped forward to take responsibility for adding your book to the time capsule. There's no record of it going in. We only saw it when they unveiled the buried items."

She went stone-cold business in a heartbeat. "Tell Twyla to get it for me."

"She did," I said quickly. "She stood up in front of a big portion of the town in order to claim it."

"I love it!" Erma Sue exclaimed, a wide grin blooming across her features. Frankie took advantage of her distraction to try to stand, but she planted a hand on his shoulder and shoved him back down. "I spent so many years trying to teach that girl to stand up for herself."

"But then…" It hurt to tell her the next part. "Twyla was killed in the beauty shop this past Saturday night. Someone stole the book."

Erma Sue's joy evaporated. She leaned against the counter, her arms going slack. "What's wrong with people?"

"I can't answer that," I told her plainly. I also couldn't help but think she'd had a hand in creating the situation. Erma Sue had been perfectly happy to ruin other people's lives, yet here she stood, shocked at the consequences. Desperate people did desperate things—like kill. "When I found Rowena at your house, I was looking for you. I was hoping you might have been watching over the shop and maybe you'd seen what happened. I'm trying to help the police learn who murdered poor Twyla Sue."

She shook her head sadly. "Last time I left New Sue's was for Twyla's birthday barbeque." She gestured weakly with her scissors. "Rowena dug holes all over Twyla's yard for me to fall into."

"I'm sorry," I said, meaning it.

"That is messed up," Frankie said through his dripping mop.

"She filled them with pig manure," Erma Sue continued, sliding off the counter. "Now my daughter is dead."

Okay, this had gone too far. Yes, Erma Sue had been a jerk, blackmailer, and an overall not-nice person at times. I'd leave poetic justice to the deceased citizens of Sugarland, but I'd do my best to make things right in the world of the living.

"We're going to find out who hurt your daughter," I vowed.

She fought tears as she flicked a lump of dried pomade out of Frankie's hair. "How?"

"She's pretty decent at tracking down the bad guys," Frankie admitted. "She's even got me helping."

The corner of her mouth turned up in a smile.

"You also need to find my book," she said, snipping at Frankie's hair with quick little strokes. "It would be terrible if it ended up in the wrong hands."

I had a feeling it already had.

"We're working on that as well," I assured her. "But I'd also like your help ungrounding a ghost on my property."

Her eyes flicked to me.

I had her interest now.

"It's me," Frankie said. He then proceeded to tell her the entire story while she fussed over his ends.

Told him the chair would do him good.

Erma Sue gave me the kind of look my teachers had when I'd forgotten my homework. "She dumped your ashes onto a rosebush?" she asked, firing up a razor.

"Then she hosed them in good," Frankie said as if I were a meanie like Rowena.

"It was a mistake." He understood that. He'd seen me do it.

"I don't know," Erma Sue mused, taking a razor to the nape of Frankie's neck. "She might have done it on purpose."

"Hardly," I gaped. She really did like to stir the pot.

Erma Sue directed a stink eye at me. "She might have wanted to trap you so she could keep borrowing your power and be a big-shot ghost hunter. I mean, what was she before? Nothing."

Frankie's jaw dropped. "I never thought of it that way."

"Because it's not true," I snapped. Had she forgotten I was going to help her? And since when was I ever a big-shot ghost hunter? Or a nothing?

"It makes sense." Erma Sue trailed her hands through his hair to test the cut. "You're grounded the same way Rowena trapped me."

"Only I still have to live there," Frankie said as if my property were the booby-trap-infested torture palace Rowena had created.

"I'll make you a deal." Erma Sue pursed her lips. "You two learn who killed my daughter. You bring me my book back. And I'll leave the shop for an evening, and we'll set Frankie free."

"Yes!" Frankie clapped and spun the chair in a circle.

"In one evening?" Imagine that.

We'd been trying for years.

Although one evening might be all I could stand of her after listening to her spout off with Frankie.

"That's all it takes to change things for good," she said, taking a blow-dryer to Frankie's hair. "If I can show people I have the book again…" She grinned. "They'll have to respect me. I can coax my clients into the chair again. Maybe reopen the shop with Twyla if she wants to give it another whirl."

I might be re-creating a monster.

And Frankie's haircut was…different. Somehow, I didn't think we'd gotten Erma Sue's best work.

She slammed the dryer down and clapped her hands together. "I'm coming back!"

"That may be a little premature—" I began.

And shouldn't she be more worried about her daughter?

"Don't argue," Frankie muttered in my direction. He held out a hand to Erma Sue. "Pleasure to do business with you."

She shook with him. "Believe me, the pleasure's all mine," she crooned. And I shuddered to think about what kind of deal we'd made.

CHAPTER 12

*E*rma Sue watched after us from the door as we made our way down the cinder-block hallway. "Tell anyone who asks that it was me who did your cut," she called after us.

"I wish she'd died with a mirror," Frankie said, trying to get a feel for the cut by running his fingers through it. "How does it look?"

"Um…" I glanced back at the satisfied hairdresser. "Different. Trendy," I added at the furrow of his brow.

I mean, it truly depended on what decade you were going for. If you were in the 1960s and you fancied a bowl cut, this would be cutting edge.

"It doesn't matter," he said, brushing me off. "I'm this close to being free."

"Let's focus on that." Because he was going to kill me when he saw his hair.

First we had to find Erma Sue's book. Hopefully that would lead us to the killer, and then Erma Sue would help us free Frankie.

"Things are looking up," I said, stepping out into the sunny parking lot.

Unfortunately, they didn't stay that way.

We arrived home to find a horse gone wild.

"Frisky Pete!" I admonished, grinding my car to a halt and rushing for the back porch. The horse had used my porch—the porch my grandfather had built by hand—as a chewing post. And the damage wasn't limited to the ghostly plane. My bucket of mums lay toppled, the porch swing hung sideways, and the ghost horse currently had his head thrust through my kitchen window.

Worse, my skunk was nowhere to be seen.

"Where's Lucy?" I demanded, taking the porch steps two at a time. "Pete better not have trampled her."

"Number one, Pete can't trample the living," Frankie admonished, gliding through the broken rail to stroke the beast's neck. "And B, Pete's a champion. He doesn't trample. He gallops."

He was going to be galloping on out of here if he didn't watch it.

The kitchen door stood open. I pushed in through it and stepped into a bigger mess on the other side.

"Lucille Desiree Long!" At least I'd found her.

On my kitchen counter.

She'd spilled the kitchen trash on her climb to the promised land. Not only that, she'd knocked my coffee pot to pieces on the floor. She'd scattered my sink sponges and soap. And most shocking of all, Lucy currently stood between the sink and the window, her nose millimeters away from Frisky Pete's.

Her little back foot had kicked the water on at some point, and it now flowed over the counter and down onto my floor.

"Now whose pet is out of control?" Frankie asked from outside. "Frisky Pete didn't knock over your flowers or mess up the porch swing, either."

"Just get your horse out of my house." And away from my skunk. "What have you done?" I asked Lucy, but she had no time for me. She merely lifted her dainty nose toward the horse, who nickered and shook his head.

I turned off the water, tossed a few towels onto the floor, and lifted my drippy-footed skunk away from the bad-boy horse.

"You've got to get control of your animal," I said to the gangster, who'd glided through the wall to survey the damage.

"Riiiiight," Frankie said flatly as Lucy struggled in my grip.

I wrapped her in a tea towel. "He's not worth it, sweetie."

"Anyhow, this is the deal you made to get me in the chair for that haircut," Frankie stated, heading down the hallway toward the hall table and the mirror above.

Oh, boy.

"Eee-yow!" he hollered, as if he'd seen a ghost.

One with a dreadful haircut.

"It could be worse," I called after him. He had to look at the bright side. "It's not as if you died with goofy hair."

The gangster shot back into the kitchen, eyes wide. His white Panama hat had reappeared on his head. "Look at this. It looks like I'm bald if I wear my hat."

Too bad Frankie did not make a good-looking bald man. "Well, don't wear your hat, then," I suggested.

He looked at me like I'd suggested he shave his eyebrows too. "It's. My. Hat."

"Erma Sue said your hair will grow back," I pointed out.

"She also said you trapped me on purpose." He yanked the hat down as if it would stretch to cover his shaved undersides. "None of the guys I know have ever cut their hair."

None? "I wonder why."

"Because they don't want to look stupid!" Frankie exclaimed, accidentally knocking his hat off.

"Fair enough," I concluded as he hurried to retrieve it. I could see where a bowl cut would not fit the gangster lifestyle. "But look—you have Pete!" I said, motioning to the not-so-bright horse who still had its head stuck through my window. "And we're going to get you free."

"The sooner I get out of here, the better," he said, rubbing the shaved part at the back of his head. "Your skunk is corrupting my elite racehorse."

"I think it's the other way around," I said, feeling the chill of the horse as it began to nibble on my ponytail. "Don't even think about it, Pete," I said, carrying Lucy into the parlor. "Okay," I said, perching on the arm of the purple sofa, "so how do we find the killer and get Erma Sue's book back?"

"That's the trick," Frankie said, pacing as I rubbed Lucy dry with the tea towel. "Either the person who stole the book and planted it in the time capsule is dead or left town, or they're still here but lying low. Maybe nobody knew about the book until your sister unveiled it and Twyla Sue took it. Or maybe somebody did but doesn't want to admit it."

"It had to be two different people, or else whoever took the book in the first place would have kept it, right?"

"Probably," Frankie conceded. "Unless the culprit thought it was safe underground, but once it came out of the time capsule, he—or maybe she—wanted it back."

We could go around in that circle all night. "Let's instead think of who might have taken the book from Twyla Sue."

"Most likely the same person who killed her, but we can't be sure," Frankie said, pausing in front of the trash can that held the rosebush and the dirt I'd trapped him under. "We don't have enough to go on. I mean, there's lots of reasons why people need killing. Taking the book could have been a totally separate job."

We'd pretend that was true. "Either way, finding the killer should get us closer."

My cell phone rang, and I saw it was Ellis.

"Just a sec." I held up a finger to the gangster.

"Really?" he groused. "Priorities! This is why you'd never make it in the mob," he mumbled under his breath.

That was the only reason?

"Hey, sweetie," I said, maintaining my grip on the skunk as I cradled the phone against my ear. "How's it working with highway patrol?"

"Long. Intense," Ellis said, fatigue bleeding into his voice. "Listen, I was hoping you could help me out this afternoon. Can you go check on my mom?"

That was a favor. And a complication. "Frankie and I are kind of busy here," I explained. And it wasn't as if Virginia Wydell would be glad to see me even if her house was on fire. "Can you call Beau?" I suggested. "Or Leland?" His brothers knew how to handle her better than I did.

"Beau is out of town at a folk art show. For all I know, he tossed his phone into a pond. And Leland has been distancing himself from Mom since her arrest. He's thinking of making a run for the senate."

I pulled my skunk close as she struggled to escape, her wet little feet dampening my sweater. "And Virginia is suddenly a liability?"

I'd never feel sorry for her, but that was harsh.

"My dad is also hanging her out to dry." Ellis sighed. "He's refusing to come back from Malta for what he's calling 'Mom's drama.'"

Ellis's dad had never been a great husband, or father for that matter, but this was bad even for him. "He's a hotshot lawyer, and his wife was arrested after being found with a dead body. Doesn't he think he could be helpful?"

"I've given up on trying to change my family," Ellis stated. "But I keep getting text pings for the alarm system notifications for my mom's garage door." Unlike me, she'd let him install a security system. "The door keeps opening over and over again.

Now her front door keeps opening and closing. Something's going on over there, and she won't answer her phone."

"I can't believe you get her text pings," I said. It wasn't like they were close.

"I can't, either. She wanted the Sugarland police to handle her security directly, but we don't do that. I'm the next best thing."

Poor Ellis. He got all of the work and none of the respect.

"Maybe she's just having people over." Virginia was the matron of Sugarland society. Receiving visitors went with the territory.

Ellis sighed. "I told her to lie low." Ellis and I both chuckled at that. "Seriously, though. I don't think anybody would visit if she issued an invitation. Last time I talked to her, she was really down on herself."

"Virginia?" I found that hard to picture.

"She's been getting threatening phone calls. Vandals tearing up her yard. Twyla Sue was well-liked in town." Ellis paused. "I mean, I almost hope Mom's feeling good enough to see friends," he said, "but she's supposed to be locked down and not having tea or entertaining or anything."

As if Virginia was known for following the rules.

"So you want me to check on her." And possibly interrupt her socializing and incur her wrath. Although, she was the one who should be worried about what I thought after I'd witnessed her with blood on her hands.

"Verity," Ellis pressed, "there's a killer on the loose, and Mom is the only witness."

Unless she *was* the killer.

Sure, Virginia had a reasonable alibi, but she'd also had at least twenty minutes to sneak up on Twyla Sue and slash her throat.

Still, this was Ellis. He'd supported me through some really rough times. He tended to give his best to a lot of people, including his family, and he rarely received the same support in return. But I'd always been there for him, and I'd help him today as well. "I'll check it out," I promised before I changed my mind.

Even if Virginia was my least favorite person, I had Ellis to think about. And it might be interesting to see what was going down at her house.

I placed Lucy on the floor, which was a mistake, because she immediately made a break for the horse.

"Lucy!" I dashed for her, shocked as she began climbing the trash can by the counter like a raccoon on steroids. "That's enough," I said, lifting her halfway to the promised land and moving the trash can aside with my foot. The horse whinnied and nodded his head above my kitchen faucet.

Heavens. I turned to Frankie. "You need to get a handle on your animal while I go deal with Virginia."

"You need to stay here so we can peg a killer and get me free," he countered.

"One thing at a time," I said as my skunk struggled in my grip. I let her down because, what else was I going to do? This was her house, too. Even if it was coming to pieces around an overactive ghost horse. "I mean, what's our next step, Frankie?" I asked as the ghost glided toward me.

"Heck if I know," he said, stopping short.

"Then let me fix this for Ellis." It was the least I could do after all he'd done for me. "I shouldn't be gone long," I added, gathering my purse and my keys. "In the meantime, you figure out how to fix this mess with the horse." Maybe he could call some gangsters and have a barn raising or something. On my land. No. Something else, then. "When I return and find you've...solved the horse issue, then we'll put our brains together and decide how to track down Twyla Sue's killer. Maybe I can find out something from Virginia while I'm there."

"As if a horse on the porch is your biggest problem," Frankie countered, gliding through the back wall as I closed the door behind me.

"It's high on the list," I assured him. "I have to approach this murder mystery in a methodical manner, and I can't do that with my home in shambles."

"Fine." He crossed his arms over his chest as Frisky Pete kicked over a bucket, and a flood of feed pellets cascaded across my porch.

If Frankie turned his power off right now, I'd be slipping on the porch for the next week if those didn't get cleaned up. Like the horse was trying to prove my point.

"Fix it," I pressed.

"Oh, I'll fix it good," he vowed. "But I'm fixing it for Frisky Pete and not for you," he added as I made my way down the steps.

I closed my eyes briefly and said a little prayer. Frankie said he'd make this right, and I had to trust him. I had to believe this would get better—or at least not worse—as I tried not to think about exactly what he'd be doing while I was away.

CHAPTER 13

I drove to the west side of town and down the old mill road under a canopy of fall trees awash with color. I tried to take in the reds, oranges, and golds.

I kept the windows down and tried to soak in the lovely fall breeze.

It did not help.

I toggled a few radio stations but soon gave up.

Nothing improved the trip when it came to making the journey to the Wydell estate. My visits had been mostly unpleasant, often shocking, and never welcome.

Ellis was lucky I loved him.

There was a brief moment when his mother had tolerated my presence, and that was a few years after college when I'd dated her youngest son, Beau. I hadn't existed before then, at least as far as she was concerned. And I'd been deemed passable only because I came from an old family in town and because Beau was her darling. Whatever Beau wanted, Beau received with a ribbon on top. Including marriage to a "simpleminded but pretty enough girl," as she'd referred to me.

That should have been my first clue.

My shoulders tightened as I drew nearer to the estate. I'd given in to her every whim for the wedding. She'd promised to pay for the excesses. I'd been young and naive, but smart enough to kick Beau to the curb after I'd caught him trying to force himself on my sister.

At the time, I'd believed it was the absolute worst thing that could happen.

Then Virginia Wydell had nearly bankrupted me by suing me for the cost of the lavish celebration she'd ordered. She'd slandered my name in town. She'd called it punishment for betraying her son, never mind what he'd done to cause it.

I'd lost my security, my livelihood, and my reputation.

I adjusted my grip on the wheel. I needed to try to let it go. Ellis was the one I was helping here, not Virginia.

Ellis wasn't like anyone in his family. He'd joined the military instead of the family law firm, a decision his mother had never forgiven. When he'd chosen to enlist rather than network his way to officers' training, she'd stopped calling, stopped sending letters. And when he became a police officer instead of going to law school after his enlistment was up, his mother had written him off entirely.

But Ellis didn't give up on people. Some would call him foolish to give her the time of day, but it made me see how he wouldn't give up on me or on anyone he loved. And I was proud to help him now, even if it meant I had to brave the lion's den.

I steered the land yacht up the twisting road along the river bluff until I came to a private driveway guarded by ornate iron gates with the letter *W* emblazoned in stylish monogram-style script. Only today, the gates stood open.

Strange.

If there was one thing Ellis's mother loved, it was a locked gate only she could open. I drove past the black call box on a pole. The red button glowed red, waiting to be pressed. Her system was working, just not in use.

Perhaps Ellis had been right to worry.

The rest appeared normal. So far. Towering cypress trees lined the meandering drive that wound past small gardens of native purple passionflowers and American beautyberry. Not a flower was allowed to be out of place on the Wydell estate.

Tires crunched on the road ahead as I rounded a planting that featured a perfectly spiral Japanese holly. I pulled as far to the right as I could, allowing a red truck to pass close on the way down. Bill Wershing waved, and in the back, he hauled an antique rolltop desk.

As far as I knew, Bill, veteran principal at Sugarland High, hadn't spoken to Virginia Wydell since Beau's attempt at a senior prank went horribly wrong. He and his friends had filled Principal Wershing's office with two dozen chickens after school without stopping to think what said chickens would be doing in there all night.

Let's just say it was stinky.

I rounded the next bend and was glad to have stayed to the far right side of the road because a Ford F-150 dragging a landscaping trailer took the bend a bit more quickly than it should have and nearly clocked me. In the back, he hauled a vintage wooden rocking chair mostly wrapped in an old green blanket. I didn't know if I was more shocked at that or at the salute Josephus Judson, current owner of Judson's Last Stop market, gave me as he hit the gas and sped faster down the hill.

Heavens. If I hadn't recognized Bill and Josephus as the fine upstanding citizens they were, I'd have thought the Wydell estate was being robbed. In broad daylight, too.

Something was definitely wrong. Was the house on fire?

Virginia Wydell would rather mount a stripper pole than hold a garage sale, so I knew my fellow citizens hadn't bought her antiques out from under her.

Not that any of us could afford it.

I raced to the top of the hill, relieved to find the grand white home as it always stood, with its upper and lower porches and towering Palladian windows. The storybook house had graced the property since 1982, after Virginia married into the family. Word had it, she'd been instrumental in razing the family's original home and replacing it with something off the cover of *Southern Living*.

She'd also gotten a special permit to bulldoze the old-growth trees on the back of the property. That way, the house looked down on the river, as well as the entire town of Sugarland.

I pulled past the richly blooming blue and white hydrangea bushes that crowded the circle drive and stopped short. The custom front door hung wide open.

Definitely not good.

I shut off the engine and dug my cell phone out of my purse to call Ellis. I mean, I hadn't discovered exactly what was going on, but I'd never known Virginia to issue an open invitation to her home.

Maybe he'd know what to do.

I dropped the phone cold when my best friend Lauralee's husband stepped out the front door, carrying a huge antique silver punch bowl.

"Big Tom!" I hurried from the car to where he struggled across the brick patio, followed by his construction buddy, Mike, who carried an entire set of silverware. At least, that was what it looked like.

"What are you doing?" I hurried to intercept them.

Had the whole world gone mad?

"Give me a sec, Verity," Big Tom said, wiping his bearded cheek on his sleeve as he adjusted his grip on the bowl. "This is heavy."

No doubt. It was solid from the look of it.

Virginia stood in the doorway, her mouth puckered and her eyes hard. She was dressed to receive, in a flawless pink suit, matching pink heels, and pearls on her earlobes and around her neck.

"Are you having an estate sale?" I asked. I wouldn't have believed it, and it was obvious she hadn't informed poor Ellis, but it was the only explanation for the parade of heirlooms leaving the house.

She glared at me like I'd asked to try on her underwear. "Absolutely not. Please leave. This is none of your business," she stated before turning her back and disappearing into the house, slamming the door behind her.

"What was that about?" I asked, following Big Tom to his truck. He'd set the silver service on the back, and he and Mike were busy wrapping the punch bowl with a moving blanket.

Big Tom tore off a swatch of duct tape and handed the roll to me. "She bought this from my great-aunt Matilda, and we're taking it back," he said, securing the blanket around the silver bowl with the duct tape.

"But if she bought it, then it's Virginia's now." I held the roll as he tore off more tape. I mean, I appreciated the desire to reclaim family artifacts, but you couldn't just haul things from someone's house.

And what was up with Bill Wershing and Josephus Judson anyway?

Big Tom left Mike to finish with the punch bowl and picked up the box of silverware. "Virginia bought my great-aunt's serving set *for a dollar* because my aunt was afraid." I opened the door for him, and he slid the silverware into the back seat of the truck. "Now Aunt Mattie doesn't have to be scared anymore. She can have her family heirlooms back."

Wow. So Erma Sue might not be the only blackmailer in town. But I needed to understand. "I get that Virginia is scary." The queen of Sugarland society could be vicious. "But what could she have on poor, sweet Mattie?"

"It's not for me to say," Big Tom said, slamming the truck door closed. "But are you honestly surprised?"

"Yes and no." Virginia had taken so much from me as well. She'd not only forced me to sell most of my family's treasures in order to pay for the non-wedding, but she'd taken great joy in watching me dismantle the legacy I'd inherited from my grandmother—the history I'd been trusted to cherish and maintain.

All to make me sorry for calling out her son's mistake. All to show me that I could stand up for myself and my future, but at the cost of my past and everything else I held dear.

Still, Virginia had been more interested in revenge than the actual value of the items she'd taken. "I just never thought she'd dare do it to anyone else," I admitted. I mean, what could Mattie have ever done to her?

Big Tom slapped me on the shoulder. "To tell you the truth, I thought we were the only ones before it happened to you." He left my side to make sure Mike had everything squared away in the back. "Mattie was so ashamed I wasn't even allowed to tell Lauralee about it, until today, that is."

"What changed?" I asked as Mike closed up the truck. "I mean, why is today the day you came to take Mattie's silver back?"

"You seriously don't know?" Mike asked.

"Then let it be my pleasure to inform you." Big Tom dug into his back pocket and unfolded a single sheet of paper. "This was posted all over town."

My mouth went dry as he handed me a photocopied page from a handwritten journal. "Is this from Erma Sue's blackmail book?"

"Read it and weep," Big Tom said.

Mike tested the truck door to make sure it was closed. "As far as I'm concerned, Virginia should be the only one weeping."

June 18, 1984

Oh my. Everyone remembers the silver 1910 rowing victory cup, a cherished part of Sugarland history, but not everyone knows what happened to it after it disappeared from the display case. What if I told you dirt-poor Virginia Nelson sold the cup up north and used the profit to transform herself from a mediocre duckling to a swan? It takes a lot of duck feed to finance the kind of look and lifestyle that would snag the attention—not to mention a marriage proposal—from the rich and powerful Leland Wydell. And what if I told you she bought the cup back once she had his money, and hid it in her attic so no one would ever know what she did? It's probably in her attic right now, behind Kitty Wershing's rolltop desk and Alma Judson's rocking chair. You might even find Mattie Clementine's silver serving ware up there if you went to look.

"I don't believe it," I said, breathless. Then again, I did. I just never expected this kind of vindication in a million years.

"A bunch of people broke the gate this morning," Mike said. "They demanded the cup back. It was all anyone could talk about at the diner."

Big Tom glanced up at the house. "Virginia is denying anything and everything about the 1910 rowing cup, but Bill Wershing forced his way in and found his grandma's desk. He called Josephus and me." He shook his head. "She's saying she forgot about our 'trinkets' she 'bought' and of course we can have them if we want them." he said. "But more people are going to come looking for that cup. And probably a lot of other things besides." He braced a hand against his truck. "These flyers are all over town."

Virginia could have hidden the victory cup anywhere in the house by now. It wasn't like attempting to relocate a heavy desk or rocking chair. Still, she couldn't hide it forever, not when everybody knew it was there. "She's in trouble," I said, the words rumbling low in my throat. Virginia had messed with an honored tradition in Sugarland, something most folks held dear. "Big trouble."

Big Tom nodded, running a hand over his beard. "People are

starting to share stories online about how Virginia likes to punish people who cross her. It's more than just a few of us. I mean, it's been forty years, and my great-aunt finally admitted she 'donated' her serving set to the Wydells because she couldn't afford attorney's fees after she lost a contest about the property boundaries between her land and the Wydells'. Virginia sent her lawyers after Mattie, and my aunt relented."

Mike crossed his arms over his chest. "The Lynns say they had to give up the Revolutionary War sword their six-times great-grandfather made by hand so Virginia wouldn't use her clout to block their daughter's nomination to West Point," he said. "Evidently, Tosha Lynn had the nerve to sell one of her bridal store customers the exact same mother of the bride dress Virginia had picked out for your wedding."

"But I didn't have a wedding." Not technically. I mean, Virginia had plowed forward with the wedding and reception in order to embarrass me after I'd called off the marriage the day before, but it wasn't as if that gave her exclusive rights to a dress.

"She knows how to twist the knife," Big Tom said.

"And she seems to know a lot about everybody," Mike agreed.

Gossip was currency in a small town like ours. And Virginia had the connection to a major source. "She was such good friends with Twyla Sue growing up," I said, thinking. She'd insisted I get my hair done at Two Sues' House of Beauty when I'd been engaged to Beau. "At one point she told me when they were teens together, they used to hang out at the salon." And she was a regular after-hours client of Twyla Sue if her story on the night of the murder was to be believed. Twyla Sue hadn't kept a blackmail book like her mother had, but she did operate in the heart of the rumor mill. "I wonder if Virginia heard bits and pieces of gossip and used them to get what she wanted. Or if Twyla Sue told her all the juicy details."

Big Tom's expression went stormy. "Doesn't matter how it happened; it's not right."

"I know." It was terrible the way she'd taken advantage of people for years, and from these stories, it seemed to be those who weren't in her social circle and couldn't fight back. It was starting to make sense that we'd found Virginia at the murder scene, looking for that book.

"She's kept so many people cowed for so long," Mike gritted out, "but now we're all starting to share our own secrets. Soon, she won't be able to hide behind her fancy reputation or her threats to expose people."

We could only hope.

"Go see what she has of yours," Big Tom urged.

"I think my treasures are long gone," I admitted. I'd be willing to bet Virginia had taken great pleasure in scattering my family legacy to the winds. Still… "I'm going to have a word with her," I said, leaving the men.

I hurried up onto the porch and knocked while they finished loading the truck. Mike slammed the tailgate shut, and Big Tom took the wheel.

Virginia didn't answer the door.

I knocked again. Jim and Mike waved goodbye as the wheels of the pickup crunched over the driveway. Virginia ignored me.

She couldn't pretend I wasn't knocking. She couldn't hole up in her mansion and act like this was none of my business. Not after she'd taken my things for her petty revenge games. Not when the diary page revealed she'd stolen our prized silver rowing trophy. Not when Bill had found the desk, Josephus discovered his rocking chair, and Big Tom had recovered his great-aunt's silver—precisely where the diary had said they would be.

I was done with her hiding up in her house on the hill. Done with her lying. Done with her. I tested the knob on the front door, and of course it was open.

This was Sugarland, after all.

I made a split-second decision and let myself in. I stepped into the cavernous foyer and slammed the door behind me. "Virginia," I called, listening to the crystal chandelier above me shake and tinkle. "I'm here, and I'm not going away until we have our come to Jesus." My voice echoed in the white marble foyer.

How sweet Ellis had grown up in such a cold, sterile house was beyond me.

The parlor stood to the right, family pictures in gleaming silver frames scattered across the floor. They belonged on top of the grand piano that had stood in the window for years. Only it was gone.

A door upstairs slammed.

"What are you doing in my house?" Virginia demanded, clutching the snowy white balustrade.

"Ellis sent me to check on you," I said, holding my ground. "Obviously, things are not good." I gestured to the empty spot on her carpet where the piano had once stood.

Her fingers tightened on the rail. "I'm doing as well as I always have," she said, her voice frosty and her expression hard, "but you've clearly gone insane."

"At least I'm not missing a piano." Not that I'd ever had a piano. And how had they gotten it out of here so fast? "You're in trouble, Virginia."

"Please." She scoffed, descending the grand staircase like a queen of old. "Tom wanted his sad little silver back, and I gave it to him. I'd have done it years ago if I knew he cared that much."

"It wasn't *sad*. It was heavy and thick, and—speaking of other people's things—what about the 1910 championship cup?"

She rolled her eyes as she reached the bottom of the staircase, her heels clicking like gunshots on the white marble. "That disappeared more than forty years ago."

"Because you took it."

She had the nerve to feign surprise. "That's a complete fabrication, and I'll hear none of it."

"People came for it this morning, didn't they?" I pressed.

She crossed her arms over her chest. "They broke my gate," she stated as if *she* were the wronged party.

"They know you took the 1910 championship cup because you told Twyla Sue, and she told her mom." She and Twyla had been friends long before Virginia's rise through the Sugarland social set. "That's why you were at the salon, looking for the burn book."

"It was more than forty years ago," she ground out, losing her temper for a split second before patting her hair and forcing her voice down a notch. "I was at the salon to get my hair done. That's it. And you should know I would never lower myself to going to a rowing competition on a river, much less steal the prize cup. Listen to yourself. Do you realize how ridiculous you sound?"

It was no crazier than her denial of what was happening at this very moment. "You've hurt people, Virginia." I didn't know how else to explain it. "The jig is up."

Her eyes narrowed. "I see why you're spouting nonsense," she said as if she were my demented therapist. "You think I've taken things from you." She drew her fingers across the pearls at her throat. "This is about you and your issues."

"It's not," I stated flatly. Not entirely at least. "But while we're at it, you had no business forcing me to liquidate my house, all for your petty revenge." She smirked, and I plowed on. "I realize you can't stand for anyone else to have a family history when you never did." Her nostrils flared, and her lips tightened. I felt mean saying it, but it was the truth. Her mother's history was murky, and she'd never known the identity of her father. "You had no legacy to speak of until you married Ellis's dad." Even then, she'd ripped down the family homestead and replaced it with the structure she'd built.

"You want to know if I have any of your things," she said with a dose of satisfaction that made my skin crawl.

"Do you?" This was more than a game to me. Unlike her, I was loyal to my family. I owed it to my grandmother to try to preserve her legacy.

The corner of her mouth ticked up. "I'm sorry, dear. None of what you had was exactly collectible."

"It wouldn't kill you to be kind," I reminded her.

She scanned me up and down as if she were measuring exactly how far to push me. "All right. I admit it. I went to the auction. There was one item of yours that didn't sell. It seemed a shame to leave it, never mind the silver is thin and it's entirely too small and shabby for actual use."

My throat tightened. "Show me," I ordered.

She tilted her head. "Wait here."

I held my ground in her foyer as she strode up the staircase. She returned a short time later holding a blackened mess of a bowl out in front of her. My heart leapt, and tears sprang up in the corners of my eyes.

Virginia held the delicate bowl with the tips of her fingers so she didn't have to touch it any more than necessary, but to me it was the most precious thing in the world.

"It was in the attic with the rest of the junk," she said. "Don't pretend Big Tom didn't tell you."

He hadn't. I doubted he would have recognized it anyway. In fact, I could hardly believe it as she made it to the bottom of the stairs.

My grandmother's favorite silver fruit bowl. I hadn't seen it since the estate sale. I'd thought it was gone forever.

"You had this?" I asked, touching the rim. I recognized the grapevine scrollwork beneath the muck, the indent of the L for Long. Grandma had gotten it as a wedding present and shined it every Sunday. We'd picked blueberries for the bowl and tossed them in with the strawberries we bought every Friday at the fruit stand down the road. It had been a fixture on her table since before I was born.

"It's yours if you want it," she stated as if she hadn't purposely kept it from me for years. "But seeing as I rescued it for you, I expect something in return."

"You're the reason I lost it," I ground out, itching to snatch the bowl. Everything with Virginia was transactional, even if Ellis couldn't quite bring himself to see it.

She ran a finger along the rim. "It's nothing, really. Or it shouldn't be much to you."

"Virginia," I cut her off. I was done listening to her nonsense. I was done playing her games. I'd checked up on her because I loved Ellis. I'd keep the peace with her as best I could because I'd have to live with her for a long, long time if I ended up marrying her son. But I'd reached my limit for the day and quite possibly the next ten years. "Say it plain."

She notched her chin up. "I'll give it back to you if you stop whoever has that diary that's causing so much trouble. And find out who killed Twyla Sue."

"In that order," I said flatly. She really was a piece of work. "You're trying to bribe me to help you."

She didn't bother denying it.

It was sad on about ten different levels. Most people just asked for help, and I happily agreed. I *liked* to help people. But one of the consequences of being such a mean person was that Virginia didn't understand how she could be on the receiving end of someone's goodwill.

"Talk to your ghosts; do what you do," she said with a dismissive wave of the hand. "Learn who thinks they need to post these evil lies about me."

Ha. That was the trick. "They're not lies, Virginia. You really are that evil," I said, the words just falling out. "There's a reason people believe these stories about you, or are you really that far in denial?"

Her cheeks went red. "Do you want your little bowl back or not?"

"I do," I said, plucking it straight out of her hands. "I'm taking it because it's mine."

"So we have a deal," she said, surprised.

"I hate to bust your balloon, but no. We don't have any sort of deal. I'm not going to save you from what you did. In fact, I'm glad you're finally getting your due," I added, while her mouth opened and closed like a fish. "Actions have consequences. At least they do now." She might have avoided it for years, but not anymore. I tucked the bowl under my arm. "You need to make things right. Admit your mistakes. Return what you took. And while you're at it, beg for forgiveness."

"I—"she began, her cheeks reddening.

"You'd better hope the people you wronged will be more understanding than you were when the roles were reversed. Be prepared to accept it if they aren't. But no matter what happens, Virginia, know you deserve whatever you get."

"Get out." She reached for the bowl back, but I swiveled it out of her grasp. Unlike her, I held it tight.

"Oh, I'm leaving," I assured her. With any luck, I wouldn't be back for a long, long time. "But the truth is out. Do the right thing when folks come back looking for that cup."

"It's not in the attic—" she said haltingly.

"Wherever you stashed it, you need to give it to them. You need to apologize and set things right."

"You're crazy," she said, tossing her hands up.

"You can't hide anymore. The sooner you realize that, the easier it will go for you."

Virginia stood in shock. That was fine. Maybe she would listen more carefully that way. I was only going to say this once. "I love Ellis, and that's the only reason I'm bothering to tell you any of this. You can't keep going the way you have, controlling people for your own purposes. You've raised your oldest son to care more about a senate race than his mother being in jail. Your husband didn't even come back to town when you got arrested. Your old life is set to implode," I warned her. "The fuse has been lit. You don't get to stop it. You only get to choose what you're going to do from now on."

Her bottom lip trembled. "You're unhinged."

"I've watched my life burn down, and I can tell you it's going to get worse before it gets better. Ellis loves you, and I love him, so I will do my best to help catch the pieces as they fall. But you need to start treating him better. He's the one who asked me to come check on you. He's the one who has some sense of twisted duty to a mother who has no use for him."

I walked away.

"He's a disappointment, and so are you," she declared.

I kept going, then thought better of it. I kept a hand on the doorknob as I turned to face her. "You just don't get it, do you? You think you're better than me, that I don't deserve a man like Ellis. Well, bless your little heart. *You* don't deserve Ellis. And you sure as hell don't deserve me."

I held my head high and my fruit bowl tightly as I slammed the door and left her alone in her big fancy house full of other people's treasures.

And as I tucked my grandmother's prized silver fruit bowl next to me on the bench seat of my old Cadillac, I realized that for once I was glad to have visited Virginia Wydell.

CHAPTER 14

$\mathcal{I}$ drove down that hill with a new sense of freedom. I'd done it. I'd released Virginia Wydell's hold on me. I'd let her know in no uncertain terms what I thought about her and her attitude. And I felt like I'd had my say for Ellis as well.

I never thought I'd see the day when the good citizens of Sugarland began saying "no more" to Virginia Wydell, and I was glad to be a part of it.

There wasn't a second I regretted, except I maybe should have tried to help Big Tom lug that bowl. Then again, Big Tom could probably stuff me into the bowl and run a mile carrying us both if he set his mind to it.

I pulled over near the stop sign just short of Route 4 to come back to earth and breathe. And that was when I realized perhaps I'd better call Ellis before his mother did.

I wrestled my hands-free headset out of the glove compartment. The wires lived in a near-permanent tangle, and my entire system needed an upgrade, but I hadn't been able to afford it for so long, and I'd simply gotten used to living without.

Yet another casualty of my life after Virginia Wydell had gotten hold of it.

Ellis picked up right as I'd gotten the headset on and the wires mostly sorted. "It's me," I said, trying—and failing—to douse some of the cheer from my voice.

"Verity." He sounded relieved to hear from me. Because, of course, he thought I'd taken care of his mother.

Well, I had.

In a way.

"I checked on your mom," I said, glancing over my shoulder as I pulled out onto the road. As for the rest, I wasn't quite sure how to explain Virginia's current predicament, so I settled for the facts.

Ellis grew silent as I explained how the page from the burn book had showed up in town, and the multiple repossessions it had inspired. I told him how his mother most likely had that championship cup hidden in her house, and the longer she held out, the worse it would be.

My stomach twisted in a knot for each prickly detail I felt morally obliged to add. I didn't regret what had happened or my part in it. But I did feel terrible that a good person like Ellis had to be caught up with Virginia by virtue of being born. On top of that, poor Ellis had been cursed with an extra dose of moral obligation and an unwavering sense of duty to the wretched family who didn't feel much at all for him.

"I advised your mom rather strongly to make things right with the people she hurt," I said to Ellis. Including him, I added to myself, realizing my diatribe had taken me the length of Route 4.

"I'd like to think she can do that," Ellis said, hedging.

We both knew what a step that would be.

"Either she'll take my...ah, fervent suggestion, or I may have torched any and all bridges I had left with her," I admitted. "Then set fire to the water."

He didn't speak for a long moment. At least I didn't think he did. It might have been my discount bin headset.

"Thank you," Ellis said at last. "I appreciate you taking care of her."

I let out a small sigh of relief. "I did my best." Too bad it hadn't quite turned out the way I'd planned.

"I'd have told her the same," he said. "She'd best be prepared for what is coming."

"I appreciate you trusting me." He knew I'd always do right by him.

"I do," he said, as if it felt good to say. It sure felt good for me to hear. "Still," he added, "I'm worried about her. This sounds like her worst nightmare. Even if she created it. And I think there's more to it than we know." He hesitated before plowing forward. "Three days ago, my mom gave away the piano that's sat in the front window for as long as I can remember. When I asked her about it, she said she'd donated it."

"To whom?" I asked, my fingers tightening on the wheel.

"She refused to tell me. I mean, why would that be a secret? So I did a little digging. According to Duranja's cousin, who owns the only moving company in town big enough to handle a piano, the piece went to Vincent Youngblood IV."

I was quite familiar with the three-time widower who lived up the hill from the Heritage Society. "Vincent is rich as Croesus," I said, trying to make sense of it. "He doesn't need donations from Virginia."

"My thoughts exactly," Ellis said. "We can talk about it more tonight. I'll check in with Mom after my shift, but right now I'm still on this stakeout..."

"Of course," I said, turning onto the side road near my house. "Why don't you drop by my house after?" He'd need to vent.

"How about I lure you over to my place with takeout?" he countered.

"Sounds great." He'd want to be home after a long day. "But don't worry about food. I'll take care of dinner."

And him.

I'd stop by my friend Lauralee's food truck. We could both use a nice comfort meal after the day we'd had, and we had a lot to talk about. Aside from the obvious drama with his mother, I wondered what had inspired her sudden donation. The diary page hadn't mentioned a thing about a piano or Vincent Youngblood. And she'd given up the piano before anybody knew about the prize cup.

We agreed on a time and hung up. But I wondered if there was something I could do in the meantime.

An interesting thought occurred to me, and I pulled over under a towering oak to locate the number for Vincent Youngblood IV. I'd visited him while working to solve the murder of his third wife, Julia. Perhaps I could reach out to him again and save Ellis some legwork.

After dialing, I began the slow drive through the neighborhood that led to my house, letting the phone ring and ring and ring.

It didn't surprise me when Vincent failed to answer.

I mean, yes, I'd solved his late wife's murder a year and a half ago, and he'd been grateful. But he'd also been high on my list of suspects for a time. Unfortunately, I hadn't exactly been secretive about it.

I dialed his number again. Perhaps he'd been out in the garden.

Or avoiding me.

The phone kept ringing, but Vincent still wasn't picking up. Neither was his voice mail, which made me think avoidance was the most likely scenario.

Perhaps I'd just drop by unannounced.

This was Sugarland, after all. Drop-ins were a part of life. And if I showed up on his doorstep, he'd have to talk to me or risk being seen as impolite. Vincent Youngblood IV was a lot of things, but he wasn't rude.

I'd just return my grandma's fruit bowl to the table where it belonged and check in on Lucy to make sure she wasn't having any more trouble with that horse. I could be in and out in a jiffy.

I made my way through the neighborhood that had sprung up after my family sold the land near the main road and soon came to the long drive that led to my home.

All appeared well. Dare I say peaceful. Perhaps Frankie had finally done as I'd asked. Maybe my troubles with Frisky Pete were over.

I could almost see the old racehorse, well-behaved and grazing far, far away from the house, in the field on the other side of the pond. A speck in the distance. That would be nice. Or maybe Frankie had called his gangster buddies to pick up Pete and take him to a ghostly training facility near one of the old racetracks, where he could have a real trainer who knew horses. Frisky Pete could frolic and play and do whatever else dead racehorses did.

It was about time.

I didn't even care if Frankie wanted to make his shed into a horsey haven. Lucy wouldn't go near the place, and since Frankie was the dominant ghost inside his shed, he could make the space as large and as custom as he wished.

That way, Frankie could focus on what was important. Namely, his freedom.

It would be much easier to hunt down Erma Sue's book if we weren't dealing with a horse on the porch.

I looked for signs of life at home. Perhaps Lucy asleep under the hydrangea bush near the front porch rail, or under one of the spindly peach trees.

But I didn't see her.

That was all right. She might be out back under the apple tree.

But as I pulled around to park behind the house, my anticipation faded to dread as I was greeted by a small animal that
was definitely not my skunk. Not even close. I froze for a
second in shock as a tiny, ghostly baby goat loped over to
greet me.

I slammed the car door. "Frankie!"

The gray and white speckled goat was insanely cute, with a
smushy little nose, perky ears, and big, round eyes. It leapt
around me as I stalked toward the ghost in the fedora who
stood on the porch, chain-smoking.

"Frankie," I bellowed as a second gray, glowing baby goat
danced its way down my porch stairs.

"Frankie, what have you done?" I demanded, charging up the
back stairs with my grandmother's fruit bowl under my arm.
On my way I had to dodge the fuzzball on the steps and a third
baby goat standing on the back rail next to a jubilant Frisky
Pete.

A full-sized black goat stood on a hay bale next to the horse,
eating one of Frisky Pete's carrots, while Lucy took turns
jumping up and down off my very real potted mum, smashing
the flowers and scattering dirt. She'd joined forces with a gray
and white speckled baby goat, who seemed to take great delight
in breezing straight through the mess.

The gangster turned, his hat askew as he took a hard drag on
his smoke. "I was told a goat would be good for keeping Frisky
Pete company," he hedged.

"So you figured five would be better." One on the lawn, one
on the steps, one on the back rail, mamma on the hay bale, and
the little gray speckled one diving through my potted mum.

"Six," Frankie corrected, pointing his smoke at a baby goat
standing on my gently swaying porch swing, chewing a bit of
ghostly hay. "It's…more goats than I planned," he admitted. "But
the only goat I could find was Nibbles, and I wasn't going to
separate her from her babies."

"Nibbles?" Who named these creatures, anyway?

"This is not a farm," I stated in no uncertain terms as my skunk took her turn on the potted mum, scattering a fresh round of dirt. "Your horse, your goats, they are a bad influence on Lucy!" I insisted, going to fetch her before she made a bigger mess.

"Hey, you didn't like it when Pete and Lucy were getting friendly. The goats are supposed to take the place of your precious skunk," he said, whipping off his hat and pointing it in the direction of the mamma goat. "Nibbles here is a good girl."

Lucy dodged my grasp and set up for another run at the mum pot.

"Nibbles is keeping Frisky Pete company," Frankie lectured, as if I were uneducated in the ways of goats and horses. Which I was, but so was he. "Lucy will get bored and go back to sleeping under the porch once Frisky Pete starts ignoring her."

"Any idea on when the *goats* will start ignoring my skunk?" I prodded. Nibbles and the gang had turned my porch from a party into a circus.

"You should be glad that they're having fun," Frankie insisted, taking another hard drag. "Ghostly animals—unlike me—are free. If they're not happy, they can leave."

"Well, they seem to be having a grand time here." Unfortunately for me. I stood and basically gave up on capturing the overexcited skunk. "Can you just…get them to chill out?"

"I'm the horse whisperer, not the goat guru," Frankie snapped as if *I* were the unreasonable one.

Even a horse whisperer had to see this was ridiculous. "Why did you think a goat would work *at all*?"

"It's common knowledge among horse people like me," he stated, as if he'd been a horse owner for years instead of a solid day.

I let out a small shriek as Frisky Pete stomped happy-horse style, shaking the porch on the ghostly side. That kind of energetic pressure couldn't be doing any good in the land of the living, either. Lucy made another leap onto the pot of mums. I watched in horror as it toppled sideways. She rolled past a goat, who leapt over her with glee. Dirt and flowers spilled everywhere. "You just cracked my best planter pot!" I cried.

"Bad skunk," Frankie said, grabbing a carrot from the horse ball and feeding it to Nibbles the goat.

Lucy hunched and drew her tail close. "Naughty skunk," I corrected, scooping her up with my free arm and giving her a quick kiss on the head. That probably wasn't the best thing to do when disciplining her, but it wasn't her fault she'd gotten overstimulated. "Bad gangster," I declared, aiming the blame where it belonged—on the wiseguy who had stuck a horse on the porch in the first place.

"Of course I'm a bad guy," he said, sneaking another carrot for Nibbles. "It's what I do."

"You've completely blown our agreement," I said, adjusting my grip on Lucy as she tried to scramble out of my arms. Even Frankie had to see this was beyond the pale. I kept hold of her and my temper, but just barely. "I said you could keep what you had on the porch *then*. We're aiming for fewer animals, not more."

Frankie had understood perfectly. He just didn't care.

Frankie held a finger up. "Actually, we did not define a set number of animals."

"Fix it," I barked. "Control the horse. Get rid of the goats."

"The goats *are* fixing it," Frankie protested. "See how calm Frisky Pete is now?"

He was tap-dancing on my last nerve. "Make my house peaceful again," I ordered.

"I held up my end of the bargain," Frankie said. "I let you talk to Erma Sue."

"That benefitted you too," I reminded him.

ANGIE FOX

"Only to a point. Now you have to do your part to find the book and get me free," Frankie declared.

"I'm working on it. Someone is releasing pages from Erma Sue's book." Or at least it appeared that way. "If we figure out who's doing that, it could lead us straight to the killer."

"I don't care about the killer. I care about the book," he declared as the baby goat who had so enjoyed my mums began nibbling at his coat. "I think I'm going to call you Scape," he informed the little one.

"I care about both." And about Ellis. I ducked into the kitchen and placed Lucy on the floor, sighing as she made a mad dash for the window.

Frankie followed me inside with Scape clambering at his heels. "Look," he said, "you don't need to solve Twyla Sue's murder. You just need to figure out who has Erma Sue's book. Then you'll be free of me and the horse and the goats and everything that's so terrible about your life."

"What about justice?" I asked, earning a frown from him.

"Okay, say you get justice," the gangster said, clearly patronizing me. "Say you pull a guy's fingernails out or blow up his car with him in it. It's fine, but after a fine steak dinner, you forget all about it."

He didn't get it. "I'm talking about a killer getting his or her just due."

"What's the fun in that?" he balked. "Unless they killed a friend of yours, and then it's fingernail pincers and car explosives."

"And a steak dinner," I said drolly.

He snapped his fingers. "Now you've got it."

Great. "Can I tell you what we have going right now?" I set about explaining the gist of what had happened at Virginia's house, leaving out most of the details because Frankie wouldn't care anyway. Instead, I told him about the page from the diary and how the missing piano led to Vincent Youngblood IV.

144

"I need to ask what transpired between him and Virginia that caused her to give up such a nice, not to mention high profile, piece," I said, setting my grandmother's fruit bowl on the kitchen table. "She only gave up the other stuff because that diary page came out." I'd bet anything she still has that rowing trophy, even though it'll sink her ship if anyone finds it at her house."

Frankie's eyes narrowed. "So you're going to investigate gossip instead of helping me."

In Sugarland, it was one and the same. "The gossip may lead to the book."

"Okay, fine." He ran a hand along the back of his neck. "I'll come along in case you need me to throttle anyone."

I wanted to talk to Vincent without any ghostly interruptions—not that he'd notice if Frankie sat in his lap. Besides, one or several of Vincent's late wives might haunt the estate. With any luck, they could shed light on his recent acquisition, and I'd rather talk to the spirits without the help of a jumpy gangster with no filter and a bad haircut.

So I pointed out the obvious. "You have a problem to fix right here."

"I know what you're doing," he said as I rooted around in the fridge for a quick meal for my skunk. "You're putting me off so that I have to stay here. You've gotten used to the fast life, and you're afraid it'll be boring when I go."

I was, but not for the reasons he thought. While I wouldn't miss the horse or the goats or the general mayhem, I'd miss him. Frankie, despite his attitude and his blatant disrespect for law and order, had grown on me.

I cut some carrots for Lucy's lunch and reached for an apple I'd left on the counter.

Whether he believed it or not, I was trying to help him.

"I'll see you when I get back," I said, setting the apple on the chopping board.

"You're lucky you can see me—or anything—right now."

I added a few chunks of pineapple from the fridge as well as a bit of low-fat yogurt. That would make Lucy happy. And mask the dry, high-fiber Vita-Skunk cereal. "Don't even think about cutting off my power. This is a solid lead." Or at least a way to get some real insight into what was happening. "I promise we will find Erma Sue's book."

The gangster ground his jaw. "You can't make a promise like that," he insisted, as if it hurt too much to hope. "Nobody can."

And I hated to think it, but for once, Frankie was right.

CHAPTER 15

*V*incent Youngblood IV lived in a century-old home on a wooded bluff overlooking the river. If it was possible for a Victorian to appear masculine, this one did. It had been painted in rich shades of gray and deep blue, with stunning white trim and double bay windows on both the first and second floors.

Tall windows arched up toward the kind of gingerbread trim that would make the editors at *Southern Living* swoon. And most notably, his wraparound porch was blessedly free of both goats and horses.

Vincent had inherited the house from his third wife. As I drew closer, I saw him sitting in a black wicker chair on his veranda with a cocktail in hand.

It was the hour for that sort of thing. My excursion to Virginia's unplanned estate liquidation, along with the goat bonanza on my porch, meant I'd reached the widower's house in the later part of the afternoon.

Vincent was a handsome, athletic man. His wavy black hair had grayed stylishly at the temples, and he wore a white oxford shirt tucked into belted charcoal dress slacks.

He stood and began to head inside as I parked in the circle drive.

"Wait a moment if you please!" I called, shutting off the engine.

He couldn't ignore me now that I'd made social contact.

Vincent paused, gripping the handle of the stately oak front door. It had a long window built into it, veiled with antique lace curtains.

"If you don't mind, I'd like a quick visit," I insisted, hurrying up the stairs. "I'll get right to the point," I vowed when I'd reached him.

Vincent slowly turned to face me. His steely-eyed glare would have done an emperor proud. "The point is to enjoy my evening, and I don't think I will now that you're here."

That stung. "I just want to talk to you, maybe ask a few questions," I promised, sniffing as his spicy aftershave tickled my nose.

The ice in his glass clinked as it shifted and settled. "The last time we did that, you accused me of killing my wife."

"I'm sorry about that." Actually, I wasn't, because it had led me to finding her actual killer. "But this time, I want to ask you about the piano you, ah, recovered from Virginia Wydell."

"I don't know what you're talking about," he said, stepping inside and closing the door behind him with a firm snick.

Well, dang.

He had to know he wasn't the only one who'd repatriated items from the queen of Sugarland. Surely he'd heard about the diary page? He'd ended our conversation much too soon for me to get any kind of clarity, and it wasn't as if I could walk inside after him. Popping into Virginia's had been questionable. Pursuing Vincent would be scandal incarnate.

Not to mention very, very bad manners.

"Look, I understand why you wouldn't want to talk with me...ever." I cupped my hand against the glass and called past the fluttering antique curtains. "But a page from Erma Sue's journal is plastered all over town, and it shows Virginia has extorted people. She's manipulated them out of some of their most prized possessions. I'm assuming this includes your piano. I don't blame you if you sent Duranja's cousin to take it back. However, if you could tell me how it all came about, I'd be most appreciative."

The door flung open, and I nearly fell inside onto a shocked and horrified man. "I haven't been to Virginia's house. I don't have her piano. And it's terribly rude to accost me at my own house and make assumptions about my private life."

I had to be getting close if he was trying to make me feel guilty for prying. Did my mother raise me better? Yes. But she'd also raised me to be a proud Southern girl with a backbone, and if there was ever a time to stand firm, this was it. We were dealing with a cold-blooded murder. We didn't have time to play games.

"I think whoever murdered Twyla Sue is the person who is trying to expose Virginia," I told him plainly. He had to understand the importance of my questioning. "I can show you proof if you'd like." I started talking faster as he began to close the door. "I'm just trying to put the pieces together," I urged. "I need your help. Please."

He closed the door.

Heavens.

Twice in one day.

"I just want to bring Twyla Sue's killer to justice, the same as I did for your late wife Julia," I said, appealing to his better nature.

The door didn't budge.

I should go. Admit defeat. Or at least try another day. Except the diary page was my first, best, and pretty much only lead to find Erma Sue's book and Twyla Sue's killer. Vincent's run-in with Virginia might help fill in the blanks, or at least give me another avenue to pursue.

The widower hadn't needed the diary page to spur him into recovering his property from Virginia. I wanted to know how she'd kept the piano from him for so many years when it was plainly visible in her living room, and what prompted him to go after it now.

He'd obviously been wronged like so many others in town. "I'm only trying to set this right," I said to the brass door knocker.

Problem was, he didn't trust me. He didn't even like me. Despite what I'd done for his late wife.

"Have you *seen* the diary page?" I scrabbled through my purse and found my copy, scurrying to press it against the front window.

He didn't look at me as he stalked through the well-appointed front room into his study and out of sight.

I lowered the diary page with a sigh. There had to be a way to get through to him. Then I noticed something peculiar on the other side of the glass.

An extremely familiar-looking piano. Standing right in his front window.

And he'd said he hadn't taken it back.

I pressed my face as close as I could to the glass. I'd bet my last silver nickel it was the same grand piano that had graced Virginia's front room for as long as I could recall. Same gleaming walnut veneer, same acanthus and floral molding. I mean, how common could that be? I took in the unique scalloped edging on the case, the lid, the matching bench. It was unmistakable, gleaming in the early evening light.

This was the 1912 Louis XV Steinway Virginia had covered with silver-framed family photographs—the same ones I'd seen scattered on the bare floor this afternoon.

Oh, Vincent was right in the thick of things. No, he'd been a step ahead. He'd been to Virginia's house before any of them!

"You lied to me!" I stalked to the front door and flung it open. "You're a part of it!"

"Why are you still here?" he sputtered, emerging from the study, holding his glass like a shield between us.

I strode into his front room. "You're as much a victim of Virginia as the rest of us. She took your piano, didn't she? And you took it back."

He closed his eyes briefly. "I took it back."

"She had it for years, didn't she?" I pressed. "Decades."

He took a sip of his drink that turned into a swig. "A few...decades."

"And suddenly..." I prompted. "What?"

He answered me with a pained expression.

"Look, I understand this is technically none of my business—"

"Do you?" he inquired.

Not exactly.

But this was bigger than me, and bigger than him, too. I took a seat in a comfortable chair by the coffee table and crossed my legs like a proper lady.

Even if that ship had sailed.

"I just want to understand more of what happened so that I can make sense of why someone is trying to bring up old secrets. Who would want to release that diary page?" Perhaps he'd had a conversation with someone who had given him the ammunition he'd needed to go after her. "I mean, obviously anyone who would want to ruin Virginia would do it, and that list is very, very long." Hopelessly long.

He ran a hand along the back of his neck. "I honestly don't know." He sighed. "Stop looking at me like I have all the answers. I don't. I'd rather not be dragged into this."

Too late. He was already knee-deep to Sunday. Although, it

didn't seem kind to point that out. "Whatever you have to say, I'll keep between us," I vowed. "And maybe Ellis," I conceded, "but he's not on the case, and he's very discreet, and he tends to have amazing insights." I scooted to the edge of the chair. "Look, I'm not trying to make your life miserable. I only want to help get to the bottom of this, and I really think I can."

He looked at me like he couldn't quite believe he hadn't kicked me out yet.

"You may not like me," I added, "but you know how good I am at sussing out the truth."

"You are persistent." He regarded me over his glass. "And you do seem to get things done." He took a long, slow drink, the ice clinking in his glass. "If we begin a discussion, I must have your word this conversation will stay between us."

"You realize I kept the sensitive details surrounding Julia's death private." I wasn't one to tattle all over town. It was part of the reason why people trusted me with their secrets.

He regarded me carefully. I gave him time, listening to the tick-tick of a grandfather clock, taking in the gorgeous sitting room with thick woven rugs over gleaming hardwood.

He closed his eyes briefly before he seemed to decide. "Wait here," he said before retreating through the arched doorway to his study.

He returned a short time later with a sheet of paper that had been folded neatly in three. "I found this in my mailbox the day after Twyla Sue died," he said, handing it to me.

I quickly unfolded it and discovered a copy of a second diary page, completely different from the one I'd seen earlier that day. "Why didn't you call the police?"

"Copying a diary page isn't a crime," he said simply.

No, but this one was most likely stolen after a murder. I began to read. As I did, I pressed my toes so hard into the carpet they began to tingle. It was clear why he'd rather keep this particular page hidden.

. . .

DAISY YOUNGBLOOD WAS the star guest at Virginia Wydell's Christmas Cookie Exchange this year. And not because Daisy served the best gingersnaps. No! She discovered the depth of her husband's deception with the oh-so-proper Mrs. Wydell. Scandal, scandal, scandal!

I STARED AT HIM, the paper crumpling in my hands. "You...and Virginia." I stumbled. "And you..." There was no good way to say it.

He stiffened in his chair. "It implies we were having an affair."

"Did you?" I asked, afraid to move.

"No," he stated unequivocally.

The piano bench rattled, and my gaze darted to the empty seat. "Did you hear that?"

Perhaps a spirit begged to differ with Vincent's account.

He frowned. "This conversation is over if you're going to start pretending to see ghosts."

Amazing that he still didn't believe.

The bench had stilled. For now. I'd keep an eye on it, and for the ghost who might linger nearby.

I perched on the edge of my chair and focused on the widower. "I assure you, this is all very real. Please. Tell me what happened between you and Virginia."

His mouth tightened. "I'd rather not say."

Perhaps the new owner of the diary had already gotten to him. "Did that diary page come with a blackmail note?"

"No," he said stiffly.

The killer had released one page publicly and one page just to Vincent. If they hadn't asked him for anything yet, it was only a matter of time. "If you can help me learn who is releasing

ANGIE FOX

diary pages, we can stop the killer from extorting you." He stiffened. "We can keep them from exposing any of your other private business for that matter."

It was a calculated guess on my part—the fact that the three-time widower would have more to hide. He winced slightly but didn't speak. Still, the arrow seemed to hit its mark.

He ground his jaw. "I think Virginia killed Twyla Sue and took the book."

"No," I said quickly. "I mean, yes, she was found at the scene, but she has an alibi for most of the time before the murder."

"Most of the time is not all of the time," he said pointedly. "Besides, you know her lawyer could get her out of jail even if they found her standing bloody over the body, holding the knife."

She hadn't been holding the knife, but the rest of that was true.

"If you really think Virginia did it, why were you so hesitant to tell me?" There was certainly no love lost between the two.

He stiffened. "It's complicated."

"Okay." I tried another angle. "Why would Virginia send you proof of your affair with her?"

"I didn't have an affair with her!" he thundered.

"Fine." I pivoted. "Why would Virginia release a page from the diary that tells how she stole an antique trophy and mucked up a town tradition?" A page that took away so much of her power that people were breaking down her gate to look for that silver cup.

Vincent smirked. "She's smart, and she's ruthless, and now she looks like a victim instead of a killer."

"Hardly. She looks like a queen in a fortress on the hill."

He ran a finger up his glass. "You realize she's not going to think of things like you do."

I'd realized that a long time ago. "But she called her own son to the murder scene."

"Most likely to cover it up," he said, all too accurately.

A pit formed in my stomach. Thank goodness Ellis had called the police against her wishes.

"You're making sense." Some sense, at least. "But I still can't see Virginia as a murderer." Murder was messy, particularly that one. Virginia was ruthless, but she didn't have the stomach for getting her hands dirty. Besides, she'd appeared too stricken this afternoon at the vengeance of the town. She couldn't have brought that on herself. Virginia was too much of a survivor.

Vincent leaned forward, resting his elbows on his knees. "I hate to remind you, but you have been nearly killed before when you didn't see a murderer coming."

He would have to bring that up. "The newspaper accounts exaggerate," I said weakly, not even believing it myself.

He looked down at the glass in his hands. "You want more?" He wiped away a rivulet of condensation with his thumb. "Fine. There are a lot of things you don't know about Virginia Wydell." He flicked his gaze to me. "For example, Virginia and I were an item before either of us were ever married."

I dropped the diary page and felt it flutter against my foot. "No way." I cleared my throat, recovering. "I mean, of course you were." I could see it. "You're a handsome guy. Distinguished. You have money," I added out loud before I could stop myself.

But he didn't take offense. He merely chuckled.

"Yes, she was after my money," he said, tipping his glass to me. "I was new to the area, living over in Jackson, and from the show she put on, I thought I'd hit the jackpot." He took a swig. "We went out to all the best places. We had some wild times."

"Virginia?" The wildest thing I'd seen her do was order a second glass of champagne.

He merely laughed. "We were young and in love, or so I thought."

Amazing. "Come to think of it, I talked to Virginia about you when I was investigating Julia's death, and she never mentioned you two dating."

His mouth twisted into a wry smile. "She'd probably like to forget. That was my late wife Daisy's piano she swindled from me, not mine. She did it for revenge."

I was all too familiar with Virginia's need for vengeance. "What did Daisy do to bring down the wrath of Virginia?" It couldn't have been worse than leaving her favorite son at the altar like I did.

"It was what I did," he said grimly. "Like I said, Virginia and I were young and in love. It was a whirlwind romance. I was a bad boy, born and raised out in Memphis. She was a cute, small-town girl." He stood to get himself a refill from the bar trolley. "I thought she had money. She thought I had money. Eventually I realized both of us were looking for a spouse to help support us." Ice clinked into his glass. "We were too much alike in that respect."

"Hold on a sec," I said to his back. "You were both gold digging?"

He shrugged a shoulder as he poured two fingers of scotch. "I had some ventures going that I needed to finance in order to make a go of it. She had only her…attributes. So I ended it."

"She must have had a fit." I couldn't imagine a scorned Virginia.

He turned to me and took a sip. "I couldn't let her know I was stone-cold broke. She thought she'd let her golden opportunity pass." He eased back down in his chair. "But she dodged a bullet. We were both after someone to take care of us. It wouldn't have ended well in any case."

"Maybe she really loved you," I suggested. She must have had a heart in there somewhere.

He gestured weakly with his glass. "Maybe." He took a drink. "In any case, she married Leland rather quickly after that. I was happy for her." His expression darkened. "But when

I found my first wife, Daisy, Virginia wanted her pound of flesh."

"That sounds like Virginia." She'd seek revenge on the man who'd broken up with her, whether or not he'd broken her heart.

"Unlike Virginia, Daisy was quite wealthy. And a lovely person," he added, almost in passing. "You should know I cared for her."

"Of course," I said automatically.

He nodded and took a sip. "Nevertheless, Virginia visited me, quite upset when she heard news of my engagement. You realize she'd married by then and should have been perfectly content."

"When is she ever content?" I asked.

He chuckled. "Would you like a drink?"

"No, thanks." I waved him off. "I'm driving."

He nodded. "Daisy's father bought us one of the big old houses on Battery Hill."

"Number seven?" I asked, my voice catching.

"Number twelve," he said, brows furrowing. "I was there alone, overseeing the move while Daisy and her mother shopped for her trousseau in New York. Virginia was jealous to say the least."

"She thought she'd let the big one get away," I ventured.

He nodded. "It was terrible. Virginia stormed in like a woman possessed, telling me she'd made a mistake and we were supposed to be together. I tell you, it was ridiculous. So ridiculous that I felt sorry for her, and I told her the honest truth. I was in debt, but once I married Daisy, I had a business deal all ready to go, and I'd be fine. I wasn't the man she'd thought I was. I thought I was doing her a favor, you see?"

I did, but I was willing to bet Virginia hadn't seen it that way. "No doubt she was furious you'd lied to her."

"She lied to me, too!" he said, shooting up off his chair. "In any case," he continued, color tinging his cheeks, "it shouldn't matter. She should have been happy to be rid of me. Happy to find a rich spouse. Happy to be in love. I know I was."

"That's because you have a heart." I wasn't sure we could say the same about Virginia.

He looked to the antique grand piano. "That was Daisy's pride and joy." He strolled toward it. "The movers put it in the front window at our Battery Hill house. Daisy was concert-level good. And that Steinway had been her grandfather's."

My stomach clenched. "Virginia took it."

He lowered his head. "She took what I'd confided in her and said she'd use it against me. She'd tell Daisy I was a fake, worthless. That the only reason I was marrying her was so I could get out of debt and make something of myself." He turned to me. "Or I could give her my fiancée's treasured piano, and she'd keep my secret to herself."

"Virginia likes trophies," I agreed glumly.

He rubbed a hand over the polished wood. "She said it was her way of making me pay for marrying above my station. That I'd have to betray my Daisy in order to have her."

"So you just…gave in to Virginia?"

"I didn't want to." He closed his eyes briefly. "It was the only way I could hope to marry Daisy."

"You really thought she'd call it off?" I asked. "I mean, didn't you trust that she loved you enough to go through with the marriage anyway?"

His ears reddened, and he took another sip. "Daisy was amazing. Perfect. She could do way better than me." He walked back to me, defeated. "In any case, I couldn't risk losing her. Not over a piano. Or at least that's what I told myself." He took a swig from his glass. "I was young and stupid. Virginia had Daisy's Steinway moved to her place using a company from out of town. I told Daisy the movers wrecked her piano, and we filed an insurance claim."

"Yes, but how do you hide a piano?" I stood and walked to the gorgeous piece. "Especially one like this." Surely, word would get out.

I ran a finger over the ivory keys.

He took a sip of his drink, looking much older than he had before. "Virginia assured me she had as much interest in keeping it under wraps as I did. And it's not like anyone in Sugarland is a Steinway expert." He shook his head. "But then Daisy got involved in the Heritage Society." He pressed his lips together. "Virginia used our secret as an excuse to snub my wife. She didn't invite her to any of the get-togethers outside the organization, at least none of the ones she hosted. Naturally, those events were the ones all the ladies talked about." He slumped down in his seat and ran a hand over his forehead. "One day, I guess Daisy had had enough. She decided to bake her grandmother's fudgy pecan bourbon balls and drop by Virginia's cookie exchange."

"She saw the piano."

"She blew up at Virginia, who blamed me and said I'd given it as a love token." Ice sluiced in his glass. "Daisy came home and confronted me, and I told her everything. I loved her. I really did. But then she went off on that boat, and she wasn't a good sailor. In fact, she hated that boat and anything to do with the water."

And she'd died.

"I lost her. I loved her so much, and she died thinking I didn't care, that I'd used her." He ran a hand over his face. "I was responsible for her going out on that boat alone. If I hadn't caved to Virginia. If I'd just been honest…"

"You can't blame yourself," I assured him. "You were doing the best you could." He couldn't have known what would happen. Many in the town called him heartless and sly, and I'd assumed the worst of him, too. He didn't deserve that. "I'm so sorry."

He gazed past me toward the piano. "I couldn't find it in me to care when Virginia started spreading the rumors about me— that I'd killed Daisy for her money and that I was some sort of monster. It was so absurd, and it didn't matter. What mattered was that she was gone, and me spilling our tea wasn't going to bring her back, was it?"

But in the end, it had mattered. He had to know people called him the black widower, never mind that the police had ruled his second wife's death an accident, and I'd solved his third wife's killing.

He had money and a certain amount of notoriety. He'd been a major victim of Virginia's even if he'd rather not admit it. He'd cared enough to pay the blackmailer to keep his secret, and he'd cared enough to take the piano back.

"Why *did* you take the piano back?" I asked. It couldn't have been merely for the financial value. He was more than set with money.

"Penance." He took a drink. "It reminds me of my role in Daisy's death."

As if anyone had let him forget. "Maybe it also reminds you of the happy times you had with her," I suggested. It seemed theirs had been a love match. I hoped he could learn to enjoy the instrument she'd loved so much.

He stared at it, grim. "I didn't want to make a scene before, but damn it. They could take my money and release the page anyway, and if they do, I'm at least bringing that part of Daisy home."

"You're a good man," I told him. He needed to know that.

The ice tinkled in Vincent's glass as he took another sip. He said nothing.

I stood and walked over to the Steinway. Vincent had told me his version of events, but I wondered if there might be another side to the story. I tried to think of a way to inspire the spirit to appear or at least let it know I was listening. It seemed to be fond of this piano. I touched a finger to the G key.

Bing. Bing. Bing. Bing. Bing. Bing.

I played the opening notes of "Chopsticks." It was the only song I knew.

Bong. Bong. Bong. Bong.

The piano sounded well-tuned and resonant, even to me.

Vincent set his empty glass down on the coffee table. "Stop it."

"Sorry," I said, although I didn't regret my actions at all. I kept my hands to myself as I kept an eye on the piano, waiting for any sort of ghostly sign.

Vincent eyed me, as if he were trying to take my measure. "What are we going to do about Virginia?"

"I'm working on it," I admitted. I wasn't sure there *was* anything to do. "I am going to see what she knows about the diary page you received." Virginia had turned manipulation into an art form, and she might be connected to whoever had left the page in Vincent's mailbox.

He tilted his head slightly. "I never thought I'd say it, but I'm actually glad you're digging into this. If you learn anything new, will you let me know?"

"I will," I said. As long as it helped us sort out the truth or gave him some peace.

Vincent and I had begun an uneasy truce, and I didn't want to break it. Still, I'd best remember that he wasn't my investigative partner or my friend. He'd trusted me, but only because it had suited him in the moment.

To get to the bottom of this, I'd have to go back into the lion's den. Virginia's estate.

CHAPTER 16

$\mathcal{T}$he gate still stood open in the waning light of dusk.
I made my way up the hill, taking each turn carefully, my headlights cutting through the deep shadows cast by
weeping willows and tall pines. Stars twinkled in the emerging
night sky. I didn't pass another soul on the way up.

Well, that was a nice change.

Perhaps Virginia had taken my advice and made her amends.
Maybe she'd returned the championship cup to the town, and
the good citizens of Sugarland had decided to leave Virginia in
peace.

As long as I was wishing for things, maybe Ellis was waiting
for me up top with his mother's approval, a happy skunk, and a
few dozen long-stemmed roses.

The house stood dark as I parked in the circle drive. It
appeared Virginia wasn't home.

Except for the wide-open front door.

The back of my neck tickled with alarm. My car ground to a
halt, and I gripped the steering wheel, not sure what to do.

On the one hand, an open door at the Wydell estate was...
not right.

On the other, did I want to walk into trouble?

I shifted, restless. If Ellis were available, I'd call him, no question. He'd go in with me. Or for me. I checked my phone. He hadn't sent any texts. I dialed his number, and it went straight to voice mail. He was still on the job.

I tried Leland. And Beau. Neither answered.

I couldn't just walk away now.

I cut the engine and tucked my phone and keys into my pocket. It would have been really, really nice to have Frankie along. He could go in ahead undetected. Without him, I'd be walking in blind.

Virginia was the type to make her landscapers use handheld blow-dryers set on "cool" to remove every last trace of grass clippings from her delicate flowers. She would never leave her front door standing open unless she was in trouble.

Massive trouble.

My gut lurched, and I tried to push a terrible thought away, but I couldn't avoid it. What if one of her visitors today had returned to take the ultimate revenge?

I didn't want to find my boyfriend's mother dead on the floor.

Choked to death with her trademark string of pearls.

Stop. No sense courting trouble. And who was I to think such thoughts anyway? This was Ellis's *mother.*

I had to keep that in mind, or I'd come up with plenty more nasty things people would love to do to Virginia Wydell.

The darkened entryway gave me pause. My fingers delved inside for the light switch, and I hesitated. Should I make my presence known?

But I already had. The land yacht wasn't what you'd call a quiet ride.

I closed my fingers around the mace attached to my keychain and flipped the switch.

Weak sconces lit up along the right wall, their watery light casting deep shadows down the hall and into the arched entryway to the front room. I glanced up and saw only dangling wires where the foyer chandelier should have been.

"All right," I murmured, venturing inside, refusing to close the door behind me.

The soles of my sandals clacked against the polished marble floor like gunshots in the silent tomb of a house.

"Hey, Virginia," I said, easing toward the front room, one eye on the door. I'd bolt if I had to, and I was a very good runner—especially when chased.

There was no answer.

It would be the ultimate revenge for a killer to target Virginia by releasing the town on her. Half of Sugarland would have a motive. Big Tom, Principal Wershing, and Josephus Judson for what their families had endured. Vincent for the threat of being painted as an adulterer, not to mention the years of psychological torment. The ones who had broken her gate in attempt to recover the rowing cup she'd stolen.

Anyone who could have taken the opportunity to sneak up the hill later, perhaps at dusk.

I shouldn't have touched the light switch. I vowed to touch nothing else. Because if I did find her dead, I had a motive, too. I'd barged into her house this morning and told her in no uncertain terms what I thought of her. And while I hadn't been threatening, I hadn't been kind, either. She could have told anyone about our little run-in. I already had. And her version wouldn't paint a pretty picture.

I found the mini Maglite attached to my keychain and flicked it on.

"Anybody here?" I asked, stepping onto the plush carpet of the front room. My light trailed over silver-framed family portraits on the floor and the indents on the carpet where the piano had once stood. My beam caught Palladian windows without curtains, a fat jade plant in a gold pot in the place where the grandfather clock had stood, and huge swaths of bare carpet.

It looked like she'd been robbed.

My throat felt thick as I swallowed. "Hello?" I called softly as my flashlight beam caught the toe of Virginia Wydell's pink pump.

Ohmygoodness.

I froze.

My light reached a slim ankle, limp on the floor. She wasn't moving.

I forgot to breathe.

"Oh, stop gasping and sneaking and poking around." Virginia's voice emerged from the gloom.

My back stiffened, and a startled yelp escaped. Okay, I couldn't help that one. "I wasn't sneaking," I insisted. My light trailed up her thin legs, pink suit, and pearls, right to her judgy scowl.

"Tell my son I'll call him when I want to call him and get out of here," she snarled.

To think I'd wasted my time caring about her lying dead on the floor. "What are you doing here sitting alone in the dark?"

She sat with her back against the wall, legs straight, glaring at me. "Did you come here to gloat?"

That would be a move from her playbook, not mine. "I came here to talk to you," I said, catching her in the spotlight of my flashlight beam. "What happened here?"

She crossed one leg over the other. "I followed your advice," she stated like it was my fault.

"I'm...proud of you?" Although, I hadn't told her to trash the place.

Virginia stiffened and climbed to her feet. "You said it wouldn't kill me to be kind."

"Well—" I began. She wasn't dead.

"You said I needed to make things right," she added, her

ANGIE FOX

cheeks reddening. "Admit my mistakes. Return what I took. And while I was at it, beg for forgiveness."

That sounded like me. But I hadn't truly been able to picture it happening. "You begged for forgiveness?"

She notched her chin up. "I asked." She walked away from me and stood near the window where the grandfather clock had once been. "I called people. Those who had upset me in the past, the people who had sold or given me things to keep me from ruining their lives." She looked back at me. "I knew it was wrong. I'm not like that."

She had been. "Why'd you do it?" I asked, for myself and for her.

She turned to me. "I think—it just got out of hand." She pressed her lips together. "One thing led to another and another."

Until she had a house full.

"I'm glad you reached out to make it right." It couldn't have been easy.

Yes, her carefully crafted image had fallen apart around her ears this morning, but she could have locked the doors and doubled down. I'd expected that, even after my little speech in her foyer.

She blinked hard. "I was not treated as kindly as I hoped."

"Did you expect kindness?" After what she'd done?

"No," she admitted with a wave of the hand. "I deserved it. I think I would have been…worse in a similar situation. Not that I'd ever let it happen to me," she added quickly.

No one asked to be treated unkindly. It just happened sometimes, more often than any of us would like.

"Is it a relief at least?" I asked. "To do the right thing?"

Her lower lip wobbled. "Not yet."

"I like that you're honest about it," I offered.

"Oh, shut up," she said, waving off the beam from my flashlight. "And stop shining that in my face."

166

I lowered my flashlight. I wouldn't push. Much. "Did you give the rowing cup back as well?"

She walked away from me. "They'll find it in the Sugarland Library when it opens tomorrow," she said, leaning her back against the wall, her arms crossed over her chest. "Your sister helped me with that."

"I'm proud of you," I told her.

She side-eyed me. "I don't want to hear it."

Fair enough.

"Still," I pressed. We had things to figure out. "Who do you think is doing this to you?"

She shook her head.

"Who wants to see you suffer?"

"Everyone, apparently," she said helplessly.

That wasn't helpful. "Whoever killed Twyla Sue is probably the person who has the book and chose to release that specific page. You realize the killer could be trying to hurt you—"

"Of course whoever killed Twyla Sue is trying to hurt me," she snapped. "This is ruining my life!"

"Exactly," I said, trying to tamp down my enthusiasm. "But we have to dig deeper. For all we know, you're collateral damage." She did not appear pleased at that, so I hurried to continue. "Vincent received a diary page that implied the two of you had an affair and Daisy found out."

She touched a hand to her head. "So he said in about ten different voicemails. Heavens, who is trying to ruin my life?"

"Who could benefit from it all coming out now?" That was the million-dollar question.

"I don't know who would benefit, but it's clear they're after me," Virginia declared. "Whoever has the book isn't letting up. They released another page less than an hour ago, and it's all over social media."

I'd missed that. "Show me."

She huffed and called up a page on her phone. I took it and

peered at the screen. Another diary page shone bright in the darkness surrounding us:

December 12, 1983

Happy engagement and a very unmerry Christmas to Daisy Jackson. It seems her fiancé has given her heirloom piano to his ex-lover, a certain Virginia Nelson, now Virginia Wydell. You'd think the newly married Virginia had everything, but it seems she wants more. Was it a love token? Hardly. Apparently the rakish rascal was protecting his love. He's always been better looking than he is smart. And what will happen if Daisy finds out what really happened to her treasured Steinway? Will love conquer all?

"OKAY, WHO POSTED THIS?" I demanded. We could track social media. This could be our big lead.

"About twenty people and counting." Virginia winced. "Someone tacked a copy up on the bulletin board outside Lauralee's food truck." She swiped the screen closed with a vengeance. "That's where the first page originated as well." She sighed. "I'd hoped the issue with Vincent could be handled quietly, but evidently not."

"I don't think it was Vincent who tacked up the page. I spoke with him right before I drove over here, and he didn't want anyone to know."

"Then why did he tell you?" she sputtered. "Never mind," she added with a wave of the hand. "Why do I tell you things? Why does anyone tell you things?"

Because I cared.

"I'd like to know how Erma Sue found out about Vincent and his piano," I said. "According to him, nobody else knew, but Erma Sue had obviously spoken with him about it at one point."

Virginia shrugged a bony shoulder. "Twyla probably told her. She told her mom everything."

"And Twyla learned it from you," I pressed.

"Maybe." She scrunched her face. "Probably." She drew a hand down her neck. "I never expected to end up in that book. Erma Sue liked me! I was like a second daughter to her," she insisted. "She joked and called me her 'better' daughter," Virginia added, as if it were something to be proud of. "I admired her power, learned from her. I appreciated what it would have been like to have a mother like her. Twyla Sue was always too squeamish."

"I'm...glad," I ventured. "I mean, it's good to know Erma Sue wouldn't have hurt you."

"Oh, she would have if she'd had to," Virginia scoffed, as if that was how life worked. "But I never would have crossed her."

A notification screen popped up on Virginia's phone.

The white square read, *It's getting worse.*

"It's from my friend Nellie," Virginia said, opening up an attached photo.

It showed the bulletin board on the side of Lauralee's food truck, now covered with handwritten notes on colored Post-its, envelopes, stray napkins, anything people could lay their hands on. She zoomed in on one:

You WITCH. I knew my mother would never have WILLINGLY voted for you.

Another read, *I knew it! I knew it! You're done, Virginia. Done!*

Then another, *All the years I let you push me around and you never should have been in charge in the first place!*

"This is a disaster." Virginia planted her head on her phone. "I said I was sorry."

I hated to break it to her, but... "I think you're going to need to say it more."

Virginia lifted her head and froze, still staring at her phone. She'd scrolled to a portion of the bulletin board with a large white note attached. "It's another diary page," she gasped.

. . .

May 1, 2019
  To do:
  Get dirt on the following biddies before Virginia's next Heritage Society election.
  Frieda Banks
  Carole Poole
  Emmie Roth...

"No, no, no…" Virginia sank down to the floor before I could read the rest.

"At least that's not your handwriting," I pointed out. It wasn't Virginia's list. Or Erma Sue's. She'd died more than thirty years before that Heritage Society election.

In fact, I realized with a start that the writing had rather resembled the looping scrawl from the diary page Vincent had found in his mailbox. "I think we're onto something."

Virginia flopped an arm over her eyes. "Will you stop shining that damned flashlight in my face?"

Her phone lay facedown against her leg, but from the flashes, I could tell the messages were still incoming.

I sat down next to her. "You'll get through it." I had. "But right now, we need to focus. I think Twyla Sue was up to more than hairdos the night you found her murdered on the floor."

She lowered her arm but kept her eyes closed and her back against the wall. "That's Twyla Sue's writing on that page. There was a second book." She glanced at me. "That's what I was looking for after I found Twyla."

"Did you really find Twyla already dead?" I prodded.

Her eyes flew open then. "Yes." She sat up from the wall. "It was awful. She was my best friend, the only person I could ever be myself around. She'd never cross me or disappoint me. She didn't have the guts. And she was nice, too." She smoothed her hair back behind her ears. "She heard all kinds of things at the salon, just like her mom. But she didn't want to terrorize people. She just...used the knowledge to help me."

"She helped *you* terrorize people," I concluded.

Her back stiffened. "I told you. I realize I let it get out of hand."

As long as she understood.

"Look, I'm sorry I didn't tell Ellis earlier. Or you," she added as an afterthought. "But it was our secret, mine and Twyla Sue's."

"Obviously someone else found out about it," I said.

She closed her eyes briefly.

But I wasn't finished. "Who else knew about that book?" I asked.

"Nobody," she insisted, squeezing her eyes shut.

"Guess again."

"I swear." She sat up. "Twyla didn't show off like her mom did. She just kept a record. In case we needed it."

"Or *you* needed it," I corrected.

"She could have used it too," Virginia insisted. "But Twyla never had the stomach for blackmail," she added, as if it were a character flaw that Twyla wasn't as hardened as Erma Sue or Virginia.

I hated to break it to her, but... "This is about you again. The killer knew about Twyla Sue's book. Knew about you. It seems this person may really have it out for you. Who in particular did you offend?"

"Everybody," she declared.

"Virginia, you need to narrow it down, or we aren't going to get anywhere."

"I'm sorry if I didn't have the sterling moral background you were raised with." She smoothed her hair back again. "My dad ran off." She flinched like I'd slapped her. "My mom expected me to mother her. I had to get by on my own. Erma Sue was like a stand-in mom for me. She taught me everything she knew. She cared. She was proud when I made something of myself."

While she terrorized half the town. Virginia had learned too well. I stood and offered her a hand when she didn't get up. "Come on. Go get your purse and keys. We're getting you out of here."

"No." She wound her fingers through the carpet. "I'll lock the door. I'll pull the drapes. I'm not going to be driven from my own house!"

And I couldn't live with myself if I left Ellis's mother a sitting duck in the dark.

"I'm not driving you out, I'm giving you a chance."

She refused to look at me.

This was worse than dealing with Frankie. At least the gangster could be bribed. "You realize a killer is targeting you," I said. She drew a hand to her chest as that sank in. "You need to lock up and leave. You need to stay somewhere safe for a while, a place where nobody bad can find you."

She stood slowly. "I've already given them everything," she said, gesturing to her empty living room.

"We don't know what else they might be after," I said, locating her purse and handing it to her.

"I have no secret hideouts," she amended, going back for her phone.

That was more like it. "Go stay with your cousins by the old mill." That was out of the way. They were family. They had to take her in. And she didn't get along with them, so their house wouldn't be an obvious hideout. "I'll let Ellis know the plan. I'm going to his place tonight. Don't tell anybody where you are. And only answer your phone if it's Ellis."

"This is"—she dragged her purse over her shoulder—"a lot to handle, on top of an impossible day."

"Someone very devious wants to hurt you, and we don't

know how or when it will stop. If I were you, I'd find a safe place to hide."

"While my world burns," she said, straightening her back.

She'd spent years stacking the kindling.

"Tell me about Twyla Sue's book," I said. "Is there some big secret that you know? Something a person might kill for? Or kill to keep under wraps?"

"Nothing that big!" she insisted.

"I want you to make a list of everything Twyla knew."

"How am I supposed to remember it all?" Virginia balked.

"Do your best," I urged.

She nodded.

"I mean it," I insisted. "You're at the center of this whether you want to be or not. You are the key."

"If they'd let me leave town, I'd be on a plane to Paris tonight."

"Virginia, this is no time for fantasies."

"I understand."

"Good," I said, leading her out of the house. "Because your life might depend on it."

CHAPTER 17

I watched as Virginia made a right onto the rural road just past the wide-open gates and sped off into the night. She was well on her way to being an outcast, even worse than I'd been.

Although I didn't want to be the one to break that to her.

I took a few moments at the end of the driveway and called Vincent. "Did you see the latest diary page?"

"I'm at home, listening to Niccolò Paganini's Caprices," he said, mildly affronted.

I supposed I should have indulged in the typical Sugarland niceties before launching into my question, or at least told him it was me calling.

As if he'd had any doubt.

I could hear a violin in the background as I made a right turn onto the road. "What's a Caprice?" I asked, figuring it wasn't too late to be social, swatting one of my headset wires when it tangled in my hair.

"A very technically demanding piece of music," he said as if I'd asked him to dip his French fries in apple sauce. "In this case, violin solos."

"Well, that's nice." That made two of us in Sugarland who weren't glued to social media. "The person who took Erma Sue's diary posted another page," I told him, getting to the point, "and this time, the information leak was directly aimed at exposing Virginia."

"Good," he huffed.

He wouldn't feel that way for long. "I'm sorry to say it also details the story you told me about Virginia blackmailing you for your wife's piano."

"Please tell me you're joking." The depth of his anguish made me wince. "That's a very unkind thing to say, Miss Long."

"I'm sorry." I slowed as I crested a hill on the rural, tree-lined road. "I saw it. It's out there."

He silently absorbed his mortification for a moment before clearing his throat. "Virginia's getting what she deserves, but what did I do to be humiliated like this?"

Well, he had been involved with her, however long ago. "It makes her look bad, not you," I assured him.

"I gave away my wife's heirloom," he snapped. "Of course I appear monstrous. I *am* monstrous! It was a terrible thing to do," he added, sounding miserable all over again.

Not to mention the insurance fraud.

I glanced up at the skeletons of trees overhead in the darkness, not at all eager to tell him the next part. "Another page also came out tonight, less than an hour ago. It's an account from Twyla Sue this time, and it's more recent, definitely after Erma Sue's death."

"I don't understand," he said stiffly.

"I didn't at first, either. But it sounds like Virginia used Twyla to get dirt on the Heritage Society ladies. Did Julia ever say anything to you about Virginia threatening or blackmailing members to vote for her for Heritage Society president?" Ellis's mom had enjoyed a ridiculously impressive win record, and now I understood why.

The violin played a haunting melody in the background. "Julia couldn't stand Virginia, and I was glad for it," he said wearily, "but, no, Verity, I don't have details for you on any conniving female issues."

He would have to put it that way, I decided, before being jarred out of my thoughts by a piano banging on the other line, completely obliterating the violin solo. It sounded like…"Chopsticks." This was the exact song I'd played to get the ghost's attention that afternoon. Or maybe Niccolò Paganini wrote dance hall tunes on the side.

"Are you…playing the piano?" I asked, trying to hide my eagerness.

I heard a leather chair creak. "I don't play."

Bing. Bing. Bing. Bing. Bing. Bing.

Bong. Bong. Bong. Bong. Bong.

My gut twisted, and my heart sang. It was definitely "Chopsticks." Certainly not Vincent's technically demanding piece of music. Oh, my word. This could be the ghost.

"So absolutely no piano on your end," I said, absorbing my shock, making dead sure I was onto something.

"This is the greatest strings piece ever written," Vincent said dreamily.

He couldn't hear it. The spirit must not have had the strength to hit the keys on our side of the veil. But it was going to town on the ghostly side.

The song switched suddenly, as if "Chopsticks" hadn't gotten my attention. The ghost on the other line began playing the first lyrical notes of "Bicycle Built For Two."

I hummed along under my breath. *Let me call you sweetheart—* no, that wasn't right.

"Is that all the news?" Vincent asked.

Hardly. Although, I knew he wouldn't believe me if I told him what I was hearing. And worse, I could gauge from his tone he was growing bored.

I had to keep him on the line.

"So is Paganini your favorite opera?" I asked, hoping it was one of his favorite topics. My palms began to sweat, slickening the steering wheel as I turned onto the highway.

There is a ghost listening to our entire conversation, and that person may be trying to tell me something! I wished it would take the easy way out and appear to me, although not all ghosts had the strength. Still, I'd listen, in whatever way I could.

This could break the case wide open. I mean, I clearly had someone—a dead someone—seeking me out when I discussed the case with Vincent. Twice. They must have something important to say. Maybe they could stop playing songs and talk.

"Paganini is a composer. Caprices is the piece. There's no opera involved. Verity, please stick to the subject. Do you have anything else to tell me?" Vincent demanded, impatient just as we were getting somewhere. "Anything about the person who may be targeting me or my late wife?"

The ghostly piano player abruptly switched mid-song —again!

I listened to the opening salvo of "Row, Row, Row Your Boat."

According to Vincent, Daisy had taken their boat out after their dispute about the piano. But would Daisy, an accomplished pianist, try to reach me through tunes from a piano basics songbook?

This could be Julia trying to get my attention. She understood how to reach me—she'd hired me to ghost hunt back when she was alive. These could be the only songs she knew.

I had to talk with her.

"I'm coming right over," I told the widower. I'd make up some excuse. I'd turn around at the next exit.

Ice clinked as Vincent slammed his drink down. "Are you insane? We are not friends, and you are certainly not invited to my home."

"We can brainstorm." I hit the gas. "We can make a pro and con list about whether or not Virginia is the killer." It was three miles until the next exit. I could turn around and make it to Vincent's in ten minutes or less. I could get the ghost talking, and the three of us could figure this out. Maybe he'd even start to believe in my abilities.

"I'm done, Verity. I'm hanging up, and you'd better not come over. I won't answer the door."

"Wait. No." He had to see it. Well, he couldn't see anything. Only I could. "Look, fine. You don't have to let me come over. You don't have to talk to me. Just put the phone down and let me listen to your music while I drive." Maybe the spirit would be able to speak or give me some other clue. "Paganini is really growing on me."

"Call me when you have something important to say. Or better yet, don't call me at all!"

He hung up.

"Ugh." I thumped my head back against the headrest, which dislodged my headset and sent it tumbling onto the bench seat next to me. Lovely. My stomach clenched, and my heart sank. Sometimes my gift was more of a curse.

I smoothed my bangs out of my eyes. The ghost had tried to speak to me. I was sure of it.

The phone rang again, and I scrambled to drag my headset back on and answer it.

"Vincent!" This time, I'd be more eloquent. I'd regain his trust.

Or at least weasel my way inside his house.

Ellis's drawl answered. "Should I be worried?"

About another man? "Hardly." I adjusted the headset. "I was talking to Vincent Youngblood about the person who could be leaking those diary pages all over town."

Ellis sounded surprised. "I hadn't heard."

"Then you might be the only one at this point." Just as I

started to give him a rundown on the latest, his radio went off.

"I've got to take this. You still want to come by?"

I loved the tinge of hope in his voice.

"Absolutely," I assured him.

"You can fill me in then," he promised.

Maybe he could help me make sense of Vincent's ghost. "How about I grab us some dinner at Lauralee's food truck and meet you in ten?"

"That's the best news I've had all day."

I had to agree. Not only was I eager for a little reassurance from my boyfriend, I could stand to run the events of the day by him. Ellis often had insights about cases, or he'd pick up on details I'd missed. He'd also known Julia when she was alive, so he might have some wisdom on that front as well.

Lauralee was busy packing up her food truck by the time I reached the town square, but like a true friend, she was able to spot me a couple of chicken fried steak sandwiches on biscuits positively slathered in country gravy, along with peach cobbler for dessert.

"I hear your bulletin board is the hottest place in town," I told her, sampling a leftover mac and cheese croquette.

"I know, right?" she said, smiling as I made an appreciative noise over her new dish. "Who would have thought the hub of Sugarland gossip would be on the side of the truck by the picnic tables." Her grin faded as she thought of the incendiary messages posted on her place of business. "I just wish I'd have seen who keeps posting those diary pages."

"Does anybody have a clue?" I asked, using all my willpower to avoid taking another sample.

"No. At least nobody I've talked with," she said, her ponytail swinging behind her as she shook her head. "But I'll keep asking," she promised, boxing up a few free fried mac and cheese croquettes and slipping them into my order.

"You're too good to me," I protested as she handed my goodies down from the truck.

"I'm just happy," she said, beaming. "Did you get my message? I found great grandma Clementine's wedding invitation tucked into the lining of that silverware chest."

"The one Big Tom took back from Virginia Wydell?"

"One and the same," she said, leaning on her elbows at the window. "I'm going to have it framed so it can go on the wall right next to their wedding picture."

"That's lovely," I gushed. So many things were being set right now that Virginia had lost her hold on the town.

We talked a bit more, but I did have to get to Ellis's before the food went cold, and Lauralee had to get home to her family, so I called out my thanks and my goodbyes and headed off to Ellis's with a happy heart.

I found him stretched out on the couch in his front room when I arrived, which was fine, seeing as I hadn't bothered to knock.

"Didn't lock your door?" I teased, entering the modest bungalow. He'd bought in one of the 1940s-era residential districts just south of downtown. It was a perfectly safe neighborhood, like the rest of Sugarland, but he was always after me for not locking my place.

"I knew I was in for a treat," he said, rising to greet me with a peck on the lips.

"You sit. I'll handle this," I said, taking the bags into the kitchen to plate.

He followed. "I saw the leaked diary pages," he said, peeking into the bag while I grabbed two heavy plates.

"Have you talked to your mother?" I asked before telling him the events of the day.

"Yes," he said, forgetting about the food. "I'm worried about her. I'm wondering if the murder was a setup. If the killer knew

Twyla Sue's schedule and planned for my mom to find the body."

"Or they could have known your mom's schedule," I pointed out, plating the sandwiches.

He appeared even more glum at that. "She got her hair done there every third Tuesday of the month for as long as I can remember," he said, pouring the sweet tea.

So anyone in Sugarland could have known that, and anyone with a grudge against Virginia could have acted on it.

"She's at my uncle's farm by the mill," he added as he picked up our plates and headed out of the kitchen. "Their place is remote, and they'd see anyone coming." He bypassed the black metal table in his dining room and opted to deposit our meals on the glass coffee table opposite his black leather couch.

"Good," I said, joining him. "I'm glad your mom is safe."

"Thanks for that," he said, taking my hands. "I know she hasn't been kind to you, but I appreciate you making sure she wasn't alone in the dark, a sitting duck for a killer."

"You're welcome," I said, accepting a kiss. "Of course, you know I did it for you."

"And because you couldn't help yourself," he said, kissing me again. "You have a good heart. It's one of the things I love most about you." And darned if we didn't forget all about dinner.

For that little while, I felt good again. Life made sense when it was just Ellis and me.

Later, as we ate our cooling takeout, he kept one of his arms around me. The food was still quite good because it was Lauralee's cooking, so neither of us wanted to stop eating long enough to talk much. But it seemed like a good opportunity to tell Ellis about the piano music I'd heard coming from Vincent's front room.

Ellis's fingers tightened on my shoulder as I detailed what I'd heard. "I think the 'Chopsticks' opener was to get your attention."

"Agreed," I said, reaching for the last bit of fried mac and cheese. It was creamy and gooey and crispy. "Otherwise, 'Chopsticks' is too much of a coincidence." I shook my head. "I wish I could have talked to the ghost personally. Only Vincent won't let me back over there tonight to get any kind of clarity."

Ellis ran his fingers through my hair, and I plunked my head on his shoulder. "Vincent has been through a lot today. Maybe you should let him calm down, and you can try again tomorrow."

"He had a year and a half to calm down after the last time I tried to get him on board with the ghost thing, and he won't budge. Besides, he hung up on me tonight without me even telling him what I'd actually heard." I shifted to look up at Ellis. "It's not like I can break into his house and go looking for a ghost."

"Darned straight," he agreed. "We've been over this."

We had.

He dislodged my head. "Maybe the songs themselves are clues. What do 'Chopsticks,' 'Bicycle Built for Two,' and 'Row, Row, Row Your Boat' have in common?" he asked. "Other than they are beginner tunes."

"Well, we can probably assume 'Chopsticks' was to break the ice, so to speak," I began.

"So the actual message likely starts with 'Bicycle Built for Two,'" he finished. "Okay, so what are the lyrics to 'Bicycle Built for Two'?" he asked, reaching for his phone.

"I don't know," I said, leaning on him as he searched. "I tried to sing along in my head, but I think I got it wrong."

He pulled up the lyrics on his smartphone screen.
Daisy, Daisy
Give me your answer do
I'm half crazy
All for the love of you
It won't be a stylish marriage

I can't afford a carriage
But you'll look sweet
Upon the seat
Of a bicycle built for two

Goose bumps trickled up my arms. "It's Daisy." His first wife. "She had the money. He didn't." It seemed she might have known all along and married him anyway. Vincent had said it was a love match. "It was her piano."

"So maybe she's letting you know who she is, and that she was fine with Vincent's secret," Ellis said.

"And then she played 'Row, Row, Row Your Boat.'" My heart thudded heavily in my chest. "She died taking the boat out."

Ellis stared down at me. "Maybe it wasn't an accident."

I stared back at him. "Maybe Virginia killed her."

"Not where I was going," he said sharply, breaking eye contact.

But it was a possibility. "Vincent could have done her in as well," I suggested, with less enthusiasm. "Although, he did seem to care for her, and he'd get half of her money in a divorce anyway."

"Half," Ellis repeated, as if that were the damning part.

It was still a lot.

"Did your parents ever have a boat?" I asked.

Ellis stiffened. "When I was younger. Are you saying my mom chased her down and sank her?"

No, but Virginia would have seen Daisy get upset and go to confront Vincent. If she had access to the dock, she could have watched her take the boat out. And then...?

"Daisy could tell me," I said, not exactly eager to spell it all out to Ellis.

I wished the ghost could track me down and have a conversation. Or that I could go over there right now and ask.

"Maybe she'll be waiting for you on your porch when you get home," Ellis said, opening his arm to me once more.

The last thing I needed was another ghost on my porch.

"Maybe," I agreed, settling back against him. I'd rather seek her out. What I needed was an excuse for Vincent to let me inside. "Care to go over there with me tomorrow?"

He blew out a breath as if willing the tension to leave his body. "I have to be at the stakeout at 6:00 a.m. tomorrow." He drew a hand through my hair. "I don't think I'd be much help with Vincent anyway. You gained his trust this afternoon, at least for a little while. Long enough to learn why my mom was blackmailing him."

I wanted to claim the victory, but it felt incomplete.

Ellis tipped my chin up gently. "I'm sorry I snapped at you."

"You didn't," I corrected. He'd been emotional, but not short.

He planted a soft kiss on my forehead. "We'll figure it out."

He always had such faith in me and in us. "You have to admit, we're at a dead end here. Unless someone saw who's been posting these pages around town."

His expression clouded over. "I called Duranja about that, and they're looking into it, but so far, they don't have any leads. Nobody saw who posted the pages on Lauralee's community board."

Dang. "And there are no cameras set up anywhere?" For once, I wished there were.

"This is Sugarland. Not New York," Ellis said, and I was glad to have it that way.

"True." I kissed him on the cheek.

"Maybe another diary page will come out," he said reluctantly as I rested my head again on his shoulder. "Maybe the next one will give us more of a clue."

"Or lead to further disaster."

"I know," he said, wrapping an arm around me, as if he could protect us both from the storm. "That's what I'm afraid of, too."

There had to be a better way, something more to do to track down the killer. Only I didn't have access to the police investigation of Twyla Sue's murder and neither did Ellis. The diary pages, presumably possessed by the killer, had been posted right under my friend's nose before being distributed on social media.

"I can call Melody," I suggested. She worked at the library in the town square, very close to where Lauralee parked her food truck. "She might have seen something," I added when Ellis didn't respond.

I looked up to find him snoring. The poor man had fallen asleep sitting up.

I eased out of his arms and helped him stretch out sleepily on the couch. "I'm listening," he murmured, a part of him always on the case. But he'd had enough for one day, and it was time to let him rest.

His fuzzy blanket lay tossed over his video game system. I retrieved it and tucked it over him. Then I cleaned up the dinner plates and cups and threw out the trash we'd left on the kitchen table.

I'd planned to stay, but Ellis needed his rest. And Frankie might need a kick in the pants when it came to cleaning up my porch. While I'd asked him to fix the issue with the goats and the horse, he tended to do things his own way. That usually meant a way I wouldn't approve of.

I ran back to the car for the Southern breakfast burrito I'd had Lauralee add to the bag, and left a love note on the refrigerator to help direct Ellis to his breakfast treat.

It was all I could do for him and his stakeout. And I found I already missed him terribly as I kissed him gently on the forehead and slipped out the front door.

CHAPTER 18

*E*llis needed rest and quiet, and I could have done with the same. But when I pulled into the parking area behind my house, I realized I wasn't going to be that lucky.

Frankie was supposed to fix the issue on my porch. He'd promised to put an end to the lunacy with the goats. He owed me some peace and quiet, or at least a little progress in that direction considering the work I was doing to recover Erma Sue's book and help him get free.

Instead, I pulled up to Scape the goat sleeping under one of my grandmother's heirloom rosebushes, which Nibbles was doing her best to decimate.

At least it wasn't half gone on the side of the living.

But it was little comfort.

I'd asked Frankie for one thing. *One.* A bit of consideration. A reprieve from his constant scheming.

And as I stalked up the stairs toward the monster of a horse still tied to my porch, I discovered something worse. My skunk, my sweet, obedient angel of a skunk, stood riding the porch swing with a knobby-legged baby goat, a goat who should be gone from this property and *not* gadding about teaching Lucy new tricks.

"Lucille Desiree Long!" I admonished, but my skunk ignored me completely in favor of happy grunting and directing doe eyes to the speckly goat. Of course Lucy couldn't resist showing off for her new friend, taking them both higher with each swing.

"This has got to stop," I declared, laying down the law to the hardened gangster, who sat knees-out on a round stool in front of the hay-chewing horse, hammering wood and constructing what appeared to be a lopsided trough of some kind. "Since when are you a farmer?"

An icy-cold presence pierced my shoulder, searing my bones and shooting chills down the rest of my body. "Help!" I shrieked, swatting at the menace.

I whipped around to find a large donkey nose where my shoulder had been. I rubbed frantically at the spot the ghost had touched, as if that would help, and struggled to find my voice and my breath in the wake of my shock from the phantom touch.

"Why—?" I bent over and tried to compose myself as the donkey inched forward.

"He-haw!" It dipped its head with each step.

Oh, heck no. I backed up fast, careful not to touch the ghostly hay bale or the horse ball or the pile of ghostly horse pucky steaming up my porch. I was trapped. Cornered! "Has the entire world gone crazy?" I demanded, ducking out of the way as the ghost donkey once again tried to bop his head against my shoulder and rest it there.

"Why are you getting so bent out of shape?" Frankie demanded, standing. "You should be flattered. Hoté likes you!"

"Donkey Hoté does not belong on my porch!" I shrieked as it went after me again. "It's a menace." And it was obviously too dumb to realize touching me would shock us both all over again.

"*It* is a he," Frankie said, resting the hammer on his hip, "and Hoté is here to calm Frisky Pete. It's science."

"What kind of pseudoscience is that? You were supposed to get rid of the animals, not add more! Since when are you Farmer Frank?"

"I find the animals soothe me," he said, gazing philosophically at the horse, who tried for a carrot from the hanging horse toy and still hadn't seemed to figure out the trick. Frankie plucked a carrot and fed it to Frisky Pete. "Besides, I have to do everything I can to manage Frisky Pete's mental health. He is a champion." The gangster accept a nuzzle from Hoté, and I shivered.

"What about me?" I asked, thinking Lucy might have a better chance at the track than a horse who couldn't even find a carrot.

Frankie frowned. "It's your fault for taking so long to free me that I had to find a new line of work. Bootlegging, robbery, and extortion aren't exactly easy to do from your back porch."

"Now you're just trying to drive me crazy," I ground out.

"That's merely a side benefit," Frankie said, sitting back down to work on his sad attempt at a trough.

"Can we just stick to the issue?" I pleaded.

"Yeah." Frankie stood, knocking over the stool and flinging his hammer down onto the porch. Frisky Pete jumped, Hoté ran to nuzzle up to him, and I rolled my eyes. "You're gone all day, and you didn't come home with Erma Sue's book or any way to free me. You expect me to bust myself finding a good home for Frisky Pete and his friends when I can't leave your property. All I have to do is take them with me if and when you ever get me out of here, but that doesn't make you work any harder. You criticize my goats when your skunk is the instigator. And all you care about is your precious porch. You can't even come home and be happy with a snurfle from a perfectly nice donkey.

Well, I'm done. I'm done making it comfortable for you to act like the queen of the castle while you put me off and trap me here and criticize my animals. I want action! Throttling! And if I don't get it, let's just say I'm in the market for a herd of alpacas."

"You wouldn't," I gritted out.

He loomed over me and lowered his face an inch away from mine. "I have the names all picked out."

We stared each other down like dueling cowboys in the street.

"I am working on it," I hissed.

"Work faster," he ground out. He backed away, keeping an eye on me like I was about to pull a fast one. "Next time, I'm going with you."

"Fine," I snapped. As long as he took care of his end of the bargain.

"Fine," he barked, shrinking down into an orb and zipping out into the night. Leaving me with the horse, a donkey, six goats, and a joyous skunk.

"Fine," I repeated to Frisky Pete, who nickered at me. "Frankie's the champion," I grumbled to myself, adjusting the bag on my shoulder. "A champion jackass," I added with an apologetic nod to Hoté, who looked as if he might follow me into the house.

I hurried up, stepping over another steaming pile of ghost pucky on the way to my back door. Horse or donkey, I couldn't tell.

Only when I turned the knob, it didn't open.

"My door is locked," I declared to Hoté, who lowered his head and watched me intently. My limbs stiffened.

My door was never locked.

Lights blazed from the kitchen window.

I hadn't left them on. I never left them on. And it had been broad daylight when I'd headed out.

Someone had been on my porch. In my house. Someone

189

who wasn't a dead gangster or a farm animal. I backed away slowly, almost colliding with a wandering baby goat.

Okay, I could call Ellis and hope I could wake him up.

No telling where Frankie had flitted off to.

I dialed the number for the Sugarland Police Department instead, my finger hovering over the green button to start the call. With Ellis at home, there was nobody on the force I wanted to talk to right now. And one I was especially interested in avoiding.

It couldn't have been a burglar because…well, we didn't have those in Sugarland. No, this violation of my personal space had to be related to the person I was pursuing, a person who had slashed a woman's throat in cold blood.

A person who might kill again if cornered.

The good news was I might be closer to finding the killer than I'd realized.

The bad news was the person might be waiting inside.

But why lock the door? I had to find out.

I wouldn't venture far inside, and I could run like the dickens. My car was close by.

I dug through my bag for my keys and slipped my house key into the lock.

I said a quick prayer I'd find my kitchen empty, my grandmother's silver bowl safe on the kitchen table.

Bracing myself, I swung open the kitchen door. Ready to fight. Ready to grab Lucy and run through a dead farm animal or three if it meant making a clean escape.

"You," I uttered low in my throat when I spotted the intruder in my kitchen.

Virginia stood stock-still, a grim smile touching her lips. "I've been waiting for you."

CHAPTER 19

*V*irginia held one hand behind her back, her expression hard.

She'd been waiting for me.

"What are you doing here, and what do you have behind you?" I demanded.

No way she could be the killer. No way could she be ready to jump me in my own house.

She made a move toward me, and I grabbed a kitchen chair and tossed it at her. It skidded sideways, and she dodged it. "Verity!" She jerked her hand out from behind her back and revealed an overflowing can of beer. She shrieked as it splattered all over her. "Eek!"

"You—" She glared at me with half a can of beer running down her white silk shell and pale pink skirt. The can of Pabst Blue Ribbon fell from her hand and clattered onto the floor. "You're supposed to be gone tonight."

"I thought you were trying to kill me," I exclaimed, keeping the table between us.

She clutched her fingers into fists. "If I wanted to kill you, I'd have done it already. Believe me. My life would be a lot easier without you in it."

Indeed. "Then why are you hiding out in my kitchen?"

She tossed her hands up with a snarl and a curse and fetched the terry cloth towel folded neatly on the island. "Ellis said you would be at his place tonight," she insisted, frantically drying her hair.

"So you figured you'd have a beer and a hang at mine."

She stopped cold. "I like beer," she admitted, pink tinging her cheeks.

As if that was her biggest secret.

"Okay, but why break into my home and scare me to death in my kitchen?" It seemed a rather dramatic solution, even for her.

She sighed and gave up on her sopping body. "My best friend has been murdered. My only real friend," she added quietly. "A killer is after me." She tossed the towel onto the floor and began wiping up the mess with her pink-pumped foot. "My idiot cousins-in-law are holding a grudge and wouldn't let me in their house." She glanced up. "Can you believe they pretended they weren't home? I saw them all run upstairs."

"Yikes." Although, it didn't exactly surprise me she'd burned all her bridges.

She brushed off her hopelessly wet skirt. "I figured the last place anyone would look for me would be at your house."

She'd figured that right.

Me included.

She walked wearily to my refrigerator and pulled out another Pabst Blue Ribbon. She turned to me and popped the tab.

"Make yourself at home," I said with a level of tart I usually saved for Frankie.

"Do you want one?" she asked, holding it up. "I bought a six-pack."

"No," I said as she returned to my kitchen table and took a seat. Now was the time to run her off. Or drive her...somewhere. "How many of those have you had?"

"Just the one," she said, taking a long sip with pink-glossed lips. "Well, I spilled most of it on myself," she added, brushing again at her wet skirt.

"Where's your car?" I pressed.

"Parked out in the field behind your pond," she said nonchalantly.

"You have had a day," I said, finding it ironic to see her sitting at the table with my grandmother's fruit bowl at the center.

She squeezed her eyes shut. "Look, as long as you're here, I need to tell you something. I—" Her voice caught. "I didn't tell you and Ellis the whole truth the night you found me with Twy...with the body."

"I figured," I said, retrieving the chair I'd tossed. She eyed me with trepidation as I planted the chair across from her and sat. I knew better than to think she was nervous about me. She was afraid to be honest about whatever she'd neglected to mention before. "You know you can trust me."

Her fingers fluttered over the beer can. "Twyla Sue was beyond help when I found her," she insisted. "I was so shocked, I —" She paused to gather herself. "When I saw her mother's burn book missing, I knew what the killer was after. But only two other people knew about Twyla's book. I wanted to see if it was still there."

Now we were getting somewhere. "Who else knew?"

She wet her lips. "The mayor's sister, Nellie Holcamp. But I left her behind at the fundraiser the night Twyla Sue died. She couldn't have done it."

I'd have Ellis double-check on her whereabouts. "Who's the other person?"

She shrugged a bony shoulder. "Your friend Lauralee. She

saw the book fall out of Twyla Sue's purse two years ago at the supermarket."

"I'm sure she's in the clear." In fact, I'd bet Lauralee hadn't realized what she'd seen, or she would have told me.

Virginia spread her hands. "I didn't say I had the solution. Only that I did try to check on the book so we could narrow down the murder suspects."

"Are you sure you didn't want it for yourself?" I prodded gently.

"Maybe. As a memento," she hedged.

Sure. A keepsake that doubled as a blackmail book. "You don't expect me to believe that."

She gave a ragged sigh. "Twyla Sue and I understood each other in a way no one else could."

That was one way of putting it. "When you needed dirt in order to win a Heritage Society election, Twyla Sue was there."

"Yes," she said a little too eagerly. "Twyla Sue was as good as her mother when it came to digging up the dirt. Only she never really used it."

"She told you," I corrected.

She looked down at her beer on the table. "Of course she helped me. Why wouldn't she?"

I leaned back in my chair. I didn't understand Virginia sometimes. Not one bit.

Still, I could see how she'd gotten tangled in the twisted awfulness that had gone down at Two Sues' House of Beauty. Twyla Sue had accepted Virginia in a way nobody else would. Erma Sue had been like a mother to Virginia, a girl who'd had no power or standing and had craved both.

"You realize it has to stop," I said, folding my hands on the table between us.

She smoothed a lock of wet hair away from her forehead. "I hadn't realized how far it had gone until people started showing up at my house." She stared at the table. "Then when I tried to make things better and apologize, it made some people angrier."

They had the right. "You hurt them," I stated simply. "You don't get to control how they feel about that."

She whipped a glare at me, and just as quickly, I saw it fade. "I want to," she admitted.

"Yes, but do you want people's honest reactions—good or bad—or do you want to stuff it all down and get what you want, never mind if it's fake and forced? I mean, that's what you're saying you're done with."

"So my life is fake and forced," she huffed, not denying it.

"You can twist my words, but we both know what I'm saying." I was only trying to help her be a better person.

"You're just trying to design yourself a better mother-in-law," she grumped.

"That would be a nice side effect," I said, the corner of my mouth twitching up. I admit it warmed my heart that she saw Ellis and I headed toward a future together.

"I'm not a monster," she said, as if I'd accused her. "You don't know what it's like growing up with nothing. People look at you different when your dad's run off and your mom's a drunk. When you live in a house with plywood walls. When you have one friend and if she doesn't like you, then nobody does."

"You're right. I don't know what that's like," I admitted. Even at my lowest, I had my family's ancestral home, along with a good family and a best friend.

She took a deep breath. "I saw the kind of power Twyla Sue's mom had, and I wanted that, too. I didn't grow up having any respect. I had to earn it."

I folded my hands together. "Respect and fear are two different things."

Still, I could understand what she was saying. The late Erma Sue had ruled the town with blackmail and threats and grown rich and powerful because of it. Would it have been entirely crazy for a young, poor girl to want to do the same?

It wasn't right or fair or good. But it had happened, and there was no getting around it.

Virginia's cheeks tinged pink. "You don't know what it's like when it gets out of hand. You have to keep going, keep everything in line or..." She tossed out a hand. "You saw what happened when I gave in. Everything came crashing down."

"Can you blame them?"

"No," she snapped before focusing hard on her untouched drink. "I thought about that a lot tonight. When it was dark and I was by myself. I thought how I wished I'd never taken anything."

"I'm glad to hear it." To be honest, I didn't know how things would end for Virginia now that the town was onto her. Realizing she was wrong could never make up for years of tormenting good, hardworking people, but it was a start.

She braced herself. "I realize you won't believe me when I say this, but I'm sorry I reacted so poorly when you called off the wedding to Beau. Truly."

I felt the anger bubbling up. The frustration that I'd lost so much of the heritage that had been entrusted to me. "You reacted very poorly." It was the understatement of the year.

She stood. "I was wrong to force wedding choices on you that cost a lot of money and only made me happy."

My chair clattered behind me as I took to my feet. This was where she had it dead wrong. "It wasn't even about the wedding."

She folded her hands primly in front of her. "I was wrong to think you should marry Beau after he assaulted your sister at the rehearsal dinner."

"Yes," I snapped. "Yes, you were."

Her expression grew pained. "I was afraid of looking bad, and I was afraid he'd lose you." She made a weak gesture with her hand. "I just thought if you kept at it like I have, we'd all get what we wanted."

"What would I get, a rich life with an abusive husband who didn't love me?"

Her gaze snapped to mine. "Beau loved you. He still does. You know it."

Maybe in his own way. And he was working toward a more honest life. Still… "Any romantic feelings I had for him are dead, and they're not ever coming back."

She lost some of her fire. "You said that to me on the night before the wedding, and I hated you for it. I wanted you to keep going. I'd kept going. I expected it from you, too."

"Why?" Why couldn't she just let it be? Leave me alone. Realize she was wrong and he was wrong and let it be done.

She hesitated for a moment before tilting her head slightly. "I saw myself in you. A girl trying to make it. A girl who loves this town and the people here."

Oh, please. "You can't say you love this town and then do what you did to the people in it."

She crossed her arms over her chest, defiant. "I started off like you at your very lowest. Dare I say lower than your lowest. You may not want to see that, but it's true."

That was where she had it all wrong. "I have no doubt you've been laid low, Virginia." I had a feeling she was at one of her lowest points right now as well. "But you've got to wade through the muck and the pain. You have to let it change you for the better. Do you understand what I'm saying?"

She chewed her lip. "I might." She dropped her arms. "I'm sorry I hurt you. I am. And I'm going to do everything I can to make you believe me."

"First key is to stop trying to make people do anything," I cautioned.

For a moment, it looked like she might cry. Then she burst out with a shaky laugh instead. "I'm hopeless, aren't I?" She gazed at my grandmother's fruit bowl, the one she'd kept as a trophy when I didn't live my life on her terms. "I'm broken," she declared.

Well, sure. "We're all broken in some way." It was part of life.

She let out a long, ugly sigh. "For what it's worth, I'm glad you're with Ellis. I see how happy he is with you."

"Ellis is one of the most caring men I've ever met. One of the most loyal, too." He'd become who he was in spite of the way she'd questioned his choices at every turn. "You should try to get to know him. Like, the actual him." Not the son she'd wished he would be. "Appreciate him. Accept him. Thank him for caring about you."

She gave a small wince. "Ellis is the only one taking my calls."

"I'm sorry." I truly was.

She fluttered a hand at her throat. "I mean, Beau is at that artist retreat, and for all I know, he tossed his phone into a fire and called it performance art," she said, trying to joke. "But Leland…that stings," she admitted.

"He's running for senate," I said as if that justified it. There was no sense kicking her when she was down.

"I meant Leland III," she admitted. Her unloving husband had been absent this whole time as well. She ran her fingers along the edge of her silk blouse. "He's still in Malta."

"I see." He couldn't even make it back after his wife had been arrested for murder. "You still recommend marrying for status and sticking it out?"

Her fingers found the pearls at her neck, and she gripped them. Hard.

"You deserve to have people in your life who stand behind you. People who want what's best for you and will help you get it."

She lifted a slim shoulder. "I don't even know why you're helping me."

I didn't like to see anyone suffer. It was my strength and my curse.

"Listen, it's getting late." And I was tired. "I think you should go on over to Ellis's to spend the night," I said, returning my chair to its place at the table.

She cringed. "I parked in a big mud puddle. And I've been drinking."

"I'll drive you," I said, gathering my purse and opening the door.

Lucy came barreling inside and did a spin on the kitchen floor.

Virginia didn't notice. "Can I sleep here tonight?"

"No." When she opened her mouth, I added, "I mean, we're good." Sort of. We were better than usual. "But you're in much better hands with Ellis." He was the police officer, not me. And I needed a break.

"Please," she said, glancing over as Lucy buried her mouth in her food bowl and crunched away. "I just want some peace."

I stared her down. "I don't have an extra bed or a sleeping bag." In fact, I didn't have much, thanks to her. "But you can have the purple couch and a blanket."

She nodded quickly. "Thank you."

I stepped past her to lock the kitchen door and pick up a few skunk kibbles from the floor by Lucy's bowl. Virginia followed me to the foyer, where I shook out the blanket on the couch. Lucy liked to make her nest there, but she'd be sleeping with me tonight anyway.

I spread the blanket out next to a couch pillow and let Virginia have at it.

"Thanks again," she said, settling in.

"Good night," I answered, sparing her a nod as I headed up the stairs to my room, my little skunk toddling after me.

CHAPTER 20

$\mathcal{I}$ awoke to the smell of coffee and smiled for a sleepy moment, thinking of the way Ellis liked to wake me with a steaming mug of dark roast. Then the happy cloud dissipated, and reality sank in. Virginia lurked downstairs, and there was no telling what she was up to.

Lucy toddled ahead of me, tail swishing as I grabbed my robe.

We found the dethroned queen of Sugarland society in my kitchen, arranging the sugar and cream on a plate. The silk blouse and skirt she'd slept in were a wrinkled mess. She smelled like beer, and she'd finger-combed her hair.

"Coffee?" she asked, pouring me a cup. They were Ellis's brand of beans, but she didn't comment.

I accepted the mug on the way to let Lucy out the back door. My skunk clambered across the farmyard of a porch and dashed down the steps, joined by the speckled baby goat.

The gray donkey began strolling my way, and I slammed the door.

That situation had not improved overnight.

"I tried to make up the couch, but it's a little dark in there,"

Virginia said, rubbing her stiff joints as she eased onto a seat at the kitchen table. When I sat across from her, she nudged the plate of cream and sugar my way. "The light switch in the parlor doesn't work," she added, awkward in her attempt at friendly banter. "I'll bet Ellis could take a look at it."

"There's not a light in the parlor," I pointed out. At least not one that worked on a switch. "You forced me to sell the chandelier."

"Right." She shifted uncomfortably in her seat. "I—I have a lot to make up for."

I added a spoonful of sugar and stirred. "One day at a time."

She nodded, staring at her cup. "I was thinking last night, maybe I can go home soon. Maybe the killer isn't after me."

"That's wishful thinking," I said, taking a sip. Her coffee was actually quite good.

"Hear me out," she said, scraping a scraggly lock of platinum hair behind her ear. "I spent all afternoon yesterday confessing my sins and trying to make things right. People were upset. But this is Sugarland. A lot of people were more gracious than I had a right to expect. Nobody tried to hurt me or kill me. The only big mystery left, the only wrong to be righted, lies with the secret Vincent kept from his wife and what happened after she fled to the boat."

"You started that," I said, lest she forget.

"I was wrong to coerce him into giving me the piano. But I still say he killed her. I mean, if he didn't, who did?"

"That's the question. Maybe she truly was just a bad sailor." I wished I could have gotten through to the ghost in Vincent's living room.

She gripped her cup with both hands. "Twyla Sue thought he did it," she insisted. "Erma Sue thought he was running around on Daisy."

"Did either of them have proof?" I asked. When she hesitated, I pressed. "Think about it. Think hard."

"I—" Her voice wavered. "Not that they showed me."

I stared at her over my coffee cup. "I think Daisy tried to communicate with me last night. In fact, I'm pretty sure Daisy haunts that piano you gave back to Vincent."

Her eyes widened, and her cheeks tinged pink. "No."

"Yep, you unwittingly brought a ghost to live with you." She deserved what she got. "I swear the piano bench moved when I went over to see him. And when I talked to Vincent on the phone last night, I could hear his piano playing, but he couldn't."

She gasped. "Daisy loved that piano."

Like Erma Sue had loved her stylist chair.

"She played 'Chopsticks,' 'Bicycle Built for Two,' and 'Row, Row, Row Your Boat,'" I said, wondering if Virginia might have any more insight into what I'd heard last night "You knew Daisy. Did any of those songs mean something special to her?"

"I can't think of what." She drummed her fingers on the table as she thought. It was a very un-Virginia-type move. "Daisy must have walked in on him or something," she insisted. "I told you he was up to no good. I mean, the man killed Daisy in cold blood," she said sharply as if it were fact. "He followed her out onto the lake and drowned her."

According to Virginia, who liked to bend the truth like Play-Doh. "You said yourself you have no proof."

"No," she snapped.

"You just assume he did it." I'd followed her hook, line, and sinker a few years ago to my regret. I'd learned to look at the facts since then. The main fact being that the Sugarland police were extremely good at their jobs, and they had cleared Vincent of any involvement. "But you," I said to Virginia, "you had every reason to jump to conclusions and make him look bad."

"You're always asking people to believe you with no clear proof," she shot back.

That was only because a good portion of my evidence usually resided on the ghostly plane.

"Think about it." She scooted her chair closer. "Sometimes you just *know*. Or if you don't want to take my word that Vincent's a low-down dirty criminal, go ask Daisy."

"You make it sound so easy." Unfortunately, ghost hunting was rarely a simple maneuver. "Even if Daisy is haunting her piano twenty-four seven, I can't get close. Vincent's not going to let me in his house to talk to a ghost, and I promised Ellis I wouldn't break in anywhere."

"Why not?" she balked. "You need to go where you need to go. It's for the greater good."

"It's illegal," I reminded her. Although Virginia wasn't exactly keen on rules.

"Pish-posh," she said with a wave of a well-manicured hand. "You have a gift, Verity," she said, as if it were my responsibility to use it, come hell or high water. "You can do what nobody else can—you can learn the truth about why Daisy died. At the same time, you can ask her exactly what she was trying to tell you last night. And you can ask her if I'm in any danger at my house."

"Is that all?" I drawled.

She stood and began to pace as she sorted out the exact reasons why I should break the law, disappoint Ellis, maybe even make any evidence I discovered inadmissible in court.

"Look at it this way," she said, turning back to me, "Daisy started a conversation. She's basically inviting you in. She's made a lot of effort to get your attention, and you owe it to her to hear her out."

"No." I wasn't going down the primrose path with Virginia, of all people. "Absolutely not. And it's time for you to head on over to Ellis's house. You'll have it to yourself all day."

"Fine. I'll go to Vincent's," she said, heading to the sink to rinse her coffee cup.

"That's not what I said at all." I stood and followed her. "You are not going to go over there and stick your nose in everything and mess this up. Vincent is fragile and angry—"

She snorted. "Wait until I get done with him."

No. "You going over there and confronting him, or telling him my ghost story about his dead wife, will only make things worse. In fact, I already regret telling you."

I regretted even speaking to her this morning.

I regretted letting her stay.

I regretted saving her butt at her house last night.

She finished rinsing her cup and held out a hand for mine. "Today is Tuesday. Vincent meets the boys from the yacht club every Tuesday morning to play cards and drink Bloody Marys—not necessarily in that order," she added with a judgmental air. "I will merely stop by his house while he's away."

"And do what?" I demanded, hands on my hips. It wasn't like I could stop her. I couldn't even get Ellis to stop her. He was on his stakeout by now.

"I'll investigate," she said simply, drying her hands on a towel. "I'll do your job for you," she said pointedly. "It's not like I have anywhere else to go."

That was ridiculous. "You can't do my job for me. Only I can do my job."

"Then do it," she challenged.

I watched her as she neatly refolded the towel and tucked it over the handle of the dishwasher. "You're one hundred percent sure Vincent is gone this morning," I stated, keeping the warning in my voice.

"Let's call it ninety percent," she said cagily. "Because if I had a talkative ghost at my house, and I was onto you, I wouldn't leave my place unless it was on fire."

"He's not *onto* me, as you so eloquently put it." At least I didn't think so. I hadn't told him about the ghost playing the piano. "Besides, he doesn't believe in ghosts. He thinks I'm overly impressionable and maybe a little mental."

I dared her to make a comment about that.

She wisely pursed her lips. "Are you coming with me or not?" she asked, striding to the parlor to fetch her purse.

"Definitely not," I declared, and I let her walk out my door.

It wasn't as if she'd be able to talk to a ghost without me. It wasn't as if she'd be able to do much investigating.

I sat back down at the kitchen table and wrapped my hands around my cooling coffee cup. I would just sit here and not think about how I was letting Virginia break into the widower's house. I'd try not to think of how she could be blowing the case, destroying evidence. I'd try not to worry how she could get Ellis kicked off the force by scandal alone.

I cringed.

"I'm going after her," I said to Lucy, belatedly realizing she was outside. Most likely causing trouble. Everybody was up to something except for me.

"I'm going," I said out loud to myself, fetching my bag. "But I'm not confronting Vincent if he's there," I vowed. "I'm not breaking in if he's gone. I'm merely going to keep Virginia out of trouble." And maybe, if Daisy was there, well, perhaps I could get her to come out on the lawn to talk.

That would be wonderful.

But that was it.

* * *

I DRESSED as fast as I could. Virginia had a head start, and she was most likely up to no good.

Her car was gone from the other side of the pond when I left, but when I arrived, I was shocked to find no sign of her.

The house stood dark as I parked in the circle drive. I couldn't guess where Virginia was, but it appeared she was right about Vincent being away.

It would be a nice opportunity to talk to Daisy, assuming I could get close enough to that piano. And avoid her husband.

First, I had to make certain I was alone. I skirted along the gravel drive at the side of the house, to the rear, along the edge of the cliff overlooking the river. The back parking area stood empty. That was where Vincent had left his car in the past.

When he was home.

I'd knock at the front door to make sure. Just because the house appeared dark didn't mean he wasn't upstairs or tucked away in the study. And if he wasn't, well, maybe I could find Daisy at her piano and persuade her to join me on the porch.

I peeked in the front window and saw no light or movement in the front room or any room leading off it. No ghost at the piano, either.

First things first.

"Vincent," I called, knocking on the door, "are you home?" *Please don't be home.* "It's Verity. I just need a second."

Or more like five or ten minutes alone with his late wife.

He didn't answer.

"Daisy," I called, moving to the front window. I didn't see a ghost, either. Nor any movement at the piano. Although I doubted the keys or the bench had actually stirred last night. If they had, Vincent might not have been so dismissive of my questions.

"Bing. Bing. Bing. Bing. Bing. Bing." I sang the notes for "Chopsticks" as I tapped them against the window. *I'm here, Daisy.* "Bong. Bong. Bong. Bong. Bong. Bong." *Ready and waiting.*

I watched the piano keys and the carved bench for any hint of a tremble, just in case. I listened for any sound, no matter how faint.

The only noise I heard was the slam of a car door.

Panic shot through me. *He's home!*

I whipped around to see Virginia, of all people, leaving her car in the circle drive.

"Let me take care of this," she said, bustling up onto the porch. She'd parked her cream Cadillac behind mine.

"I was hoping you'd realized what a bad idea this is," I said.

"It isn't," she retorted, peering in the window next to me. Suddenly she slapped her hand against her side. "Dang, I forgot my purse."

"You don't need a purse. You're going back to your car to wait while I talk to the ghost. Keep an eye out," I suggested, hoping that giving her a job would keep her busy.

"Nonsense. We're going to get to the bottom of this," she said, proceeding to the front door.

"It's locked," I insisted. I hoped.

Please let Vincent be one of the few in Sugarland who locked their doors.

"You can tell he's not from here," she said, trying the handle and finding it blessedly bolted.

"Told you," I said, my relief turning to horror when she drew a packed key ring out of her skirt pocket.

"Good thing I stopped by the Sugarland Heritage Society," she said, selecting a gold one.

"Those are not your keys," I declared as she inserted it into the lock.

"They were mine when I chaired the Holiday House Tour. Aren't you glad I made emergency copies…just in case? Told you we wouldn't break in," she declared as the front door clicked open.

"I'm pretty sure the police would disagree," I insisted. A key didn't equal permission. "Look, you can't…" I said as she turned the knob and cracked open the door. "I promised Ellis."

"I didn't," she said, peeking inside. "Look, we're doing Vincent a favor. You can talk to Daisy and prove to me that he's not an evil murdering bastard."

"You don't expect me to join you in there."

"You'd rather play 'Chopsticks' against the window?" she inquired before slipping into the house.

"No. I'm not going inside, and you'd better get out of there."

She'd left the door wide open for me. I watched her hurry toward Vincent's study. "What are you going to do in there?" I asked, resisting the temptation to follow her. Instead, I hurried to the front window to track her. It was obvious she had an agenda she hadn't told me about. I should have tackled her on the lawn when I first saw her. "Stop it. Now!" I ordered. "You're going to get out of there. We're leaving, and—" A shadowy figure took form in front of the piano.

I stared as it took the shape of a young woman. She wore a flowered dress with a wide puffed skirt. A large belt cinched her waist. As her form became clearer, it shimmered in tones of gray. Still, her face lay in shadow. It didn't appear to be Julia. Vincent's third wife had been much taller.

"Daisy?" I called through the glass.

The ghost beckoned me with a dainty hand.

I cursed under my breath.

"Can you come out on to the porch?" I called. "I'm not allowed inside."

The ghost didn't acknowledge my request. She merely beckoned me again.

It was sort of an invitation.

A ghostly invitation to break a very real law.

I tried once more. "I heard you playing the piano last night. I can see you now. I'd like to talk out here if we can."

Virginia emerged from the study with a stack of letters in one hand. "What are you doing?" I called past the ghost. "You're *stealing* from him?"

I should have known Virginia would have an ulterior motive for coming here. I should have known not to trust her or believe her when she'd promised she was trying to change.

"Oh, calm down," she ordered, stalking straight for me. "I'm taking what's mine."

I watched in horror as she walked straight through the ghost, who burst like a soap bubble.

208

"That was Daisy!" I protested. At least I thought it might be Daisy. Virginia had stomped on her spirit just like she had in life.

"You actually did it," Virginia said, from the other side of the glass as if she were surprised. As if my way of not breaking the law, and doing what was right, and *keeping my word* could actually work. "What did she say?"

"Nothing. You popped her!" I exclaimed. Then I gasped because I saw her forming again, this time standing inside the piano.

That was one way to avoid being trampled by Virginia Wydell.

"Can you come outside?" I asked again.

"Sure." Virginia shrugged. "I got what I came for."

"Not you." I'd deal with her later.

The ghost hadn't taken form as well as before. She had no hands this time, still no face. Frankie used to have energy problems that caused parts of him to disappear. I wondered if her piano playing last night had been too much of an exertion.

"What do you need from me?" I asked, willing to watch, to listen, to do what it took to communicate with the ghost.

She simply stood inside the piano, the edges of her arms shimmering, then disappearing into vapor.

"She won't move from inside the piano," I said to Virginia, who'd joined me on the porch.

"Daisy always was too shy," Virginia remarked.

The energy of the ghost surged, and she became clear at once as she glared at Virginia. "It's Daisy all right." Virginia certainly had a way with people—both dead and alive. Daisy's hair flowed out behind her as if carried by an invisible wind, and her slim hands once again beckoned me inside.

Heavens. "I'm going in," I said to myself before I changed my mind. "Daisy has made it clear I'm invited." Even if I couldn't prove it.

"She's the wife of the property owner," Virginia said, bustling in after me. "That counts."

"She isn't anymore." Although I wasn't sure what the rules on that were. Tennessee property law hadn't seen fit to extend itself to ghosts.

I'd only be inside for a second. I'd find out what Daisy wanted to tell me, and then I'd leave.

But by the time I walked through the door, she'd disappeared again.

"Daisy?" I called, hurrying to the piano. "Are you still here?" She didn't have to appear. She could simply speak to me.

Only she wasn't talking.

"I'm going to check the study again," Virginia said, clutching her large purse to her side. She must have retrieved it from the car while I was busy with Daisy. But why? Then a terrible thought occurred to me. Virginia had an agenda. That much was clear. If she was bold enough to take a packet of letters from Vincent's study, she wasn't above planting evidence.

"Stop," I ordered.

She shook off my demand like a duck in the rain and kept going.

But I was faster. I dashed toward the study and beat her to it.

"What?" She pulled up short as I blocked the door.

I stared at her.

What if I had it wrong this entire time?

What if Virginia was in deeper than I'd imagined? Ellis's mother had never been violent—she'd never needed to be in order to get her way. Twyla Sue had been her friend. I didn't see why Virginia would want to hurt her.

But Ellis's mother had certainly had the opportunity to kill her old friend.

It was Virginia we'd found at the scene. It was Virginia who had gone through the dead woman's purse to find her journal as the body cooled. Ellis and I didn't search the beauty parlor after we'd found the body. And while Virginia had been arrested shortly after, she could have stashed Erma Sue's book, or even both of the diaries, and recovered them a short while later when she was out on bail.

She could accuse Vincent all she wanted, but only the killer possessed the journal stolen from Twyla Sue, as well as Erma Sue's legendary burn book.

Virginia clutched her purse to her chest.

"What's in there?" I demanded.

"It's none of your concern." She bucked the question, nervous.

All she had to do was distract me with a juicy ghost hunt while she planted the evidence in Vincent's study.

But if she was going to do that, it would have been easier without a witness. Without me. Unless... "Why did you ask me to come?"

"Go talk to your ghost," she said, attempting to muster a bit of warmth. Failing miserably. "It's what you do best," she insisted.

"I'm really here as an objective third party," I said, the horrifying truth settling over me. "I'm here to watch you find the books that only the killer would have, right?" I challenged. "Or maybe I'm supposed to search the study so I can 'find' them myself."

She knew I'd be a credible witness. That I'd report to Ellis and to the police that I saw Erma Sue's burn book and Twyla Sue's journal in Vincent's study. Nobody would expect me to help the woman who had tried to destroy me, and that would be the perfect cover. An innocent man would be punished, and Virginia Wydell would achieve the ultimate revenge against Vincent Youngblood IV.

Because of me.

CHAPTER 21

"I am not a killer," Virginia snapped. "How many times do I have to tell you that?" She reached into her purse. I didn't know whether to stand my ground or run.

"Stop where you are," Vincent ordered. He emerged from the kitchen with a revolver in his hand. He pointed it at us.

"He's the killer," she declared.

To me, he looked like a man defending his home. An angry man, and rightfully so.

"Let me see your hands," he said, stone-faced.

I raised mine away from the doorway while Virginia dropped her purse and did the same.

"What are you doing in my house?" Vincent demanded, putting himself between us and any means of escape.

"She wanted to ghost hunt," Virginia declared, throwing me under the bus.

His gun arm stiffened. "I knew it was a mistake to speak to you, Verity. Much less let you in my house."

I didn't know how I was going to get out of this unless I came clean. And even then, it was a stretch. "This is going to sound crazy," I said, bracing myself, "but Daisy played the piano for me last night. I think she was trying to tell me something important. I came here to talk to her."

"Daisy played 'Bicycle Built for Two,'" Virginia added, as if to draw attention away from her sins.

"Don't," Vincent ordered. "I don't know how you know our song, but don't you dare try to manipulate me with memories of my dead wife." He tightened his grip on the revolver. "I won't let you sully our song!"

Oh, my word.

"You and Daisy?" I cut in. They had a song! I exchanged a glance with Virginia. We might be getting somewhere.

As long as Vincent didn't decide to have us arrested.

Or plug us with his revolver.

"I saw Daisy right there by the piano," I added, hoping he'd believe me now he knew I couldn't possibly be making this up. "That's why I came inside."

He pointed the gun at me, his eyes wild and his anger quick. "There's. No. Such. Thing. As—"

Virginia shrieked and pointed to the living room behind him. "Look! It's Daisy with a sailing rope knotted around her neck. You killed her!"

"What?" I demanded. I didn't see any ghost there.

Vincent whipped to look behind him, and Virginia used his split second of distraction to go for the gun.

I got there first.

He shouted as Virginia kicked him in the gut, and I grabbed the gun out of his hand. Ellis had taught me how to disarm a man fast, and I already had his weapon by the time he stumbled sideways into Virginia.

"Both of you stay back!" I ordered, pointing the gun at them.

Vincent stood doubled over, glaring at me. "For the last time, Verity Long, I did *not* kill my wife!"

Virginia shot him a death snarl before directing her ire at me. "Have you lost your mind?"

"You stay right there," I said, backing toward the piano. "Both of you." I wasn't about to let either one of them try to rush me. There was no telling which one killed Twyla Sue, if it even was one of them. But, either way, I wanted to be the one with the gun.

"You can't possibly—" Virginia stated, taking a step forward.

"Don't think I won't shoot," I said, daring her to push it. "Do you think anyone in this town would blame me if I did after everything you've pulled?"

"I wouldn't," Vincent muttered.

"Quiet, you," I ordered.

Virginia threw her hands up. "What are you going to tell Ellis if you shoot me?"

Some days, I thought he'd understand.

Vincent stared me down. "You break into my house," he gritted out. "You accuse me of murder. I don't know how many times you've tried to pin something on me."

Hey, now. "I didn't accuse you this time," I pointed out.

"She's only holding us at gunpoint because you killed Daisy," Virginia spat. "Then you killed Twyla because she knew. I read it in her journal."

"Why would Twyla Sue put that in her journal?" he demanded.

She pointed at Vincent. "She put it in her journal because it's true. You killed Daisy."

He looked ready to throttle her. "You're a twisted black-mailer who killed her hairdresser, and now you think you can pin it on me!"

"Wait!" I shouted over the din. "I hear piano music." It was faint, but I heard it. "Shh...Daisy might be playing another song."

"Nobody's playing a song," Vincent barked.

Maybe he didn't want me to hear it. "We won't know unless

you stop shouting," I said, drawing closer to Daisy's piano. The music was faint, but there.

"No." Vincent strode for me.

I held up the gun. Was I honestly going to shoot him?

No.

I couldn't.

He strode past me and slammed the lid down over the keys. "There are no ghosts. There is no music!"

He was getting on my last nerve.

"Daisy," I asked, keeping an eye on the shady duo, "I'd love to hear what you were trying to play for me." I had a feeling it was important. Why else would the ghost reach out? "I'm listening. I promise."

Vincent rolled his eyes. "You think you're listening to a ghost playing piano," he said flatly.

"Shhh!" I insisted. I almost heard it again.

We couldn't keep messing this up. I'd already seen Daisy's hands fade away. We couldn't assume the ghost had infinite energy.

"Let Verity do her thing," Virginia hissed over the faint tinkling of the piano.

"Quiet," I ordered as the first notes came clearly.

It was a slower, lilting melody—unlike the ones she'd played before. So much so that I wondered if it was the same ghost.

And then I recognized the old jazz song by Blind Willie Johnson.

Nobody's fault but mine
Nobody's fault but mine

The ghost took form beside the piano. She wore the full skirt I'd seen before, her face and hands dark in shadow.

If I don't tell you, my soul be lost
It's nobody's fault but mine.

. . .

I SANG THE WORDS SOFTLY, without realizing it, until the piano fell silent.

Vincent stood stiff. "Daisy loved that song," he said on a whisper.

She'd spent a great deal of her energy, but her message had come across loud and clear.

"I don't believe it," Vincent said, staring at the piano, as if he could somehow hear the music, as if he could catch a glimpse of his late wife.

The shadow of a hand touched the piano, then touched her gray, glowing chest.

"It is Daisy," I confirmed. "I think she's trying to tell us her death really was an accident."

"Ridiculous," Virginia snapped.

Vincent stood breathless. "She learned all the songs by Blind Willie Johnson. He's my favorite," he murmured, his eyes shining with unshed tears. "She only played them for me."

It seemed this song in particular meant something to her long after death. I watched the ghost glide toward her husband and hover nearby.

"She's right next to you," I told him gently.

The widower froze in place, and for the first time, it appeared as if he wanted to believe me.

"Did you stay because he's innocent?" I asked.

Virginia clucked her displeasure, but I knew the truth as the ghost nodded.

She really had loved him. Enough to endure Virginia's ire in life, enough to stay when her husband was accused of having a hand in her death.

Vincent cleared his throat. "Daisy loved her piano and her books. She could be quiet, but she had a fire in her for art, culture. Me." He braced himself against what he had to say next. "She trusted me, and I betrayed her. I hurt her beyond words." He stared at the floor. "She ran. I chased her. She fled onto the boat." He choked up. "I shouldn't have let her go out alone. In a way, I did kill her."

The ghostly piano played the opening notes to "Nobody's Fault But Mine."

"She's trying to tell you it's not your fault," I assured him.

Maybe that was the message all along. It might not be about the accusations Virginia made about him, but how he blamed himself. "She loved you, or she wouldn't have stuck around for years in order to play that song for you."

"I...I can't believe this is happening," he managed.

The ghost leaned close, and for a brief moment, I could see her face.

"She's kissing your cheek," I said.

He touched the place she'd kissed. "I can feel it," he said, amazed. He snorted. "It feels cold."

"It can," I said, watching as Daisy smiled.

"You did it," I told her by way of congratulations. She'd made things right the best way she could. She'd let her husband know she loved him, and she didn't blame him for what had happened to her.

Then she looked upward. I couldn't see what she did, but I saw her smile, and her face began to glow. She grew faint as she rose up. And soon she was gone.

"She's leaving now." I said. "Moving on," I clarified as Vincent made a small noise. "What a wonderful lady," I added to myself.

"No," Vincent said, shaking off the moment. "She's not going anywhere. She's not playing the piano. She wasn't here in the first place. " He brought his hands to his head. "You're the one playing me, and I almost fell for it!"

"It's real," I swore. "She stayed because she loved you."

He charged up to me, loomed over me. "I don't need you to tell me my wife loved me. I don't need you to pretend to care so you can get me to admit to a murder I didn't commit. I don't need you to use her damned piano against me." He pounded a fist down on the keys.

The notes slammed together, along with a distinctive *doink*.

Vincent snatched his hand back.

That didn't sound right.

I backed away with the gun.

"There's something inside the piano," Virginia gasped, bringing up the rear for once. "There something sitting on the strings."

"That's ridiculous," Vincent said, standing between her and the piano.

"Cover him," I ordered Virginia.

She looked at me like I'd asked her to chop down a tree. "What? Why me?"

Good point. I wasn't used to being the one with the gun. I glanced down at it, still not quite believing I held it in my hand.

"You're not going to use that," Vincent spat.

"How can you be sure? I'm crazy, remember?" He must have believed it, because he let Virginia yank his hands behind his back. She whipped a necktie out of her purse and secured his wrists.

I'd ask her later where she got that.

"This is insane," Vincent insisted, looking over his shoulder at Virginia and her knot job.

"I believe you didn't kill Daisy," I said to him, "but the jury's still out on Twyla Sue."

Daisy hadn't tried to speak to me when she'd first appeared today. That was fine. Some ghosts didn't speak. She could be one of them. So far, I'd only seen her move the bench and play the piano.

So if she wanted me inside, if she'd stood in the piano, there might be something she wanted to show me. And there'd been a definite off-note when Vincent had slammed a hand on the keys.

Not what I'd expect from an immaculately kept Steinway.

"Move him away," I told Virginia once she had him secured.

I approached the piano. "How do I open this puppy?" I asked. The keys were already exposed. I searched for the lid opening on the side, found it, and pulled it up.

"There's a wooden prop," Virginia instructed.

"I see it." I managed to wedge the prop in place, and when I reached inside, I felt the fluttery skeletons of bird feathers, and my eyes went wide.

"You found the book," Virginia gasped.

She hadn't touched the piano this morning. The book had to have been there when we'd arrived. The movers definitely would have noticed if it had been there when they delivered the piano. Which meant...

"Hold my gun," I said, handing it to her. "Keep him in line."

I might not shoot Vincent, but she would.

She took great pleasure in holding him captive while I drew the book from the piano.

It was the burn book, all right. Most likely taken by the killer of Twyla Sue.

"Is the other one in there?" she pressed, drawing closer.

"Focus on him," I ordered as I removed a slim green notebook from the piano.

Virginia's hand fluttered to her chest. "That's Twyla Sue's record of...events."

A fine way to put it.

"You killed Twyla Sue," I said to Vincent.

He didn't bother denying it. "I told you the killer would release terrible secrets in order to play the victim. Only this time, it was true. I was victimized. I hurt Daisy. Terribly. But I didn't kill her. Or my second wife."

"Or your third," I finished. "I know."

"Only Twyla Sue couldn't let it go. Virginia had her

convinced I'd killed Daisy, and she was going to dredge it up again. She tried to blackmail me."

"So you killed her and took the book," Virginia ground out.

"No," he snapped. "I told her I was going to make a payment, but really I went to talk to her. She had no proof. I didn't do it!" He sank back. "She said it didn't matter," he muttered, almost to himself. "She said it was written down and that would make people believe it. She'd decided to use her little journal like her mom had used that damn feathery burn book. She said it was for you." Vincent glared at Virginia.

The matron of Sugarland drew a hand to her throat. "I admit I would have enjoyed that," she said, her voice growing smaller.

He swallowed. "I threatened her. I wasn't going to stand for it. She thrust her scissors at me," he thundered. "So I grabbed them, and I slashed back. I only meant to scare her, but I caught her in the throat." His shoulders slumped. "It was terrible. There was so much blood."

"You left her there," I said.

Virginia gasped.

He shook his head, as if he could deny it. "She was already dead. There was nothing I could have done to save her." He swallowed. "I took the book she'd been waving at me. I took the original burn book, too."

"So you could use it like she did," Virginia choked out.

His gaze shot to her. "No! I didn't want to expose anybody else's secrets. I should have destroyed it, but I couldn't resist hurting you like you hurt me. The only ones I exposed were mine. And yours," he added, with a nod in her direction. He straightened. Gave her a long, hard look. "You tried to ruin my reputation. For years, you told everyone I was a killer. Well, now I am, and it's because of you."

And for the first time, Virginia stood speechless.

CHAPTER 22

We held Twyla Sue's killer until the police arrived. Vincent confessed to the chief, who arrested him. Duranja stayed behind to bag the evidence.

Although he wasn't so focused on his task that he couldn't spare a salty glare at me. "This time, I'm arresting you for breaking and entering."

"Actually, I was the one responsible," Virginia said, inserting herself between us. "I took the keys from the Historical Society. I unlocked the door and went in first. Verity was trying to get me to come out."

"I don't believe it," declared the square-jawed, stiff-backed killjoy.

I didn't, either.

Duranja sealed the bag containing Twyla Sue's journal and ushered us out of the house. "Are you sure that's your story?" he asked, pinning Virginia with a death stare at the bottom of the steps.

She notched her chin up. "Yes. It's all on me. And stop with the chest puffing. Your department already arrested me for killing Twyla Sue. Wrongly, I might add. Compared to murder, entering a home without permission is a walk in the park."

"We'll see about that," he gritted out.

It was like she was a hardened criminal all of a sudden.

"Duranja," the chief called. He motioned the junior officer over to his squad car.

"You two have a seat," Duranja ordered, pointing to the bottom step. "No leaving. And no talking," he emphasized.

"He's trusting," Virginia said, eyeing the officer's retreating form as she folded her skirt under her and perched on the stair.

He could also make good on his threat to arrest her. Or nab us both. "You honestly don't care if he stuffs you in the back of his squad car?" I asked, joining her on the step.

"At least it's not in front of a crowd this time," she said, elbows stiff and shoulders at her ears. She was afraid. At least a little. "The way I see this, it's my crowning moment. I brought my best friend's killer to justice. There's nothing Duranja can do to take that away."

Duranja huddled by a squad car with the chief, grilling a humbled Vincent.

"Thank you," I said. "For covering for me back there," I added at her moment of surprise.

"You tried your best to do this by the book," she said. "I think Duranja has it out for you," she added, shooting him a judgy look.

She had no idea.

I was still trying to wrap my head around the widower's confession. And Virginia's attitude toward her own impending date with the police.

Most in Sugarland would be delighted at the news of the deposed queen of Sugarland's second arrest, even if it was for helping to expose a killer.

I shook my head. "I never thought I'd see the day where

you'd have to get arrested to salvage your reputation in this town."

She attempted to smooth her impossibly wrinkled skirt. "We're just lucky Vincent kept those burn books. Those are the proof." She battled with a particularly deep crease. "He should have destroyed the evidence."

"He couldn't resist using them against you first," I said, capturing her attention. "He hated you so much that he incriminated himself."

Frankly, I could understand the temptation.

She raised a brow. "So I was the key to solving Twyla Sue's murder."

"Yeah," I said, wishing I could give her a scrub down to remove the smug half-smile on her face. "You're a real hero."

She slapped her hands down on her ruined skirt. "This hasn't been a cakewalk for me, either. I lost my reputation. My peaceful home." She dug her fingers into the silk. "The sense that I actually knew what was going on in my life."

"You'll figure it out." If anything, Virginia was a survivor.

"Will I?" she asked, as if she didn't quite know anymore.

I couldn't answer, so I let it go. "By the way, what did you take from Vincent's study?"

She scoffed. "You mean what did I take that made you think I'm a killer? You held a gun on me," she added, as if she were the wronged party.

"It was a dream come true," I admitted.

"Pipe down over there!" the chief barked.

We fell silent. Well, until the two officers became laser focused on Vincent once more.

"It looked to me like you stole a packet of letters," I said under my breath.

Virginia kept her eyes on the police officers. "They weren't important."

"Right. That's why you stole them."

"Fine," she gritted out. "They were love letters. Happy?"

"More like confused."

She blew a harsh breath out of her nose. "I wrote them when Vincent and I were young and in love. And stupid."

Duranja directed a suspicious stare our way, but we were just sitting side by side. I waved.

When he'd gone back to his investigation, Virginia spoke again. "I didn't want the letters to get out like the journal pages had." She sighed. "I hadn't written very kindly about Leland."

It wasn't exactly a secret that Virginia hadn't married for love. Or that Vincent hated her. "Why do you think Vincent kept your letters all those years?"

"To use against me," she stated, as if it were obvious, a thing all people did. "He threatened it years ago, back when I wanted his piano. But he couldn't use my letters against me once he learned I saved his letters too—the ones proving he's a gold digger."

What a great love story. "Then why did you steal his tie?"

"The one I tied him up with?" She tried to smother a smile, as if flattered I'd noticed. "It was an old love token. He had it in the box with the letters. I took it back."

Two more police cars pulled up, and Duranja jogged over to talk with the arriving officers. The chief remained busy grilling Vincent.

"What else were you going to grab from Vincent's study?" I asked. After the letters—and the tie—she'd strolled toward his office carrying her big purse. Until I'd stopped her.

Her jaw tightened.

"Tell me," I prodded. "Consider it part of your rehabilitation."

Virginia stared out at the trees dotting the massive front yard. "I was young, and I was dumb," she hedged.

"Virginia, I want this all out in the open now, or I swear to heaven—"

"Fine." She tucked her chin and gave her head a slight tilt. "In my younger, crazy days, I knitted him a lap throw. He still has it. Can you believe that?" she added, as if she were flattered.

"No," I stated.

"Good," she said, touching her hair. "Then nobody else will, either." She smoothed a wayward strand. "I don't want to be known as a woman who knits."

I'd always wanted to learn. Not that I'd ever ask her to teach me.

We sat in silence for a moment, watching the chief slip into the driver's seat of his cruiser, with Vincent secured in the seat behind him.

Virginia had lived with too many secrets, too many lies, for too long. All of that had fallen apart now, even if the secret of the afghan remained intact.

Duranja pointed us out to the two new officers, or maybe he was more interested in searching the house for any additional evidence. It wasn't as if we were key to the case against Vincent.

Not anymore, at least.

"I should call Ellis," I said, digging for my phone the second Duranja turned his back.

"And make it obvious you're talking when you shouldn't be," Virginia tsked.

"So now you're a rule follower," I said, giving up on the phone. Even if Ellis could answer a call from me during his stakeout, I didn't want to put him in an awkward situation by telling him what his mother and I had gotten up to this morning.

Especially not with her sitting next to me, ready and able to add opinions.

We sat in silence as the two new officers approached the house and made their way up the stairs between us.

I really missed having Ellis around when the bad guys got arrested.

I rested my elbows on my knees and looked at Virginia sideways as she inspected her ruined manicure. "What will you do now?"

"I don't know," she said, ripping a damaged acrylic clean off. "Most of my family doesn't even like me," she said, tossing the pink-painted acrylic into the yard. "Ellis included, although he'd rather kiss a skunk than admit it."

"That got personal quick." As I recalled, I'd kissed a skunk that morning. Twice.

"I don't think Ellis would talk to me if I weren't his mother."

"I'm sorry." I was. At least for the life she'd created for herself. It was no way to live.

She shrugged. "I didn't kill Daisy, but if it weren't for me, she never would have taken that boat out alone."

I couldn't disagree. "You were very, very wrong in how you treated her."

"I know," she admitted, her voice small. "I was awful. I am awful. I—" She hesitated. "I think there's something wrong with me. I'm not sure I know how to be any different. I'm too old to change now."

"From what I've seen, you're a fighter." Even if she did like to fight with me. "I don't see any reason why you can't change the things about yourself that you don't like. I mean, if you make a mistake, are you just supposed to keep on making it?"

She dug at another ruined nail. "Ellis's father wants a divorce. Can you believe it?"

Yes.

"No," I lied.

She tossed another nail into the yard. "Leland says he's kept up appearances abroad, and it was my job to keep up appearances in Sugarland." She took a savage go at another broken nail. "As if I don't know he's got a little chippie in Malta. I put up with it. I put up with him because we were building something." She freed the nail and tossed it. "Now that my name is mud, I'm no use to him anymore."

Yes, but did she truly want a man who only wanted her for appearances?

"Maybe he'll change his mind once he thinks about it," I said gently. "You could convince him to try again. If that's what you want."

She uttered a long sigh. "I—I have no idea. It's too much," she declared, smoothing a ragged nail. "All of it."

I glanced to Duranja to make sure the coast was clear. "You don't have to decide now." She needed to step back, get some perspective. With a little distance, I didn't think anybody would choose the kind of life she had, including her.

"I can't just suddenly stop being who I am," she insisted. "Nobody can." She sighed. "At the time capsule opening, when Twyla Sue saw the town's reaction to her mom's book—she was shocked. And hurt. She felt like people were attacking her and her family because they could." She jutted her chin out. "Twyla Sue was always too meek. She'd never had to be a fighter. And look what happened."

I looked at her sideways. "I'm not following."

Virginia refused to meet my eyes. "I told Twyla Sue that having the book was her chance to change things. She could make people respect her. She could have the kind of power and money that would make her mamma proud."

"Oh, Virginia." I didn't know what to say.

She stared past me into the yard. "I told her she should start with Vincent," she admitted, as if she couldn't quite believe she'd been a part of it. "He was an easy target and rich. Plus, she'd be doing me a favor." Tears glazed her eyes. "My need for revenge and my need to teach Vincent a lesson killed my best friend. How do you recover from that?" She looked to me as if I had the answer. "If Twyla Sue hadn't gone after Vincent for me, she'd be alive today."

It was tragic and wrong and awful on so many levels.

"Twyla Sue made her own choices," I reminded Virginia. "Now you need to decide if that's the road you want to keep following."

A bullhorn screech cut the morning air, and Duranja's voice boomed out over the front yard at us. "Stop. *Talking.*"

"Now he notices?" Virginia mused.

"It's not like he trusts either one of us," I murmured.

"He shouldn't." She waited until Duranja was distracted again before reaching under her rear and pulling out Erma Sue's burn book. I gasped. She'd been sitting on Erma Sue's burn book the whole time we'd been talking.

"I thought Duranja bagged that," I whispered.

"No," she said, hastily brushing off the porch dirt. "Duranja grabbed the journal first. I mean, that's what he needs most for the case against Vincent. This is what the police are in the house looking for right now," she said before stuffing the legendary, feathery *evidence to murder* into my purse!

"You need to give that to the police," I said, fighting the urge to yank it back out. I'd taken evidence before, and it didn't go well. Not at all. And that had been an accident!

Duranja whipped his head in our direction and stared us down. He obviously suspected we were up to something.

Because we were.

"Stop looking like the kid who stole the last cookie," Virginia whispered quickly. "The police have Twyla Sue's journal. That places Vincent at the scene. Besides, he confessed to Duranja on the way out. I heard him."

"But this is still evidence," I hissed between my teeth.

"Ellis said you need Erma Sue's burn book to free your ghost. So there you go—it's in your bag. See?" Now Duranja was getting out of the car. "I'm looking out for you."

"By taking what's not yours," I muttered to her as the deputy stalked toward us.

I shuddered to think what Duranja would do if he discovered the burn book in my possession. I mean, yes, I kind of needed it. I cared about Frankie, and I wanted him to be free.

But what would Ellis think if I interfered with a murder investigation? And Duranja? He'd do a happy jig while he locked me up.

"Are you going to quibble about it, or are you going to do right by your gangster ghost?" she asked, not bothering to hide the fact she was still talking.

Frankie would be proud of Virginia for swiping it. Ellis might not appreciate it if I stuffed it into a storage locker haunted by a dead beautician.

And me? I was horrified. "I can't be party to stealing."

"Vincent stole it from Twyla Sue. Now you're borrowing it to help your friend. In the end it's going back to its rightful owner. Really, Verity, I don't see the issue." She stood to face Duranja.

"You—" I stood as well.

"I said no talking," Duranja shouted when he reached us. His face had gone red, and his neck was all blotchy.

"Do you realize who you're speaking to?" Virginia demanded. "I pay your salary."

I realized I'd left my purse on the ground with a feathery corner peeking out. Now would have been the time to come clean.

Instead, I grabbed the strap and slipped it over my shoulder. I felt the book sink to the bottom. At least I was keeping it out of the hands of any living persons who could use it for evil. That had to count for something, right?

Duranja wasn't impressed with Virginia's insolence. "You're under arrest as soon as we can get two more squad cars up here." He glanced past us to the men working inside. "We're a little short on officers at the moment."

Virginia crossed her arms over her chest. "I told you Verity didn't break and enter. Are you really going to arrest your girlfriend's sister?"

Duranja looked heavenward and refused to answer, which truly was the proper way to deal with such an outrageous threat. "He's *not* Melody's boyfriend," I pointed out.

"Let's call her and ask," Virginia said, reaching into her bag for her cell.

"No!" I shot back, surprised when Duranja shouted the same thing.

I caught the flash of alarm in his eyes before he wiped his expression clean. "That's enough out of both of you," he corrected.

The color remained high in his cheeks. His breath came a little too quickly. That was…not good if my dear, sweet sister was indeed the cause. I'd obviously let them out of my sight for too long while I was working to solve Twyla Sue's murder and free Frankie.

Well, I'd fix that in a jiffy.

Duranja's radio crackled to life. "You're going to have to make do with the cars you have," the dispatcher drawled. "Dwyer is still chasing the cow that got loose on Route M."

I could almost hear Duranja's jaw grind. "Fine." He tucked his radio back on his belt. "You," he said, pointing at Virginia, "are getting arrested. You," he added, directing a finger at me, "are lucky Vincent saw you trying to pry Virginia out of his house. You're free to go, but I want you at the station for questioning in an hour." He charged up the stairs between us. "I'll deal with Mrs. Wydell as soon as I give final instructions to my officers."

Virginia and I shared a glance as he disappeared into the house.

"You have to leave now," she insisted. "You don't want him changing his mind and taking you downtown. You can't afford to get searched." She glanced at the empty porch. "But first, let's get our story straight. I did the breaking and entering. You saved us when Vincent drew a gun."

That about summed it up.

"I'll see you at the station," I said, hurrying to my car, digging deep into my bag, past the skeletal feathered fringe, to find my keys.

I had an hour.

With any luck, it would be enough time to fetch my gangster and return to the storage unit to deliver Erma Sue's book.

CHAPTER 23

I rushed home to find Frankie trotting Frisky Pete around the pond. A menagerie of animals trailed behind. If I didn't know better, I'd think he was the pied piper. At least they weren't on my porch. I slammed the car door and hurried past two lagging baby goats and my skunk, who had stopped to chase a butterfly.

It was like crashing a demented parade.

"Frankie, you've got to come quick," I called. "I've got the book!"

The gangster pulled up on the reins. It startled the horse, who ran into the donkey, who nipped the mamma goat, who leaped backward and began a full-on bouncing retreat straight toward me with three babies dancing at her heels.

"Don't touch me!" I hollered at the phantom goats, who didn't speak a lick of English or take orders well, forcing me to take refuge behind the apple tree as they hammered past.

I had to get Frankie—and them—away from here. Far, far away.

The gangster stormed up on horseback, kicking up a plume of ghostly dust. "You've got the book? For real? Show me."

I pulled it out of my bag, the sequined skull and crossbones glittering in the sunlight, stark against the pink and the feathers. "This is it." A faded yellow-ribbon page holder fluttered in the breeze.

"It's the most beautiful thing I've ever seen," Frankie gushed, leaping down off the horse like Roy Rogers. Passing straight through the apple tree. Not like he cared.

"I kind of...took it without permission," I confessed. "We have an hour to get this book to Erma Sue before I'm due to report to the police," I added, tucking it into my bag. "I'll grab your urn from the house."

"I'll stable Frisky Pete," he said, leading him by the reins as we both jogged toward the porch. "And, kid," he said, when we'd all clambered up and reached the back door, "I'm proud of you."

"Me too." I grinned.

I did it. I'd found the book. There were times I didn't think we'd pull it off.

"You stole evidence. For me," Frankie said, like a proud papa. "I think I've done my job here."

I wasn't even going to argue. Not today.

"Let's just get the book to Erma Sue," I said before ducking into the house.

No sense disappointing the gangster by telling him I would never follow in his footsteps. No bringing up the fact that I hadn't even broken into Vincent's house.

Not really.

I grabbed Frankie's urn from the trash can full of dirt in my parlor, the trash can that contained his ashes mixed with my garden dirt and topped by my grandmother's favorite heirloom rosebush. I'd kept it next to the mantel for years, but it wouldn't need to remain any longer once Frankie was free.

The bush and the dirt would go back into the garden at the back of the house. The trash can could live in the trash nook outside the laundry room. My home—my life—could return to normal.

Somehow, the thought wasn't as fulfilling as I'd imagined.

But, of course, it was what I wanted.

Our entire goal all along had been to set Frankie free. He deserved it. He wanted it more than anything. And soon he would leave me for good.

I tucked his urn in my bag and met him in the car.

He sat on the passenger side, arm spread over the bench seat, grinning ear to ear.

"I don't think I've ever seen you so happy," I said, depositing my bag on the floor of the passenger seat before kerthunking my car into drive.

"You weren't there for the great silk suit heist of 1929," he crowed as I backed out of the drive. "I stole everything down to my underwear, and it felt fabulous."

"I can't imagine," I told him.

I honestly couldn't.

Frankie stuck a hand through the window and waggled his fingers in the breeze as we streaked toward the old storage unit by the railroad tracks.

"There's one thing that bothers me," I confided, looking both ways before turning left onto the rural road.

"No." Frankie sat up straight and pointed a finger at me. "Nothing bothers you," he declared. "You are not going to start second-guessing me now."

"I'm not," I said, hitting the gas, going as fast as we were legally allowed. "It just occurs to me that a lot of people have been hurt by Erma Sue's book." I'd seen it firsthand with the secrets Vincent had revealed. The book surely contained more.

Not that I wanted to know any of them.

"I think someone stashed that book in the time capsule precisely to keep more people from being hurt," I declared, going slightly airborne as we crested a hill.

"Rowena did it," Frankie said.

"What?" I swerved a little and came way too close to a tree. The lower branches slapped my windshield.

"Watch it!" Frankie hollered. "The last thing I need is you dying on the way to getting me free."

"Gee, thanks," I said, wrestling all four tires back on the road.

He leaned an arm on the windowsill and adjusted his hat. "Suds asked around for me. Rowena's been bragging to her dead neighbors about it." He huffed. "Talk about a way to tick off your sister."

It made sense. "Well, at least Rowena did *something* positive with her anger." She'd put Erma Sue's diary out of commission.

Until recently.

"Yeah, she's a real gem," Frankie said woodenly. "And she still owes me a bottle of Old Rip Van Winkle."

It didn't change the fact that this book in the wrong hands could spell disaster for a lot of good people. And here we were giving it back to the woman who'd wielded it so mercilessly for decades.

I mean, the book was on the earthly plane instead of the ghostly one, so we had that going for us. Still, Erma Sue must still be able to use it, or at least see the pages, or she never would have wanted it back in the first place.

I passed a Ford pickup before returning to my lane and taking a second to glance at my gangster. "Frankie, we're about to give a blackmailer her power back."

His expression hardened. "We're about to close a deal. What she does afterward is not our problem."

But Erma Sue definitely had a plan for the book, or she wouldn't have bargained with us. "She's willing to tell us exactly how she freed herself from her old property. If her sister ever found out how she did it, she might be able to trap Erma Sue again. Do you understand?" This was seriously sensitive information. "And she's telling us. Her plans for this book must be huge."

He didn't bother arguing. Instead he raised a finger. "You forget. We will have knowledge on how to trap and un-trap ghosts. Therefore, she will not use the book against us."

I thunked my head back against the headrest and prepared to make our turn. "Is that all you care about? Us and our skin?"

Why had I wasted my breath? Of course that was the only thing Frankie thought about.

"It's not like Erma Sue can use the book," the ghost stressed. "She didn't die with it. Nobody did, so there's no ghostly version. She one hundred percent can't use it on the ghostly plane."

"Okay, good," I said, exiting onto the side road way too fast. "So the physical copy will merely sit in the storage locker with Erma Sue, and maybe she won't be able to open it." I mean, we could hope, right? "I haven't seen her interact with any of the objects in the mortal realm surrounding her in the storage locker." Maybe she didn't have that kind of control over her energy.

"Even if she can move a table or jiggle a door handle, that stuff's a lot easier than handling objects on your plane. The things might as well be made of solid lead and weigh as much as an armored car. Opening a book to any page, much less a specific one, is near impossible unless you're able to manipulate extreme amounts of energy. It's not something your everyday ghost can do."

"You're not just saying that to make me feel better, are you?" I asked, heading down the rural road toward the railroad tracks.

"I would," he admitted, "but in this case, I'm not."

I believed him, only because I'd seen firsthand how most ghosts couldn't move objects in our plane beyond a jiggle here or a slide there. I didn't see how Erma Sue could go paging through her book of horrors, or carry it around to threaten the dead citizens of Sugarland.

Instead, it would be housed in the storage unit, along with the discarded remnants of Erma Sue's career, a trophy for the dead hairdresser and nothing more.

And bonus—it would be out of the hands of the living.

We hoped.

"I wonder what's going to happen to the storage unit now that Twyla Sue's not paying the rent anymore," I mused.

"Who cares?" Frankie asked, leaning forward to catch a glimpse of It's Not Junk.

"What if someone else finds the book? Then the whole mess starts over again," I said, pulling into the weed-strewn lot.

"For the love of—" Frankie leapt to his feet, literally going through the roof. "Don't mess with my freedom!"

"The book needs to be destroyed," I concluded, maneuvering into a parking spot by the back door. "If not today, then soon."

Frankie glided out of the car then turned on me as soon as I got out. "You mess this up and I will haunt you like you've never been haunted before. I'll move into your bedroom. I'll open up a zoo. I'll—"

"Pipe down, wild kingdom," I said before he blew a gasket. "We are going to walk in there and learn how to get you free. Once you're free, you don't care what happens, right?"

"Right," he gritted out, keeping an eye on me as I pulled Rowena's key from my purse and inserted it into the lock.

We traveled the stark, mildewy hall in silence. Frankie, a bundle of nerves. Me, wishing I didn't have to give the black-mailer her prize. Even if she couldn't use it like she had in the past. Even if it remained buried in a storage locker full of beauty shop junk, I couldn't escape the feeling I was making a mistake.

That I hadn't looked at this from every angle.

Yes, I was giving a blackmailer her power back, or at least the tool she'd used to wield it. But she was dead, and as long as I kept the key to the storage locker, I could take back the book if she misused it.

And if the extended family decided to keep up the locker, I doubted they'd go searching through the old beauty shop Twyla Sue had packed away.

There was nothing to worry about, I told myself, except for the ghost of Erma Sue.

We stopped outside her door.

Frankie shook out his arms, as if loosening up for a fight.

"Diplomacy, Frank," I reminded him.

"Don't push it," he replied.

The door clicked open without me touching it.

Erma Sue was waiting.

She perched on her pink salon chair, wearing a sleeveless party dress and a smirk.

"Welcome back to New Sue's House of Beauty." She slipped from her chair and strolled up to me like she had all the time in the world. As if she didn't stand among the draped remains of her life. "You found it, didn't you?"

I remained in the hall. "Why do you say that?"

She lost the smirk. "Because you're fit to be tied and he's jumpy as a June bug on a string."

A chandelier formed out of the mist and covered the naked bulb on the ceiling. The sheet-draped lumps disappeared, replaced by the beauty salon stations from the old Two Sues' House of Beauty, the manicure station behind her chair.

She pursed her glossy lips and held out a perfectly manicured hand. "I'd like my book back now."

I stepped through the doorway and reached into my purse to withdraw the book that had tormented so many.

The ghost gasped out loud when she saw it. "It's still so beautiful."

"It's mine until you hold up your end of the bargain," I informed her.

Her expression went cold and still. "I've been thinking about that."

"Don't you dare—" Frankie rushed her, and I put out a hand to stop him.

"Frankie, no!" I turned to her. "If you don't keep up your end of the deal, we walk."

She held up her hands, as if she needed to fend me off. "I'm only saying this knowledge stays between us. If I learn you've told anyone else, if it gets back to my sister, let's just say there are legions in Sugarland who owe me favors. I'll use this book to make your life a living—and mostly dead —hell."

I glanced to Frankie. "She says she can use the book," I said under my breath.

"She's bluffing. Trust me," he gritted out between clenched teeth.

Sure. It always worked out so well when I trusted Frankie.

"We can keep a secret," Frankie vowed to her.

Erma Sue's eyes narrowed at me.

"We can," I agreed, not at all liking where this was headed.

She nodded, her hair falling in perfect layers as she did. It seemed she was a woman used to getting her way. "It's a matter of shifting how your ghostly energy works," she said, all business. "I can see you already have some practice. You're lending Verity your power, aren't you?"

"All the time," Frankie grumped, as if the whole "showing me ghosts" thing hadn't been his idea in the first place.

"Good," Erma Sue said, planting her hands on her hips. "That alone shows you're willing to break the rules."

"I like where this is headed." Frankie grinned.

The beautician smirked. "Before I managed to get out, I was literally trapped in the dirt, my ashes mixed with the roots and the muck under that awful gardenia bush."

"Mine's an overgrown rose," Frankie said, cocking a hip against her beauty station.

"A lovely one," I added, in defense of my grandmother.

"You're going to want to extricate your ashes from the soil, but that'll never work," she explained.

We had tried that to no avail.

"Science is a crock," Frankie agreed.

"You're trapped because you think those ashes are you," she explained, like she was describing a new concept haircut.

"They are me," Frankie said flatly. "They literally are."

I saw where she was going. "I think what Erma Sue is trying to explain is that you're not earthly anymore."

"Parts of you are," she corrected. "The parts that are trapped. You're so wrapped up in the ashes of your old life that you're literally stuck in the dirt with them. You couldn't escape if you tried."

"Oh, I've tried," Frankie said, nodding along.

"So stop," Erma Sue said. "Stop being the guy who's trapped in the dirt. Stop being the old you."

Frankie stared at her, his lip curling with disdain. "Sweetheart," he said, indulging her, "it's not like I can just stop being me." He cleared his throat and straightened his suit coat. "I'm Frankie the German. Men fear me. Women—"

"You can still be you, but better," Erma Sue said, brushing him off. "You've got to dig deep and learn who you truly can be."

Frankie stared at her. "Err…"

In a second, she was going to have to get out the hand puppets.

"It's in you," I said, cheering him on.

"Stop helping." Erma Sue waved me off.

"What a load of bull!" Frankie threw his hands up and retreated toward the counter. "You're just making stuff up as you go, aren't you? I came all the way here for this? I got you your book for this?"

I'd been the one to get the book, but I wasn't about to push a technicality when we had more important things to discuss. "Let's think about this," I said, glancing at my fuming gangster.

"How does it work exactly?" Her instructions were vague to say the least.

"Take my case," she said, crossing her arms over her chest, keeping an eye on the gangster. "I was trapped in my head. I thought my way was the only way to be respected and admired. Until I stewed under that gardenia and I looked at my life." She dropped her arms. "I realized the gossip and the rumors and the hurt I caused people—it was wrong for me to do that. I needed that kind of power over people because I didn't like who I was. I was afraid that without that armor, I was vulnerable. I was scared of getting hurt myself."

"You weren't a gangster, though," Frankie concluded, as if that were the sole reason she could have been afraid or unhappy.

Erma Sue closed her eyes briefly. "Listen to me. I had to evolve in order to escape. I had to learn to love and accept myself enough to change. I needed to leave that dead part behind me."

My gangster buddy scratched behind his ear and shifted uncomfortably. "Can't I just find my favorite gun or something?"

"No, Frankie," I said. We'd already tried that.

The beautician stared him dead in the eyes. "The ashes were the old me. Your ashes are the old you. You need to evolve. Start with a healthy dose of self-love and take a good, hard look at who you want to become besides Frankie the German. The Frankie who's buried under a rosebush."

"This is asking a lot," Frankie said as if he were doing her the favor.

"You can do it," I promised. I mean, Frankie had grown a lot as a person since I'd met him. He'd gone from a hardened criminal to a part-time jerk and a pain in my behind. But he'd shown at times that he cared about me. He'd found love with his girlfriend, Molly. He'd adopted a racehorse—that wasn't staying.

He'd even tried to make friends with my skunk. I had no doubt he could learn to love himself if he tried. "Still, there's one thing that puzzles me." I turned to the beautician. "You say you've let go of your need for power and control. You told us earlier that you want to build your client base and your business again."

She nodded, pleased. "It'll be like the original Two Sue's, only better," she promised. "More positive. People will see I haven't lost my sense of style. And they'll like the new me if they give me a chance."

That was great. Wonderful in fact. Still… "Don't you also need to fix things with your sister?"

Her expression clouded. "Of course not. Why would you say that?"

"Whoa. Hey." Frankie stepped in between us. "What's with the twenty questions? The lady is happy."

That was all well and good, but the beautician had one more thing to fix, a relationship to make right. "I'm just saying there's this whole power dynamic where Rowena is trying to trap and torture you, and you never apologized for stealing her boyfriends or giving her a complex about her body," I explained to the glowering beautician. Surely she realized. "You also messed up Rowena's hair."

"Leave the bad hairdos out of it," Frankie said, smashing his hat harder onto his head with one hand and making a gesture like he was going to hold me back with the other.

That wasn't the point. "I'm just saying that Erma Sue grew and let go of her need for power, but she forgot about her sister."

The beautician stood stiff and frowning. "Well, Rowena *is* still after me."

See? I'd gotten her thinking. She was starting to realize she could make more positive changes. "Rowena will continue to be angry and vengeful until you fix things," I insisted while Frankie made slashing moves against his throat.

The beautician ground her jaw. "You're right."

"I know I am," I said, pleased.

"I need to end this once and for all," she vowed.

"Verity…" Frankie warned.

For heaven's sake. Couldn't he see we were changing her mind? Maybe this talk about emotions would help him understand his own feelings. "You need to show Rowena you love her," I said to the beautician, who stood breathing hard and shaking. "That you don't need this power dynamic between you anymore."

"I don't love her. I despise her!" she shouted. "Rowena made my afterlife a living hell."

"Okay, well…" I hadn't imagined anger issues would be part of the new, evolved Erma Sue. "It's good to let your feelings out," I said, going with it. "Of course, you also realize you're beyond revenge and—"

She took a step back and scrubbed a hand over her chin. "Maybe I was right that I need to be feared in order to be safe."

What? "No." Wrong direction. "You were *not* right. You've grown and—"

"I actually have to go with Erma Sue on this one," Frankie said pragmatically. "I mean, what if Rowena shows up here and Erma Sue's all lovey-dovey? She's a sitting duck."

"I am, aren't I?" Erma Sue asked, eyes wild.

"I'd nab you if I were her," he agreed.

"Frankie, go find something to do," I ordered.

"As if I'm the one messing this up," he said, tossing his hands up and walking straight through the beauty desk.

He'd better not try to steal anything back there.

Erma Sue was breathing hard, even though she didn't need to draw a breath at all. She stared at me as if seeing me for the first time. "Take the book out of your bag," she ordered.

Well, that was sudden. "I'm not sure you're in the right state of mind—"

"Do it," she ordered again, gliding straight for me.

I hesitated, watching her expression darken. My refusal was making it worse.

I glanced toward Frankie, who from the sound of it had begun rooting around behind the beauty desk. He'd better not be stealing anything.

I drew the burn book out of my bag. I supposed I could always take it back if she misused it.

The gangster let out a shout, and I heard a snap of metal from behind the beauty desk. "Whiskey trap!"

"Darn it, Frankie," I said, moving to assist him.

I couldn't take him anywhere.

Erma Sue blocked me.

"Why are you setting traps like your sister?" I demanded.

She tilted her head. "I forgot that trap was back there," she said absently. "But I have to say Rowena's methods come in handy," she added with a quirk of the lips. "You were right about me. I do need to be feared in order to be safe."

"Hold up," I said, retreating. "Think. You've changed," I insisted. "You don't want to be trapped in a gardenia bush."

"Oh, I've evolved, sweetheart. I have all kinds of new ideas," she promised. And before I could ask her what she meant, she lunged at me with a pair of scissors.

CHAPTER 24

I screamed and dropped the book. The door slammed closed behind me.

"Stop!" I demanded, tossing a standing hair dryer at Erma Sue. It passed straight through her and clattered to the floor next to her beauty chair.

She loomed over me, gripping the deadly shears. One slice and I was finished. "Frankie, cut my power. Now!"

She could slash me, kill me, as long as I stayed connected to her world.

"I'm kind of busy here," I heard from the other side of the beauty desk.

"Frankie!" I demanded as the stylist turned her attention to the gangster in the trap. She zipped away from me and straight through the workstation that hid my housemate, her scissors raised. "Frankie, watch out!"

"Hey," he barked. Then he cried out.

"Frankie!" I shoved the beauty desk out of my way, sending it crashing into Erma Sue's trademark chair. She screamed in horror, but the real terror lay behind it. Frankie lay facedown, his arm trapped in a ghostly cage bolted to the floor, his hand still gripping a bottle of Old Rip Van Winkle. She'd stabbed him in the back, and his grayish blood spread heavy and quick. "Oh no." He wasn't moving. He wasn't even moaning.

"He's dead," the beautician said with grim satisfaction. "Again."

Erma Sue stood over the body, her scissors dripping blood.

My heart sank. I could still see her, which meant I was still connected. It would take Frankie at least an hour to wake from a second death before he could shut off my power.

If I even lasted that long.

The beautician stalked toward me, eyes alight with fire. Excitement.

She enjoyed seeing me squirm.

Talk about a relapse. And it hadn't even taken much. Just me and my dumb questions.

"You don't need to hurt me." I retreated fast, reaching for the doorknob. Even if she was convinced that she needed power and control. "You're a blackmailer, not a killer." At least I hoped. The knob refused to turn. "I gave you what you wanted!"

"Not yet," she snapped. "But you will." Her glossy lips pressed tight. "Pick up the book."

It lay next to my foot, the skull and crossbones glinting in the weak light cast by a single naked bulb—the pink feathered monstrosity that had caused so much suffering and sorrow.

"What? No." I stiffened. If the scissors-wielding madwoman wanted me to take hold of the book, that was reason enough to refuse. Then I realized with sickening clarity what she really wanted. "You can't touch the book in the earthly plane, but if I die with it—"

Heavens.

If I died holding the book, I'd bring it onto the ghostly plane with me.

It would technically be mine, but she could take it. She could have it whenever she wanted. All she'd have to do was stab me with her bloody scissors to incapacitate me for a while. She could threaten to hurt the people I loved. She could kill me over and over again in order to knock me out and keep it longer. Whatever way she chose to torture me, hunt me, take the book from me, it would forever exist on the ghostly plane, where she could use it and abuse it. Forever.

She'd have her true weapon back. Her power.

And I'd be dead.

Unless I figured out a way to get out of here alive. Out of a windowless cinder-block room with a locked door. Even if I escaped, I didn't have any illusions about outrunning a murderous ghost.

She had a weapon. I didn't.

I scanned the small room for something I could use to defend myself. The beauty counters lay bare. A manicure station in the back near the treadmill featured a magnifying light and an old bottle of polish remover decorated with pink rhinestones, but all of these things were in the world of the living. I didn't see anything I could use in the spirit world, even if it would hurt like heck to pick it up.

Erma Sue lunged at me with the scissors. I dodged to the left, tripping over the book.

"Did you read the part in the book about your grandmother?" Erma Sue taunted.

"I did not," I said, nearly forgetting to breathe.

"It's good," she assured me as I scrambled behind the beauty table opposite the one I'd toppled. "Not everything in the book is an evil, bad secret."

I had bigger problems at the moment, like staying alive.

"Might as well let her tell you herself," Erma Sue said, closing in on me.

I needed to find something I could stab with, shoot with. But there was nothing except spiderwebs behind the workstation. Frankie always carried a gun. But he was on the other side of the room.

A wall of cold slammed down on me, and the beauty desk fell backward against the cinder-block wall. With a crash of glass, the mirror shattered on the other side.

I crouched down low. Erma Sue ripped out the drawer next to my face and peered at me from the other side. "I don't care if you make me tear my entire place apart. You're dying with that book."

The only way I could see that happening was if she stabbed me and I fell over on top of it. Would that count?

She rounded the desk with her scissors, forcing me away from the rear wall.

Holy heck. That was exactly what she intended to do—drive me back toward the book.

I ran for the door again and kicked the book away from it. Prayed I could get out this time, but the door didn't budge. She slashed down with her scissors, and I ran to the far right side of the small storage locker.

I needed a plan. A way out before she ran me down, trapped me for good. Only I didn't see anything I could use to kill the ghost or even delay her for a while.

I scurried behind the toppled desk with the dead gangster behind it. "I'm sorry. I'm sorry. I'm sorry," I said as I gripped him by the suit coat and rolled him over. I felt the touch like a cold, sickening, bone-deep invasion. I dug past his silver cigarette case, searching for his shoulder holster, pocketing his lighter just in case. If I could get his gun, I'd have to use it fast. While I could handle ghostly objects, it was extremely uncomfortable to do so. And my touch also caused them to disappear fast.

"Let the dead lie," Erma Sue thundered, driving the scissors down. She got me in the arm, and a new kind of pain seared me.

I felt the sickening icy invasion of the ghostly blades at the same time as warm blood welled up from the gash in my arm left behind by the metal blades. I let go of Frankie's shoulder holster, giving up on the gun as Erma Sue slashed at me again.

I dashed from behind the toppled beauty table, gripping my arm in an effort to stanch the bleeding wound, and clambered behind the manicure station. On my way I knocked over a metal trash can that clattered loudly against the concrete floor.

Erma Sue loomed over me. "I won't hurt you if you just pick up the book," she snarled.

She wouldn't just hurt me. She'd kill me.

But I had a plan. Sort of. I snatched the bedazzled bottle from the manicure desk.

Erma Sue whooshed up from behind the nail station, slamming the scissors down onto the table where my hand had been an instant before.

I hurled the metal trash can at her. It soared right through her, but I took advantage of her moment of distraction to vault over the table and streak past her toward the door, toward the book. I had only one option left.

It was dangerous, and it was stupid, and it might get me killed anyway.

Frankie would have approved.

I didn't, but I didn't have any better options. Erma Sue had hurt me, bled me, and she'd do it again. She'd weaken me. The next blow might make it impossible to fight back. She could go on for eternity. I had one shot.

I grabbed the book.

She lunged with the scissors.

I turned the metal trash can upright and stuffed the book inside.

She tripped me, sending me slamming down on top of both.

I tried to roll off, but a heavy force kept me pinned. She cackled as I ripped open the bottle of very real nail polish remover I'd stolen from the manicure desk. With a burst of desperate strength, I raised my body off the trash can just enough to dump the contents of the bottle in. I soaked the book and myself, but I got the job done.

I tossed the bottle at her head and shoved myself back onto my butt.

I reached into my back pocket for the ghostly lighter I'd lifted from Frankie's coat. It throbbed with otherworldly energy I could feel through my clothes. I welcomed the pain because that meant it hadn't disappeared. Yet.

I grabbed the lighter, flicked the ignition, and tossed it in.

Flames shot from the trash can.

"Nooo!" Erma Sue dove for the inferno, her hands passing through the flames, the book, and the burning feathers that flew up on a wave of sparks and smoke.

She'd dropped the scissors, and I kicked them under the mess of boxes at the back of the locker, my ears ringing from the pain of ghostly contact. Once she got over the shock of what I'd done, she'd kill me for spite, and I still had to figure out a way to get out of there.

The smoke from the fire was beginning to fill the room, and when I turned back, I realized the beauty desk was on fire.

Ohmygosh.

I ran and grabbed the gray blanket off the treadmill and threw it on the flames to smother them.

Then the blanket caught fire, too.

"Oh, come on!"

I searched for anything else I could use as the smoke grew thicker, and my eyes started to water. I doubled over in a fit of coughing, and it was hard to inhale after that.

"My chair!" Erma Sue cried as it began to smolder.

I dropped to the ground, struggling to draw a breath. There was no escape, no way out. This would be my death spot. In Erma Sue's storage unit for eternity.

No. I could still try to make the door work. I reached for the knob, choking back a sob when it refused to turn. The smoke grew thicker. It burned my throat. It seared my lungs.

I kept hold of the knob. It was my only hope, even as spots formed in front of my eyes and my vision dimmed.

CHAPTER 25

J woke up in the back seat of a squad car with Duranja
staring down at me. "Don't talk," he ordered stiffly. "I
know that's tough for you," he added grudgingly. Perhaps he
was glad to see I wasn't dead.

His radio crackled. *Fire at It's Not Junk down by the river. All
available units report.*

That would bring the lookie-loos.

"There really was a fire." My head swam as I tried to sit up.
He nudged me back down.

Until that moment, I wasn't sure if the lighter had existed
anywhere but on the ghostly plane. I'd brought an object
over from the spiritual side to our world only once before. It
had been the first time I'd touched a ghostly artifact, an old
locket. The encounter had been brief and startling, and I
didn't know how I'd done it. I sure hadn't counted on it
happening again. In my desperation, I'd hardly dared to
hope.

"The ambulance is coming. The fire department is already
here."

He kept a hand on his gun as he watched the road.

Out the window, I could see black smoke billowing up into the sky. Sirens wailed in the distance.

"A real fire." My throat felt raw and tight.

"It's Not Junk has gone up in a blaze of glory." His stiff jaw looked twice its usual size from my vantage point below. "You owe my uncle Albert about twelve deer heads and a bobcat. Don't be surprised if my aunt drops by next week with a pie."

"I—" I rubbed my parched lips together. He must have seen me slip inside. He must have gotten me out. "Why?" I struggled to make my throat work. "What are you doing here?"

He gritted his jaw. "Let's try, 'Thank you, Officer Duranja. You saved my life, Officer Duranja.'"

"Right," I managed.

Boy, did I hate owing him one.

And I still didn't want him dating my sister.

I felt hot, so hot. Then cold all of a sudden. My teeth started to chatter.

He grabbed a blanket from near my feet and laid it over me. "I followed you because I was setting you up. You lied to me back there. And Virginia, of all people, covered for you." His brows furrowed. "Seriously, what is that about?"

I had no idea.

He shook his head, like he couldn't comprehend whatever grand plan I'd cooked up with the former queen of Sugarland. "I knew you were up to something. So I gave you an hour of freedom and the chance to lead me right to it."

I closed my eyes. I never suspected he was onto me.

At least he was one of the good guys. Technically.

"So what were you doing?" he asked.

I eyed him warily. No good could come out of telling Duranja that I'd destroyed a piece of evidence.

I'd tell Ellis instead.

I cleared my throat. "I had a question for Erma Sue's ghost," I scratched out.

"So you admit you were in Twyla Sue's storage locker," he crowed as if he had me dead to rights.

"Yes," I said, trying to lace my answer with attitude. I ruined it when I started coughing. "Ghost hunting."

"That's always your story, isn't it?" he huffed.

"Yes, because it's the truth." Even if he was too bullheaded to see it.

His nostrils flared. "I've had you pegged for a lot of things, but I never pictured you as an arsonist."

"Excuse me?"

"That fire started in the late Twyla Sue's storage locker," he bit out. "It's the one right next to my uncle Albert's. You just admitted to being there."

"There was a fire in the trash can, and it spread. I wasn't trying to burn down the building," I insisted.

"But you did," he said, as if the next logical step would be for me to admit it.

I kept my mouth shut.

"You're a menace." He crossed his arms over his chest. "I can't believe I promised Ellis I'd look after you." He cocked his head. "I wouldn't have agreed except your sister asked as well."

"Now you're just trying to torture me," I said, closing my eyes again.

* * *

I AWOKE IN AN AMBULANCE, wearing an oxygen mask. I recognized the EMT as the son of one of Lauralee's neighbors.

"Just relax," Samir told me as he took my vitals.

Duranja sat in the seat opposite, watching me like I planned to bolt out the open back doors. I could see the fire chief talking to two of the firefighters, their faces smudged and their gear blackened with soot.

The chief caught Duranja's eye and walked over.

"We contained the fire to just the one locker. The lockers on either side are smoke damage only," he said, adding a tip of the hat to me. "Hiya, Verity. Glad you made it out safe."

"Don't talk in front of the arsonist," Duranja instructed the chief.

He scratched his cheek, leaving a streak of black. "That's the thing, Alec. Verity said the fire started in the trash can, and we can confirm that. But my men and I can't find a source of ignition."

"Meaning...?" he prodded.

"There's absolutely no proof she tried to burn anything down or that she even started the fire."

"That's easy enough to fix," Duranja snapped. "Verity, empty your pockets and your purse."

I had left my purse in the car. But I turned out my pockets and left them hanging open. I had nothing.

Duranja placed my purse on my chest like a beacon of presumed guilt.

"This isn't the time for an interrogation," Samir stated as I attempted to empty my bag. "You don't have to do this, Verity."

"I do," I said, lowering my mask, which displeased the EMT even more. "Help me?"

Samir nodded. "Okay. Just take it easy."

I nodded. I had nothing in my purse that could start a fire, and I'd be glad to prove it. Samir shot judgy looks at Duranja as the EMT helped me unload a hairbrush, my wallet, Frankie's urn.

Duranja's eyes narrowed as we placed each of the items on the ambulance counter. He especially didn't appreciate the fact that I carried an urn. But Duranja's biggest disappointment came next.

I had no matches, no lighter, no way of setting a fire.

"I don't believe it!" he barked.

"Will you stop traumatizing my patient now?" Samir asked, adjusting my blanket.

Like Josephine's locket, Frankie's lighter had enjoyed only a brief stay in our dimension. The same touch that brought it into our world caused it to disappear. It was probably back in Frankie's pocket already.

"She set the fire," Duranja insisted.

"It doesn't look like it," said the chief.

"What?" Duranja asked, hopping down out of the ambulance. "Are you saying it was spontaneous combustion?"

Samir and I exchanged a glance. "Might be," he said.

The chief shook his head. "There was a lot of hairspray and combustible stuff in there. The fumes can build up. Then if you have any kind of accidental spark…" He snapped his fingers. "Boom. It's rare, but it happens."

"Can nobody back me up here?" Duranja demanded.

"You need evidence," the chief said.

Duranja looked like he might burst a blood vessel.

At least there was an ambulance nearby.

I smiled to myself as Duranja stalked away, grousing about the injustice of it all. He'd get over it. And he'd no doubt be after me again for something else. But today, I was safe. I'd made it. And for that, I was thankful.

* * *

DURANJA DIDN'T ARREST me that day, although I heard later that he'd wanted to get me on trespassing.

Instead, I ended up at the Jackson Regional Hospital overnight for smoke inhalation treatment and general observation.

Frankie appeared in my room an hour after I was admitted, his jacket still smoking. He waved his hat to disperse the aftereffects of the fire, displaying the neat, round bullet hole in his forehead. Not to mention his bowl cut. Dying again had not improved his hair, although I wasn't about to tell him that.

"Damn," he swore. "I bite it and you burn the whole place down."

"How'd you know?" He'd been out of it.

"Erma Sue is fit to be tied," he said, planting the hat back on his head. "She's grounded again—trapped in the ashes of her old beauty chair." He popped his hat back on his head. "Looks like she's got some personal exploration work to do before she gets free."

"What about you?" I asked.

He shrugged. "I'm perfect the way I am."

We'd work on that.

He strolled toward the window and took a look out. "I just hope she stays grounded for once." He cocked a thumb in his belt. "I don't want that crazy lady around my Frisky Pete. Anyway, I should thank you for not eating dirt back there. With you dead, I'd be stuck in your backyard forever. Or worse, I'd be trapped in a storage unit with my urn and *ghost* you. Not to mention a crazy beautician. Right when I find out how to get free."

I leaned back against the pillow. "And here I thought you cared."

"Sure, let's go with that," he said, brushing a few smoldering cinders off his jacket.

"You are going to have to step it up if you want to be free," I said, hoping he'd at least think about it. "Maybe go against your instincts. Try being good for a change. Think about why you want to lie and cheat and steal."

"Because it's fun," he said flatly.

"Promise me you'll try," I said as Melody burst in the door.

"Oh, my goodness, Verity," she gushed, walking straight through Frankie, who startled at the impact and leapt sideways like he had the heebie-jeebies. She gave me a giant hug. "I'm so glad you're okay and that Alec was there to save you!"

Yeah, he was a real hero. "He was there trying to set me up so he could arrest me," I said as she pulled away.

"He's doing his job and so are you," she lectured. "I don't know why you two can't get along."

Did she want that in an alphabetized list, or did she truly not understand her new man's desire to see me behind bars?

Frankie appeared behind her. "I say you should go against your instincts on this one," he snarked, repeating my words back to me. "Kiss and make up with Duranja. Try being 'good' for a change."

"I'm not trapped," I told him.

"Hi, Frankie." Melody gave a general wave, covering all directions the ghost might be. "I'm helping you," she said to me, as if trying to prove Frankie's point. As if her desire to "help" made everything all right.

I'd never been happier to see Lauralee bluster through the door, loaded down with a picnic basket and dragging a wheelie cooler. Because that was what you brought to the hospital. She'd made me a blueberry, flaxseed, and spinach antioxidant smoothie along with a kale and strawberry salad, saying both were good for recovering from smoke inhalation. She treated us all to a pot of fresh green tea—also supposed to be good for me —and she couldn't stop talking about what a hero Duranja had been for braving the flames to save me.

Okay, so Lauralee wasn't perfect.

Ellis arrived after a long day on the stakeout, and he spent the night watching over me. I explained to him what had really happened, and he told me that the arson squad would never believe fire by ghost lighter. He did tell me that the owners of the property had been looking for an excuse to offload it for years. An insurance claim had already been filed, and they were happily negotiating with the railroad company to raze the remains and offload the land for a hefty profit.

I wondered what would happen to Erma Sue's chair.

Duranja wanted the incident fully investigated, but so far, he was the only one.

Meanwhile, Vincent had confessed to the murder of Twyla Sue. He claimed he'd met with her only to take the burn book and end her tyranny before it started. However, when the situation had gotten heated, she'd made threats and ended up dead. His lawyer had put in a plea of temporary insanity, which would have a better chance of sticking if his target had been Virginia Wydell.

At least the jury of his peers would have sympathized with that.

Virginia was charged with breaking and entering, exactly as Duranja had threatened. She made bail and returned home to her stripped and empty house. To be honest, I wasn't sure what she was going to do next. She had a choice ahead of her, a big one. Who did she want to be?

She could stack up perceived slights and spend her life getting revenge against people, or she could take life as it came and try to be happy. It would be scary for her to be vulnerable, to let people like or dislike her on their own terms, but it would be worth it.

A lot of my neighbors said I should have gloated more about Virginia's downfall. That I should have lectured her harder or even publicly shamed her for what she'd done. I disagreed. That was what Erma Sue's sister, Rowena, had done, and it hadn't worked out so well for her.

Rowena was what happened when you let revenge take over your life. There was no doubt Rowena had been wronged. She'd been hurt. She'd deserved to be treated so much better than she had. But in seeking justice, she'd poisoned her heart. She couldn't let go of the past, and she'd let it ruin the rest of her life, not to mention her afterlife.

To me, it wasn't about letting Virginia off the hook for hurting me. It was about having my peace. That was more important than forcing someone else to learn a life lesson, especially if it meant lowering myself in the process.

Ellis also spoke with his father. He tried to get him to come back to town, at least for a while, to help support the family. His dad declined and told him the divorce would go through. My boyfriend seemed almost relieved at that, and confided it wasn't entirely unexpected.

And Beau? Well, he'd abandoned his artistic getaway, along with his phone and his luggage, to find complete freedom at a nudist retreat in the mountains. I hoped he'd at least brought his bug spray.

When I'd recovered sufficiently, Ellis drove me home from the hospital. I sat in the passenger seat of his cruiser while Frankie took the more familiar seat in the back, behind the wire mesh. "I'm going to forget about you and my mom taking the burn book," he said with a glance in my direction, "seeing as what you did was for the greater good."

"Even he has to admit it feels good to bend the rules," the ghost said.

"Frank—" I cautioned.

"What?" He shrugged. "Baby steps."

He'd have a long way to go with Ellis.

"So let me get this straight," Ellis said. "Frankie has to learn to be a better person in order to free himself from his ashes."

"Yes," I said, glancing back at the ghost, "like shedding his old self. He needs to learn not to be defined by who he was in life."

"Men feared me," Frankie said by way of defense. "Women loved me."

"And Erma Sue evolved enough to free herself," Ellis

reasoned. "But she was still...her. I mean, she also tried to kill you."

"She regressed," I told him.

"It was Verity's fault," Frankie insisted. "She makes people think too much."

"I was only trying to help her," I added, carefully rubbing the edges of the healing scissor stab on my arm. It itched.

"You convinced her she needed the book," Frankie said. "Killing you was a practical way to get it." Ruthless but reasonable.

I supposed it had been easier initially for Erma Sue to reform since she'd died without the book. She no longer had her weapon, or any real way to hurt anyone. Until I'd arrived with her ultimate temptation, and a bit of unsolicited advice.

"The only thing I wonder is what the book said about my grandmother." Now it was gone, and with it, my chance to find out.

Erma Sue wouldn't tell me, even if I wanted to track her down. Which I didn't. No sense seeking out the angry ghost who wanted to haunt me.

Ellis turned into the long drive that led to my house. "Maybe your grandma will come back if there's something she needs to tell you. Maybe it would be better to hear it from her anyway."

I looked out at the spindly peach trees I'd planted the spring before last. "You say that as if I can talk to any ghost I want."

"No," Ellis said as we meandered down the side drive, "but she loved this house. And you. Maybe she'll turn up when you least expect it."

She did. And she might. That gave me hope.

CHAPTER 26

A week later, I was back to breathing normally, but my house would never be the same.

The first truck had arrived at my house the day after I got out of the hospital, bringing with it my great-grandmother's dining room table and silver service. A dealer had bought them right out of my house. Turned out they never sold, so Virginia bought them back.

I'd spent the night in the dining room despite Ellis's protests that sleeping in his bed would be better for my health. In the end, he'd helped me drag the futon back down from the bedroom upstairs so I could sleep next to the table where my family had shared so many meals, so much laughter and memories.

But Virginia hadn't stopped there. She tracked down a pair of old paintings, the ones my great-grandparents had made of the house and the buildings back in the 1920s when it had been an actual working farm. The peach orchard stood tall out front, and even a few chickens pecked near the hydrangea bushes along the porch.

I warned Frankie not to get any ideas.

In the following week, Virginia returned my grandmother's vintage Fiestaware, the hall table, and the painting dated 1823 of a man nobody knew anymore. It comforted me, nonetheless.

I found myself walking the bottom floor of the house for hours, just admiring the changes. My house, coming back to right again. Not the way it had been, but more whole all the same. More mine.

When I called Virginia to acknowledge her efforts, she told me she was trying to change, one day at a time. She'd even attended the impromptu town celebration of the return of the 1910 victory cup, which had resulted in an immediate challenge to Jackson to renew the tradition. I'd seen Virginia on the fringes of the crowd while I helped Lauralee serve a massive influx of happy revelers needing a comfort-food fix. My friend's business was becoming a go-to place, a true Sugarland treasure, and I couldn't have been happier for her.

Virginia also said she had a surprise for me once she could schedule installation.

Today was that day.

I walked through my stately dining room and into the parlor, where a pair of electricians stood on tall ladders, reinstalling the chandelier I thought I'd lost forever. The flat crystal gleamed, freshly rubbed down in a solution of white vinegar and water. I'd done it myself, and experienced a joy I hadn't felt in ages. Reclaiming my grandmother's favorite piece in this house made me feel closer to her. I could almost sense her approval.

When I was a child, we'd sit together and watch the chandelier throw patterns of light on the antique white and gray carpet underneath. We'd watch for rainbows.

I stood on that carpet now.

I'd kept the purple couch because it held so many memories of its own. Only now it sat next to the solid wood side table my great-uncle had brought back from Mexico in the 1920s.

Frankie's rosebush still held its place of honor in the trash can by the mantel. That might change soon as well.

I heard the front door crack open, followed by Melody's voice in the front hall. Sound didn't echo as much now that the house was growing full again. Still, I heard her call, "Is the chandelier up yet?" She bustled inside. "Did I miss it?"

"You're just in time," I said, my smile fading as she walked in with a clearly uncomfortable Duranja.

He acted like he'd been dragged into an enemy camp, which I supposed he had.

Melody clapped her hands together. "I'm so excited," she said, bringing her clasped hands to her chin, tears in her eyes. "Grandma would be so proud."

"I'm not sure about that," I said, looking up at the massive fixture. It was even larger than I'd remembered. Grander. "She would have preferred I never lost it in the first place."

"That wasn't your fault," she insisted. "But this? This is your doing. You got it back. You made it right."

I couldn't help but smile. "Take a look at this," I said, walking her to the kitchen, leaving Duranja to talk lighting installation with the workmen.

Melody's eyes lit up when she saw Grandma's silver fruit bowl, polished and gleaming on the table. "You filled it with apples, just like Grandma," she gushed.

"From the tree out back," I said with more than a hint of pride. I'd also included a pear, a non-perfect, yet perfectly ripe, sweet pear from the fruit stand down the way.

Everything was working out just fine. Except...

"Did you have to bring Duranja?" I asked, glancing back to find him talking electricity like Frankie talked guns.

"Well..." Melody hedged. "He spent the night, so it's not like I invited him specifically." At my gasp, she quickly added, "Don't tell Mom."

"I wish you hadn't told me," I said, in all honesty.

"I talked to Ellis this morning, and we both think we need to do a double date," she said, laying down a double whammy.

"I'm busy."

Melody selected an apple from the bowl. "I already heard that from Alec," she said, taking a bite of the fruit. "But I'm not taking no for an answer." She looked at me shyly as she chewed. "I really like him," she admitted, "like I haven't liked anyone in a long time."

Uh-oh.

"You're going to get to know each other whether you like it or not," she insisted. "It's important to me." She cocked the wrist holding the apple and surveyed me. "Besides, how bad could it be to make a new friend?"

I wasn't sure I wanted to find out.

But I was saved from responding by a large crash on my porch.

"Just a sec," I said to Melody, who hadn't heard a thing.

She returned to the chandelier and Duranja while I walked out the back door to find a riot on my porch. Lucy chased a ghostly man in overalls, who chased Nibbles the goat. Meanwhile, another baby goat knocked over a pail of feed, sending bits cascading everywhere. And worse. I gasped. "Frankie! Catch that guy! I think he stole Frisky Pete!"

The horse's rope lay on the floor, mangled. They'd even taken his treat ball.

"That's just farmer Dave," Frankie said fondly, shimmering into existence next to me. "He's agreed to help take care of Frisky Pete while I focus on getting free."

"Are you serious?" I asked. "No funny business? I mean, you actually want to concentrate on the important things for once?"

"Yeah," Frankie said as the farmer cornered Nibbles just past the porch swing and tossed a lead over her neck. "I mean, these animals. I love these guys. They're what makes life worth living."

"But—"

"Don't call me dead," he warned. "For now, and only for now, I'm sending Frisky Pete to live on a farm with Dave and his partner, Stu, who is one of the top horse trainers outside of Kentucky."

"So it's like a dead animal ranch," I ventured.

"Training facility," Frankie corrected. "With goats. It's where I got Nibbles in the first place. Scape and Nibbles missed their home. That's why they were acting up."

"I thought you said it was my skunk's fault," I mused as Nibbles began attacking farmer Dave with kisses and head butts.

"They need to go home, and Frisky Pete was too attached to leave him behind. Stu is going to start training him for the Timberland Stakes, and as soon as I get free of here, I'm going to be out there every day doing drills with him."

I'd be glad to take him. "That's a good goal." Much better than stealing or bootlegging. Although, as Frankie would be the first to tell me, old habits die hard.

"I mean, maybe this is a new direction for me," Frankie said. "Like, I'm growing or something."

He did love that horse. And the goats. And the donkey.

Not to mention my skunk.

"Are you feeling any freer?" I asked.

"Not yet," he admitted.

Still, it was a start. "Erma Sue did it. She got free even though she still had sister issues to work on."

The gangster screwed up his face. "I don't have a sister."

"What I'm saying is better doesn't have to mean perfect."

"I'm going to count on that," he said, adjusting his hat low to cover the bullet hole on his forehead.

"We'll work on it," I promised. We'd do it together.

Farmer Dave walked Nibbles up the ramp and into the truck. Her babies scampered up the ramp one by one until they were all on board, and my porch stood blessedly empty.

"Oops," Frankie said as the truck drove away. "I think he's missing a goat."

"And I'm missing a skunk," I said, worried when I didn't see Lucy.

I thundered down the steps with Frankie on my heels. "It's not like she could have gotten into a ghost truck," I said. "It would hurt to touch."

"She's here," Frankie said, leaning to look under the porch.

We found her snuggled up near Scape.

I let out a sigh of relief. "We'll take him back later." After the workmen finished with the chandelier.

"He's a ghost," Frankie said. "He can go home whenever he wants."

Right. I'd forgotten. "Soon that will be you, buddy," I said, straightening.

"Soon," Frankie agreed.

He looked off into the distance toward where the truck had gone. "You know, farmer Dave told me he has a friend who stops by from time to time. Goes by the name of Delia Long."

"That's my grandmother!" I gasped.

"I hear she's due for a visit," he said casually, as if not to get my hopes up.

I clasped my hands to my chest. "It would mean everything to me if I could see her again."

Frankie lowered his chin. "I usually say this when I'm about to off someone or maybe slam their fingers in a car trunk, but in this case, I mean it in a good way. You deserve it."

"Thanks, Frankie. You've given me hope," I said.

Hope that I'd see her again. That she'd see how well I'd taken care of her home, that I could tell her how much I loved her and missed her.

"Me too," he said, with a sniff. "We got this, kid."

And, for once, I knew Frankie had gotten it right.

Note from Angie Fox

Thanks so much for heading to Sugarland with Verity and the gang! I hope you enjoyed this latest adventure and that you don't turn around tonight and encounter a ghostly baby goat in your living room. Those little guys like to travel, and they tend to invite themselves...everywhere. (Pro-tip: they love carrots. And socks. And basically anything you have.)

The next book is called Dread and Buried. *In it, Verity and Ellis's double date with Melody and Duranja ends just as Verity predicted—in murder. And while our favorite party of four survives, Verity soon discovers a link between the modern-day killing and an unsolved mystery nearly a century in the making.*

Thanks for reading and for being your wonderful self!
Angie

NEXT FROM ANGIE FOX

The adventure continues with
Dread and Buried
Southern Ghost Hunter mystery #12
By Angie Fox

ABOUT THE AUTHOR

 *New York Times* and *USA Today* bestselling author Angie Fox writes sweet, fun, action-packed mysteries. Her characters are clever and fearless, but in real life, Angie is afraid of basements, bees, and going up stairs when it's dark behind her. Let's face it: Angie wouldn't last five minutes in one of her books.

Angie earned a journalism degree from the University of Missouri. During that time, she also skipped class for an entire week so she could read Anne Rice's vampire series straight through. Angie has always loved books and is shocked, honored and tickled pink that she now gets to write books for a living. Although, she did skip writing for a week this past fall so she could read Charlaine Harris's Sookie Stackhouse books straight through.

Angie makes her home in St. Louis, Missouri with a football-addicted husband, two kids, and Moxie the dog.

Made in the USA
Coppell, TX
09 June 2022